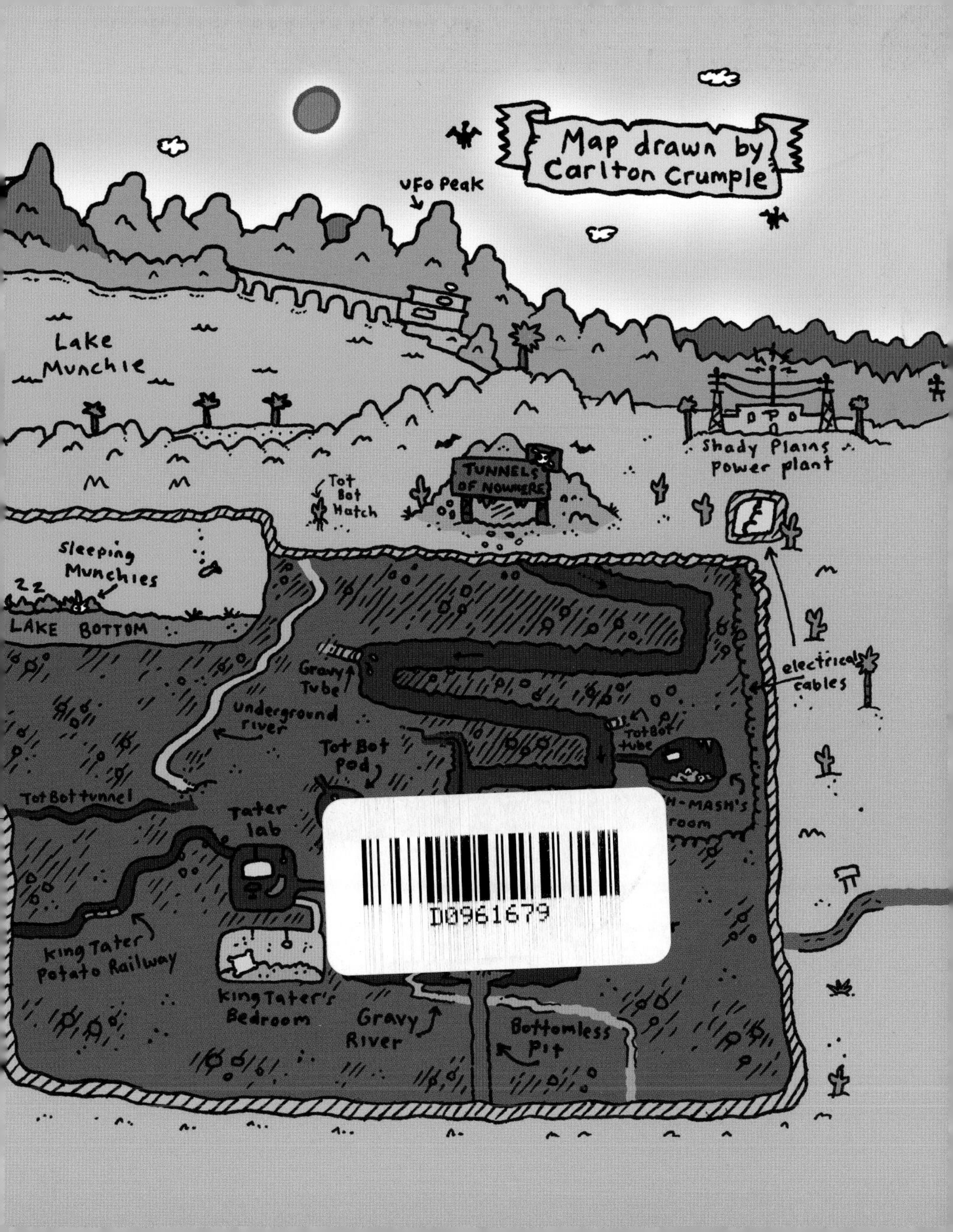
Map drawn by Carlton Crumple
UFO Peak
Lake Munchie
Tunnels of Nowhere
Shady Plains power plant
Tot Bot Hatch
Sleeping Munchies
LAKE BOTTOM
Gravy Tube
Underground river
electrical cables
Tot Bot tube
Tot Bot Pod
Tot Bot tunnel
Tater lab
King Tater Potato Railway
King Tater's Bedroom
Gravy River
Bottomless Pit

TATER INVADERS!

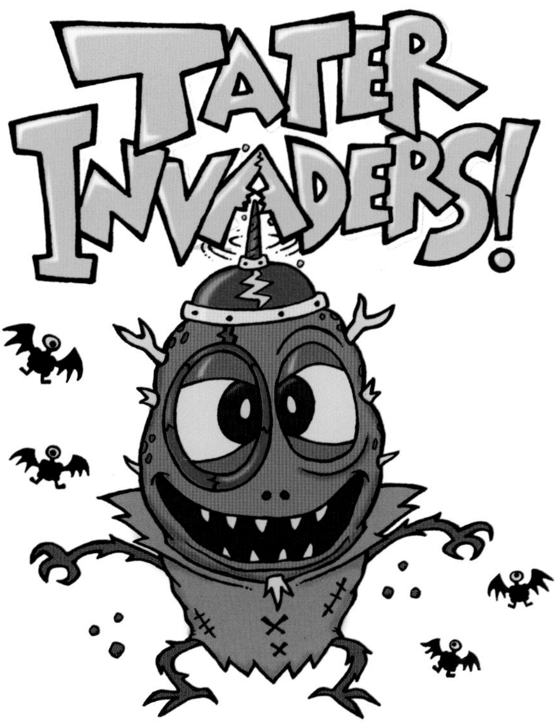

Read all the books in the
Carlton Crumple Creature Catcher series:

#1 Catch the Munchies!
#2 Tater Invaders!

Coming soon:

#3 Reptoids from Space!

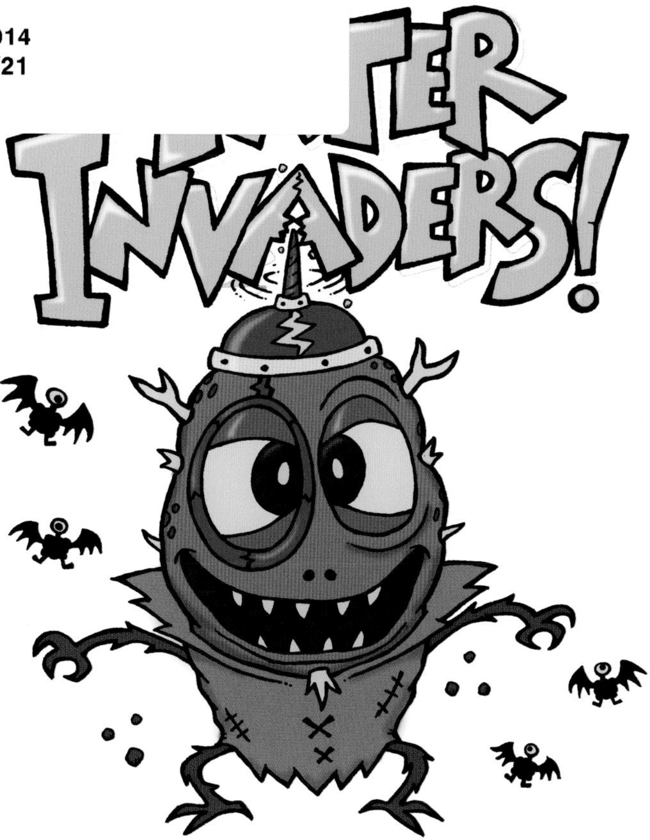
TER
INVADERS!

Written and Illustrated by David Fremont

Color by Jimbo Matison

PIXEL+INK

PIXEL✛INK

Text and illustrations copyright
© 2021 by David Fremont
All rights reserved
Pixel+Ink is a division of TGM Development Corp.
Printed and bound in October 2020 at Leo Paper, Heshan, China
Color by Jimbo Matison
Book design by Sammy Yuen
www.pixelandinkbooks.com
Library of Congress Control Number: 2020940462
ISBN: 978-1-64595-006-6
eBook ISBN: 978-1-64595-007-3
First Edition
1 3 5 7 9 10 8 6 4 2

For my mom and dad, thank you for believing in me.
And Dad, here's your side of taters!

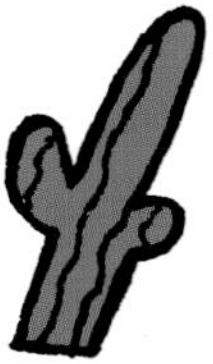

CHAPTER 1

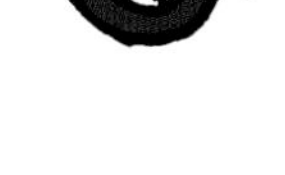

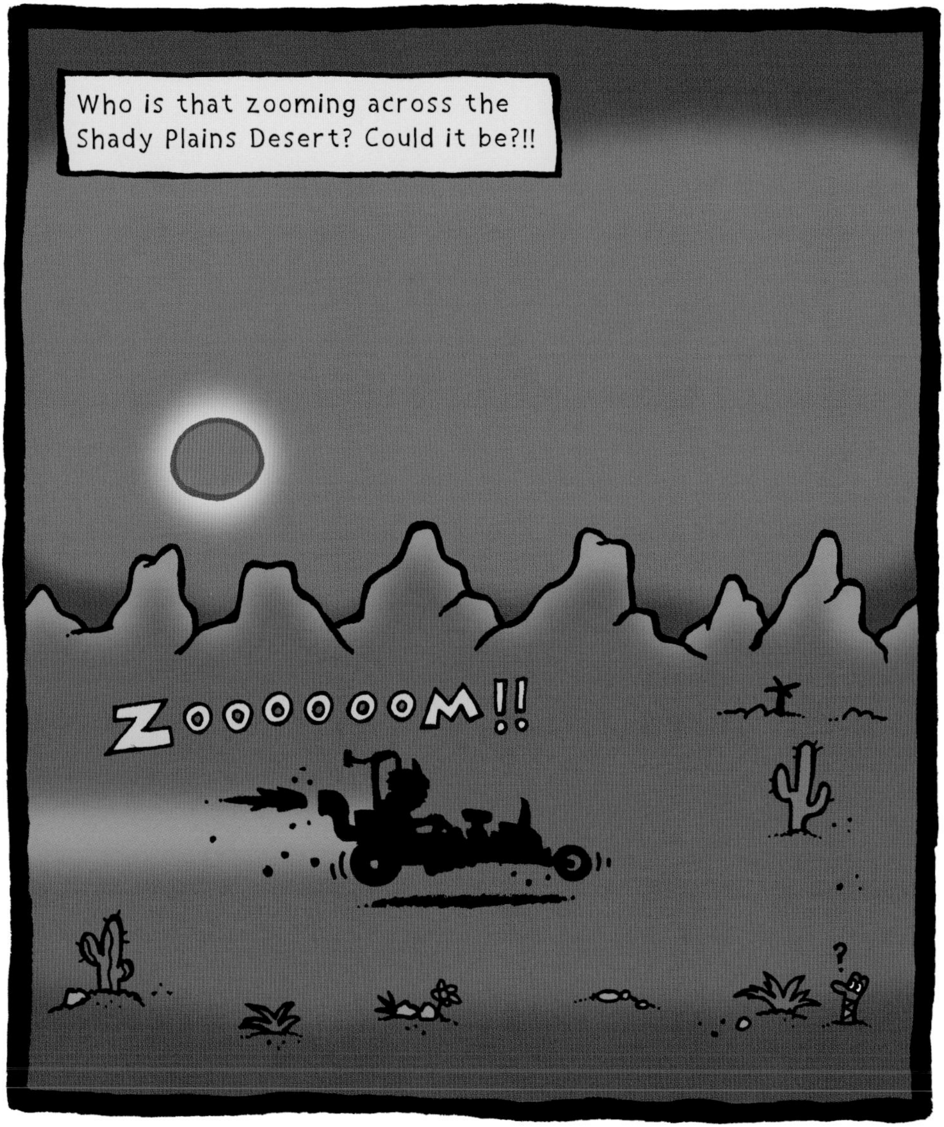
Who is that zooming across the Shady Plains Desert? Could it be?!!
ZOOOOOOOM!!

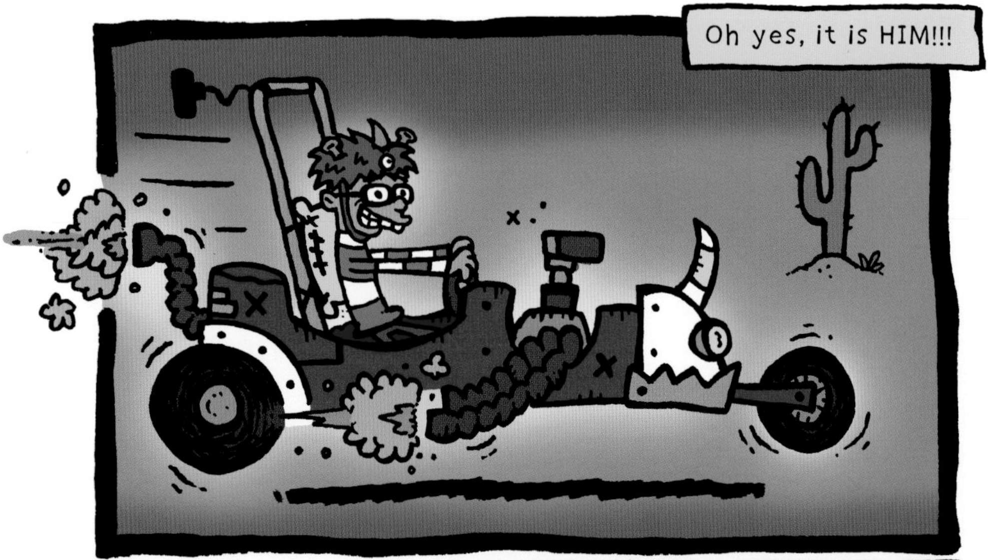

Oh yes, it is HIM!!!

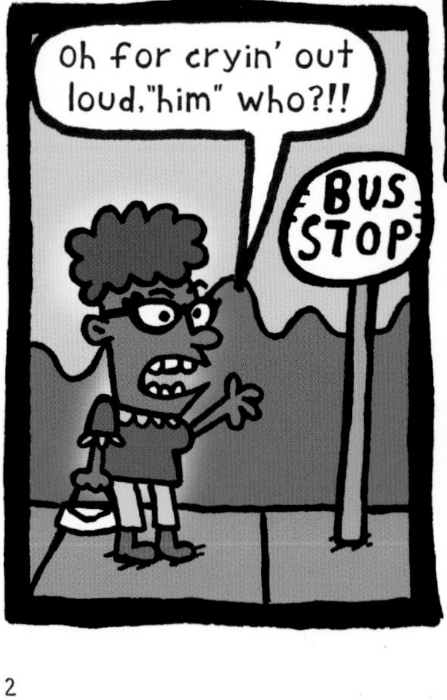

Oh for cryin' out loud,"him" who?!!
BUS STOP

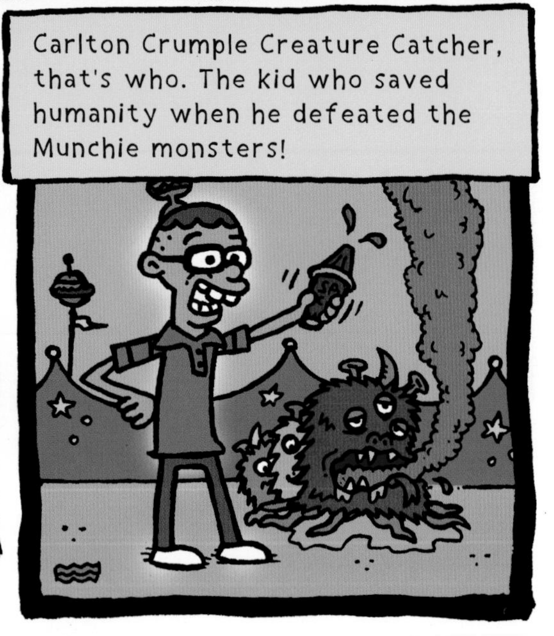

Carlton Crumple Creature Catcher, that's who. The kid who saved humanity when he defeated the Munchie monsters!

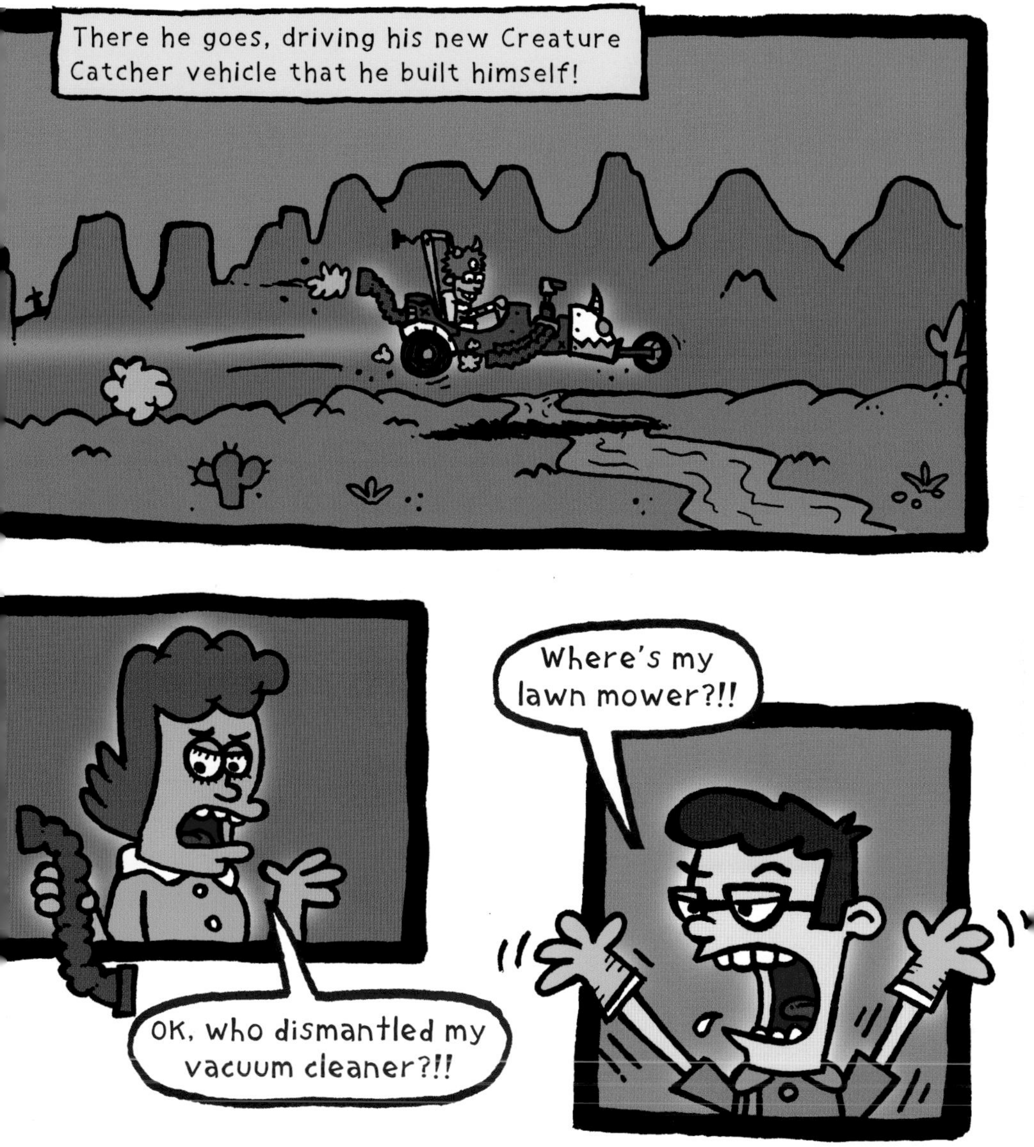
There he goes, driving his new Creature Catcher vehicle that he built himself!
OK, who dismantled my vacuum cleaner?!!
Where's my lawn mower?!!

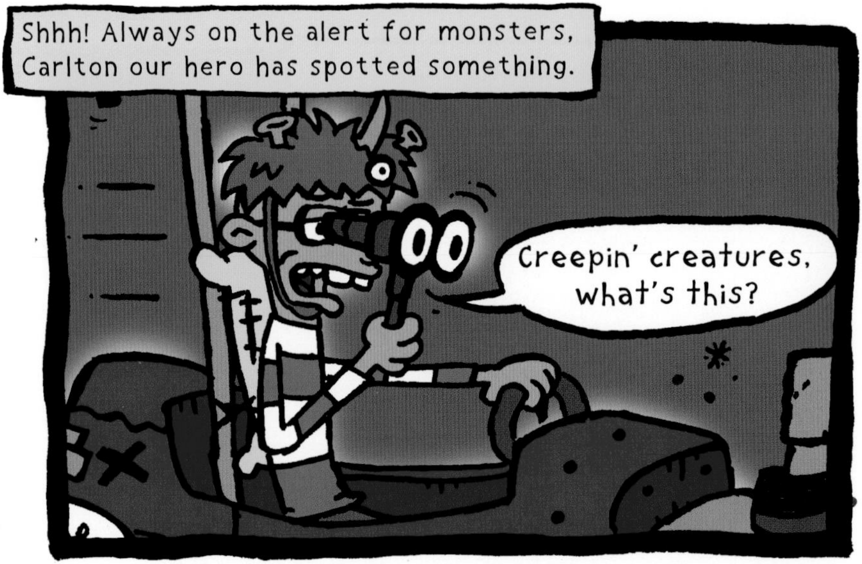
Shhh! Always on the alert for monsters, Carlton our hero has spotted something.
Creepin' creatures, what's this?

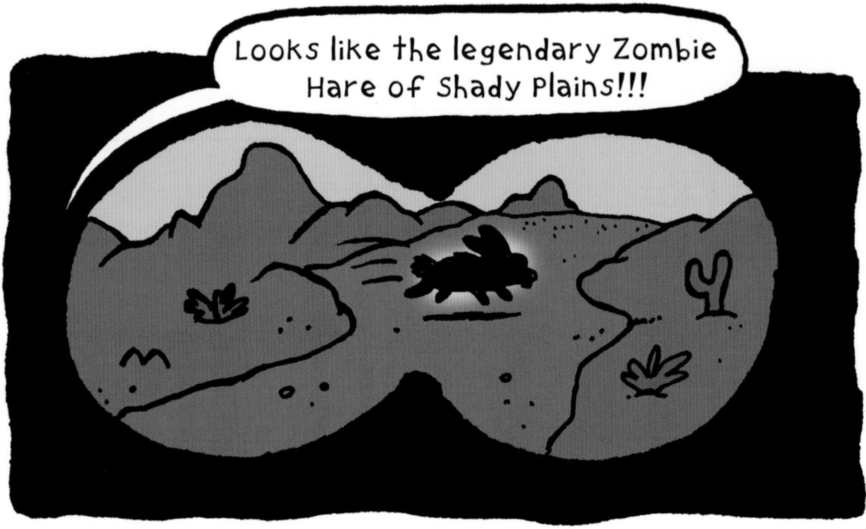
Looks like the legendary Zombie Hare of Shady Plains!!!

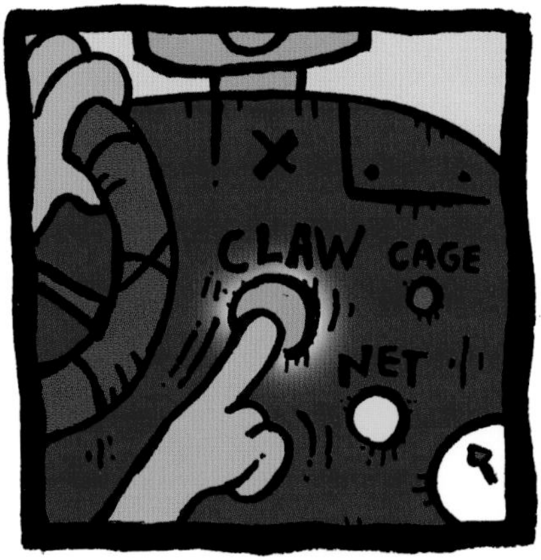
CLAW
CAGE
NET

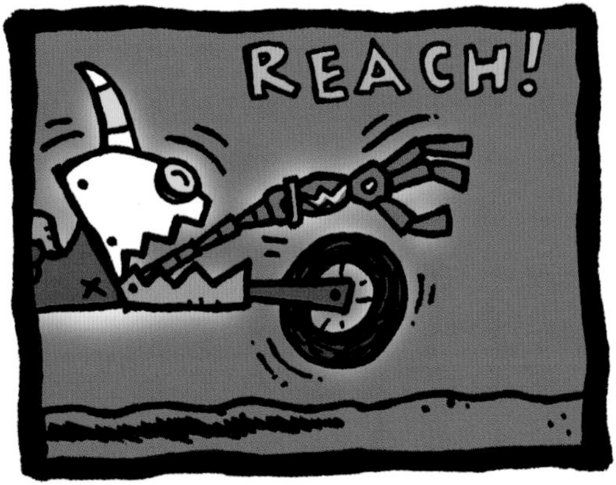
REACH!

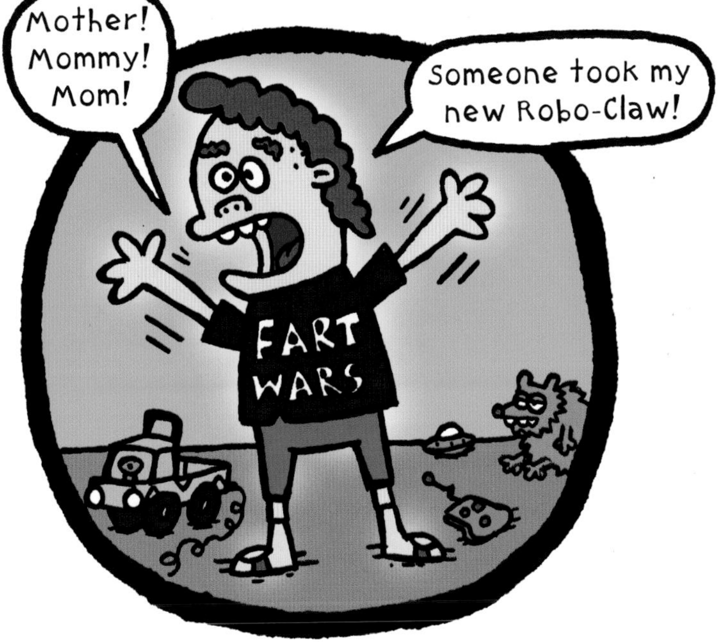
Mother! Mommy! Mom!
Someone took my new Robo-Claw!
FART WARS

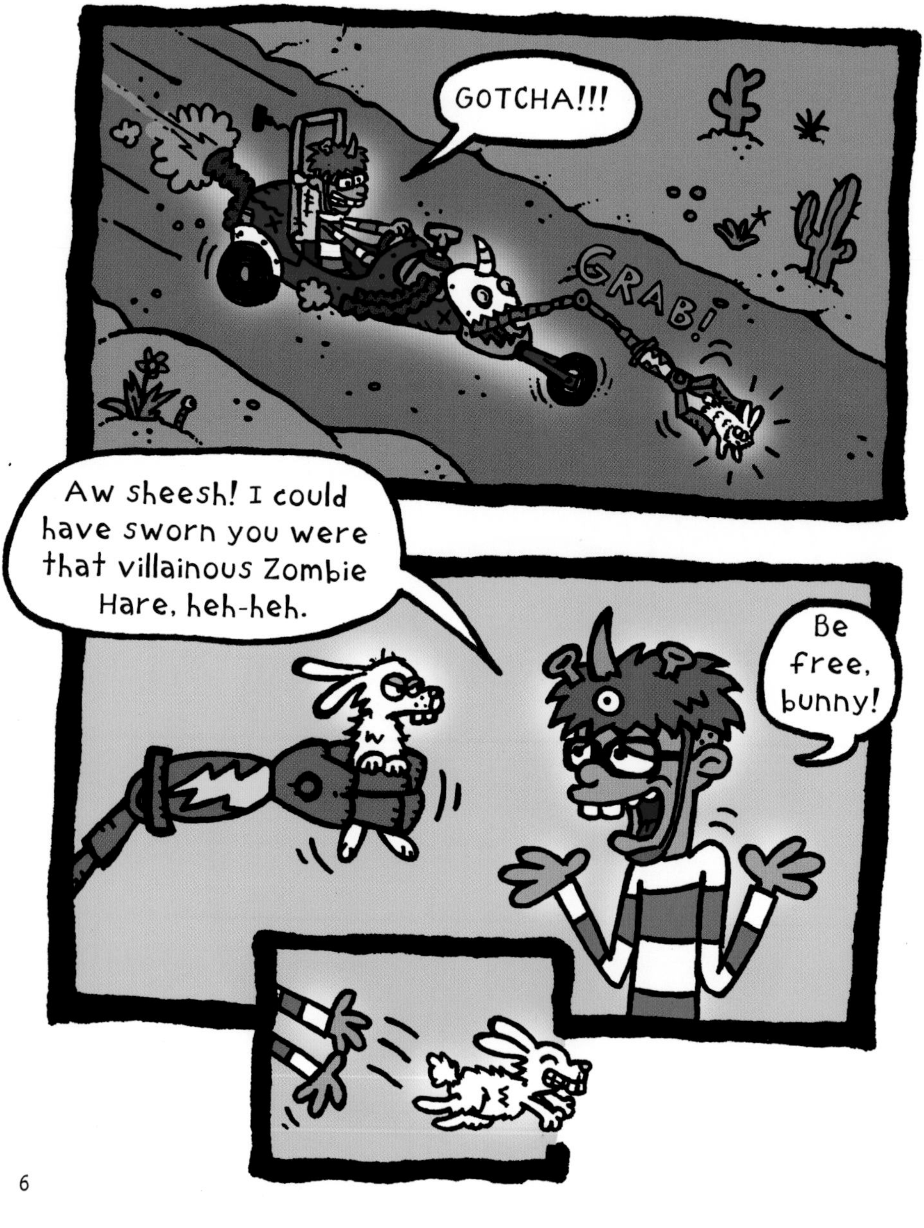
GOTCHA!!!
GRAB!
Aw sheesh! I could have sworn you were that villainous Zombie Hare, heh-heh.
Be free, bunny!

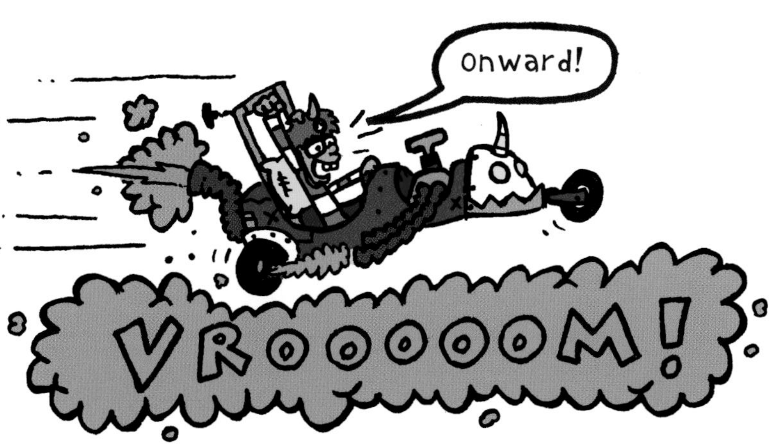
Onward!
VROOOOOM!

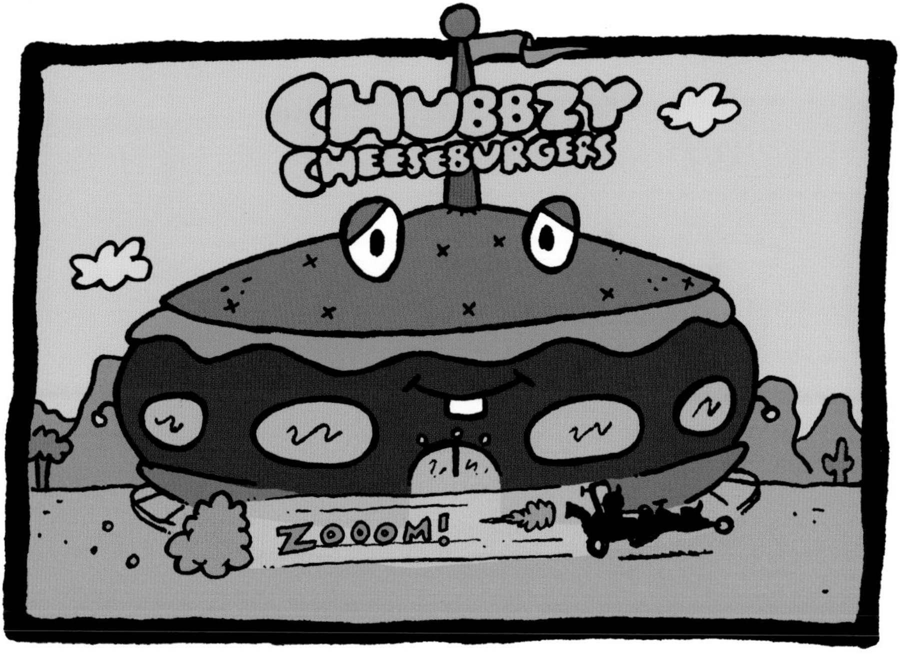
CHUBBZY CHEESEBURGERS
ZOOOM!

Hey, you crazy kid! Slow down or I'm calling the cops!
Yep.
Speaking of cops, Carlton works for the sheriff as an official Creature Catcher!
SHADY PLAINS POLICE
RRRRRRR!!!

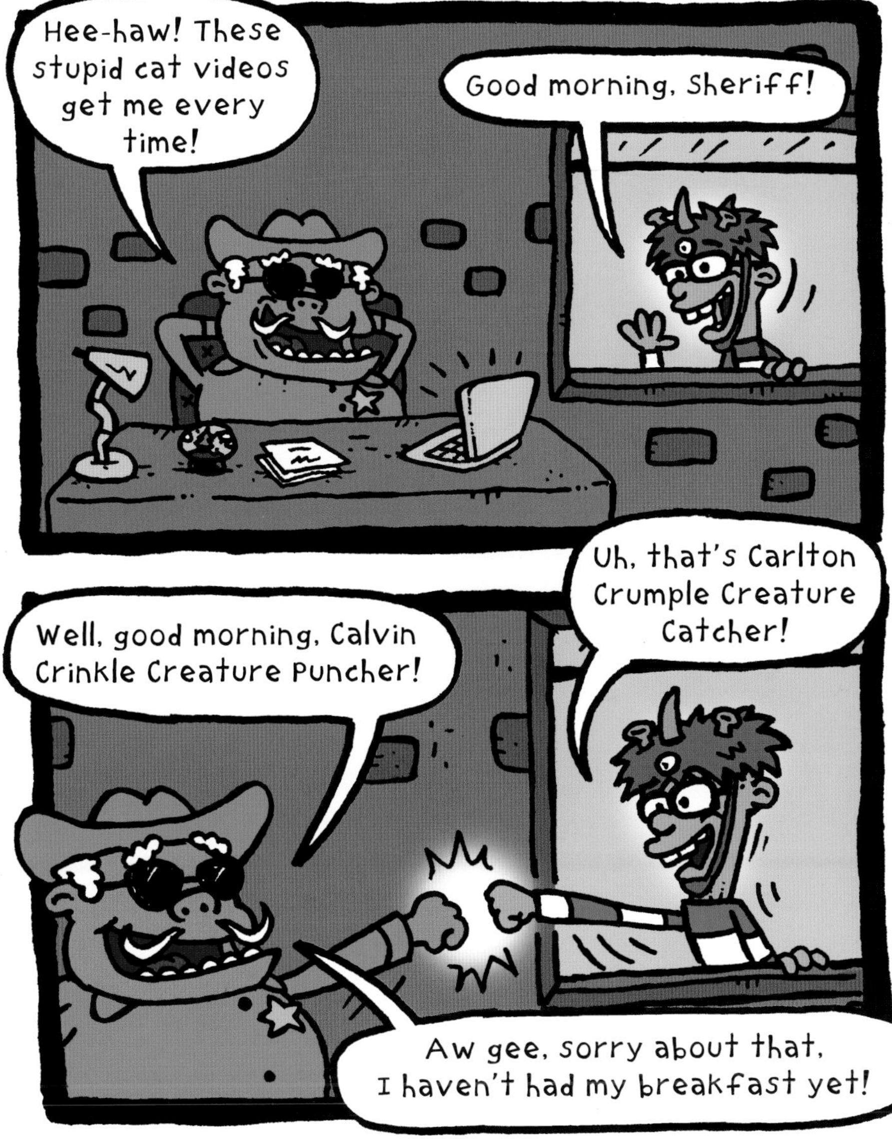
Hee-haw! These stupid cat videos get me every time!
Good morning, Sheriff!
Well, good morning, Calvin Crinkle Creature Puncher!
Uh, that's Carlton Crumple Creature Catcher!
Aw gee, sorry about that, I haven't had my breakfast yet!

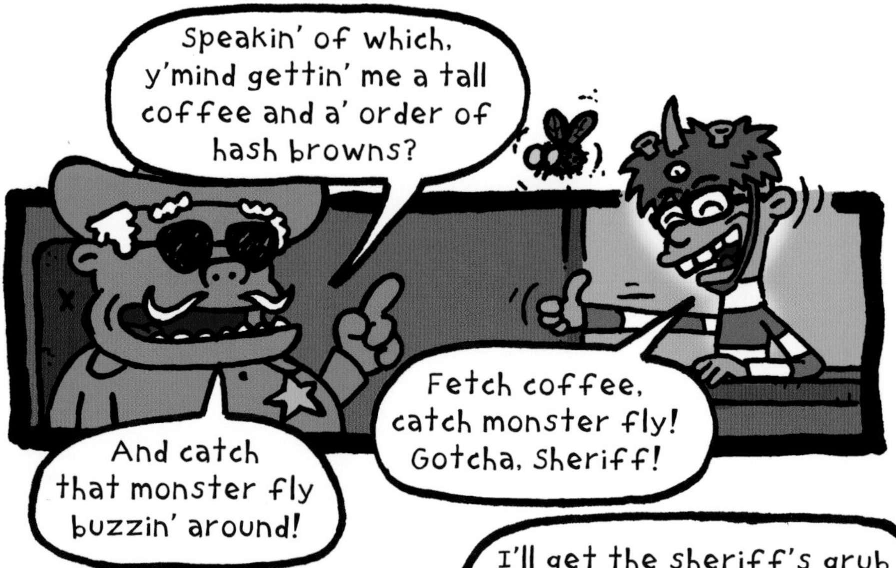
Speakin' of which, y'mind gettin' me a tall coffee and a' order of hash browns?
And catch that monster fly buzzin' around!
Fetch coffee, catch monster fly! Gotcha, Sheriff!

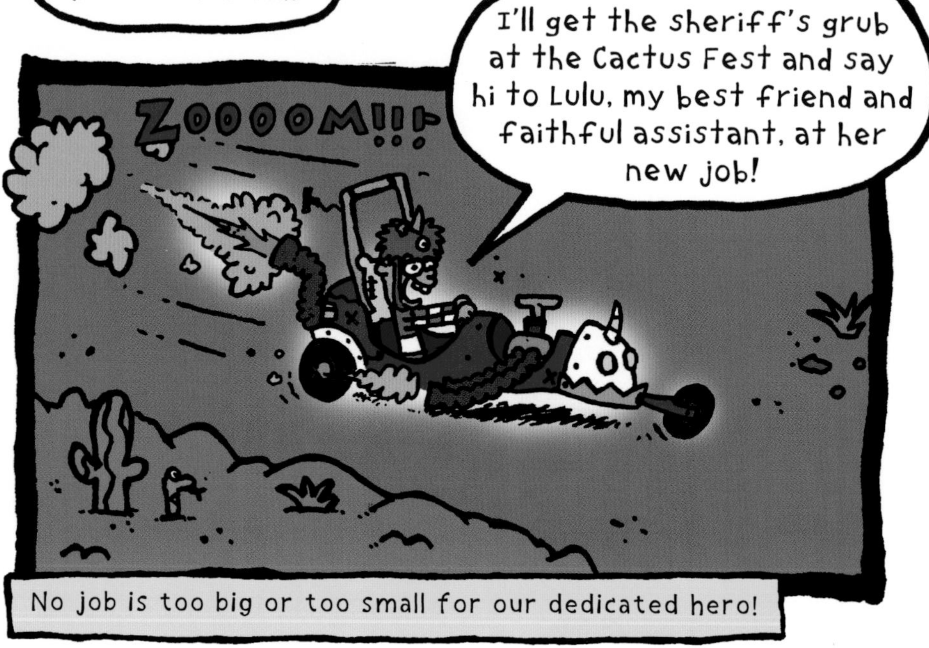
I'll get the sheriff's grub at the Cactus Fest and say hi to Lulu, my best friend and faithful assistant, at her new job!
ZOOOOM!!!
No job is too big or too small for our dedicated hero!

CHAPTER 2

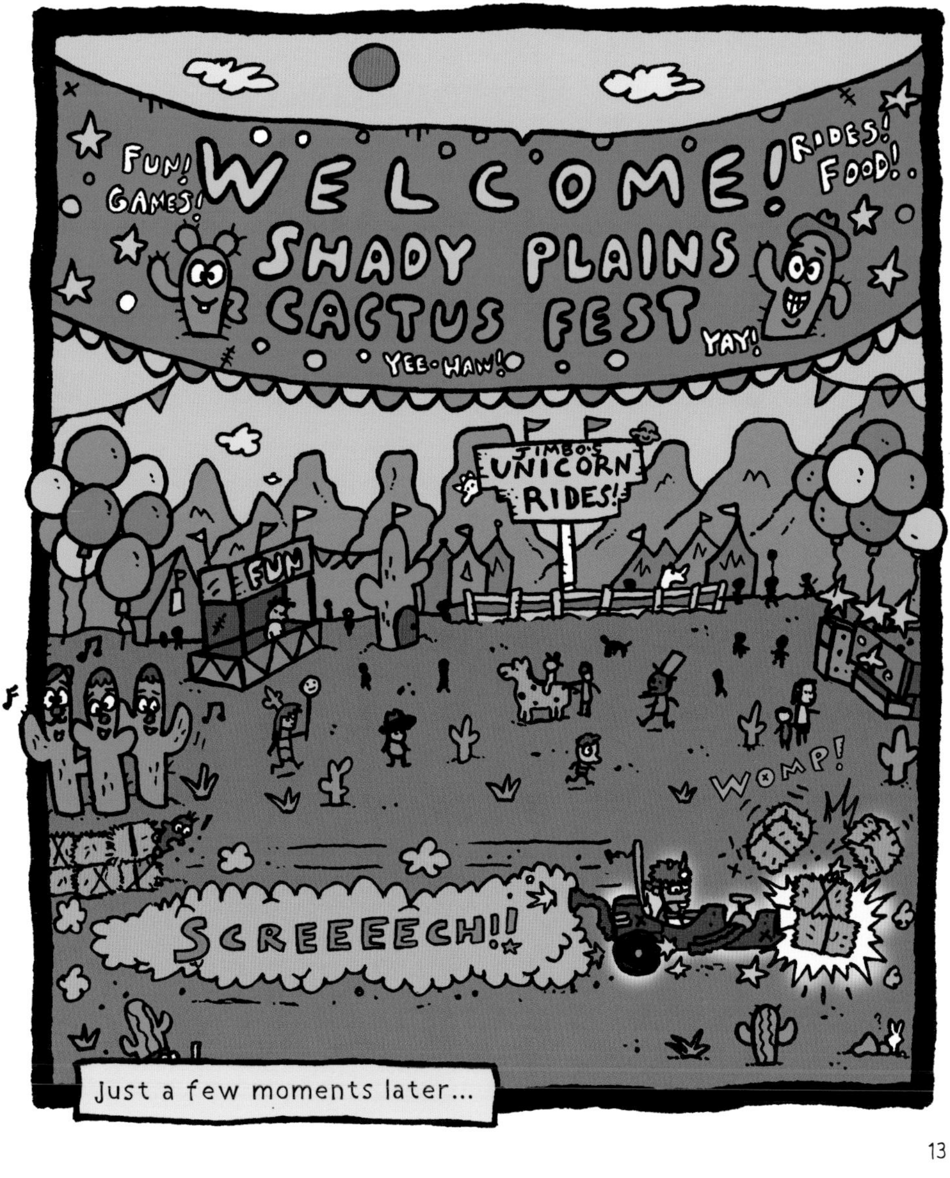
WELCOME!
SHADY PLAINS CACTUS FEST
FUN!
GAMES!
RIDES!
FOOD!
YEE-HAW!
YAY!
JIMBO'S UNICORN RIDES!
FUN
WOMP!
SCREEEECH!!
Just a few moments later...

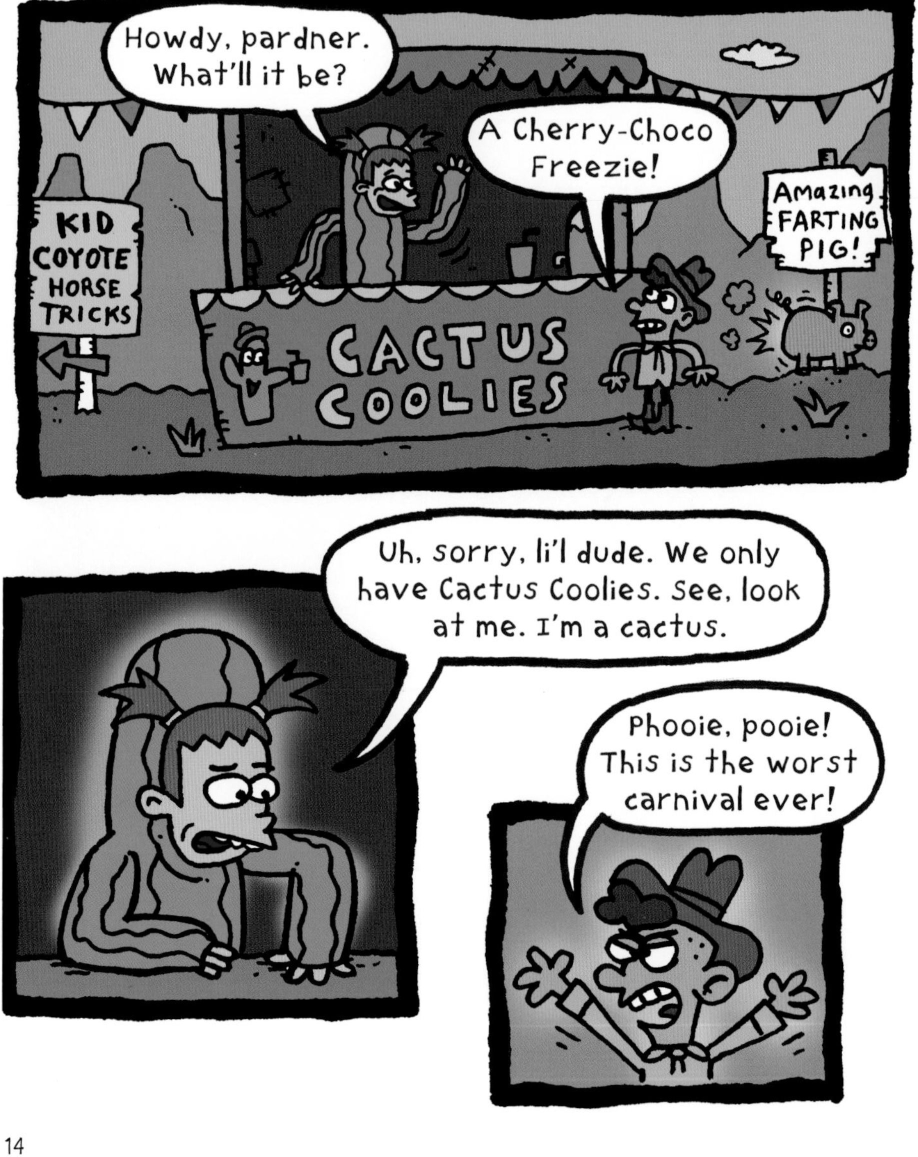
Howdy, pardner. What'll it be?
A Cherry-Choco Freezie!
KID COYOTE HORSE TRICKS
CACTUS COOLIES
Amazing FARTING PIG!
Uh, sorry, li'l dude. We only have Cactus Coolies. See, look at me. I'm a cactus.
Phooie, pooie! This is the worst carnival ever!

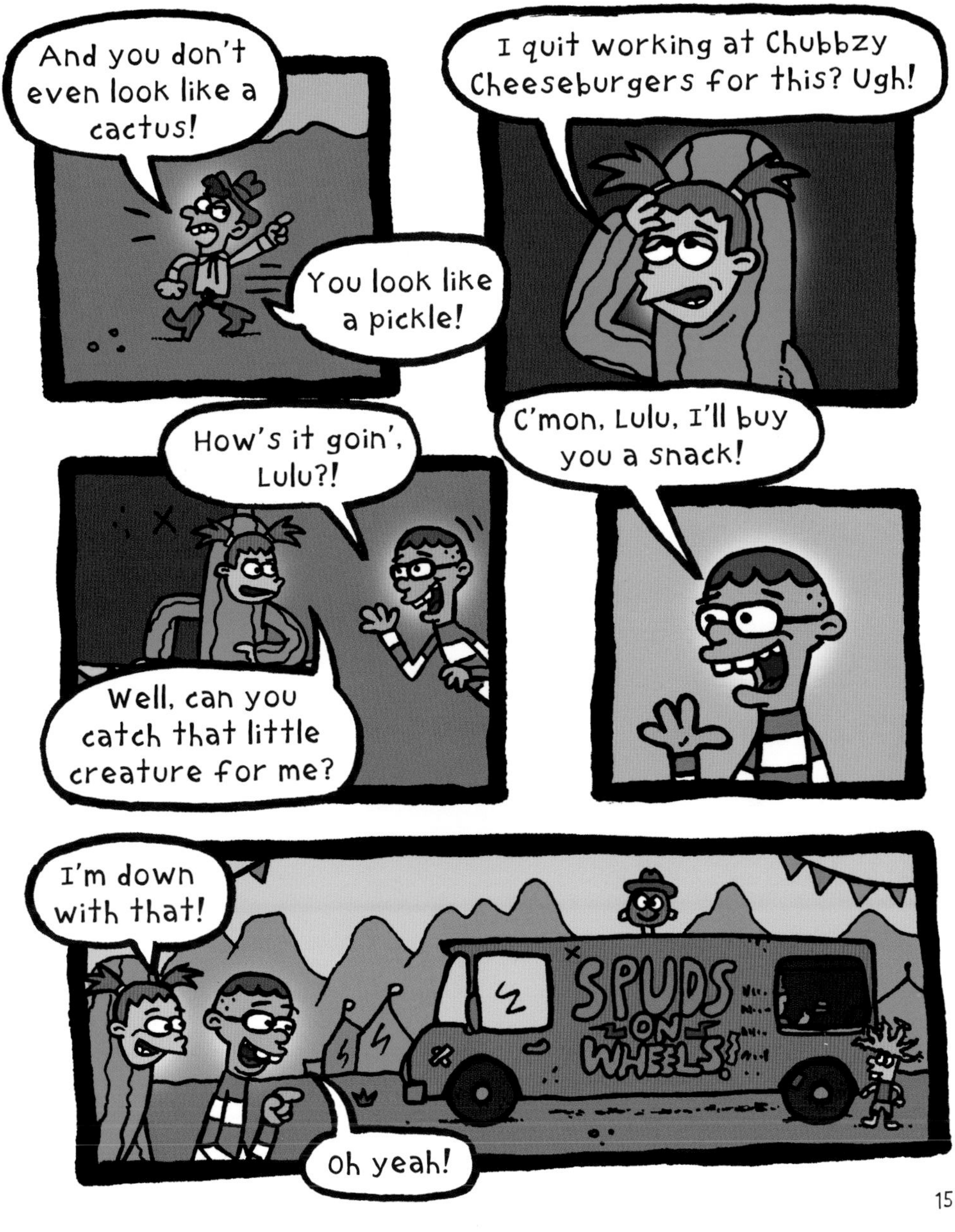
And you don't even look like a cactus!
You look like a pickle!
I quit working at Chubbzy Cheeseburgers for this? Ugh!
How's it goin', Lulu?!
Well, can you catch that little creature for me?
C'mon, Lulu, I'll buy you a snack!
I'm down with that!
SPUDS ON WHEELS!
Oh yeah!

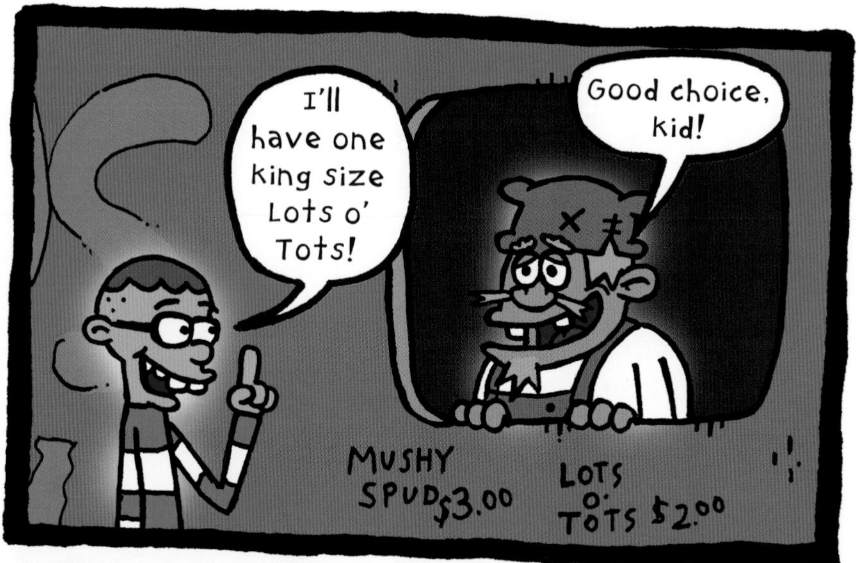
I'll have one King size Lots o' Tots!
Good choice, kid!
MUSHY SPUD $3.00
LOTS O' TOTS $2.00

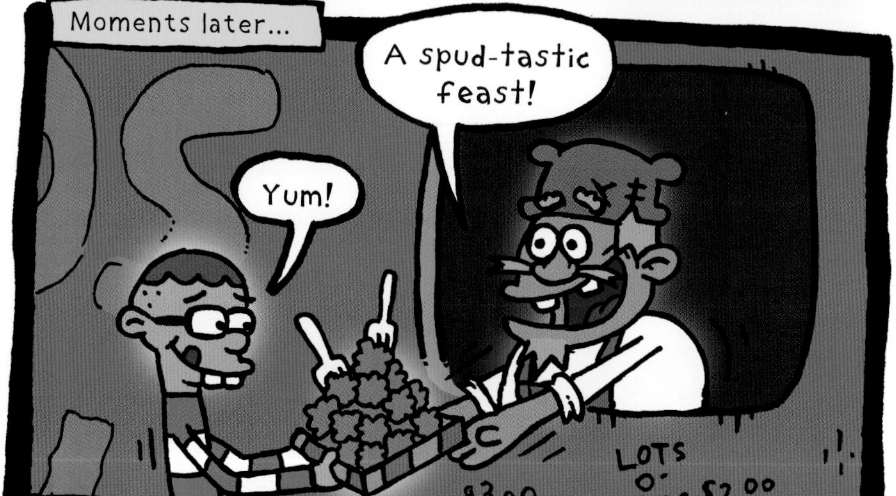
Moments later...
Yum!
A spud-tastic feast!
LOTS O' TOTS $2.00

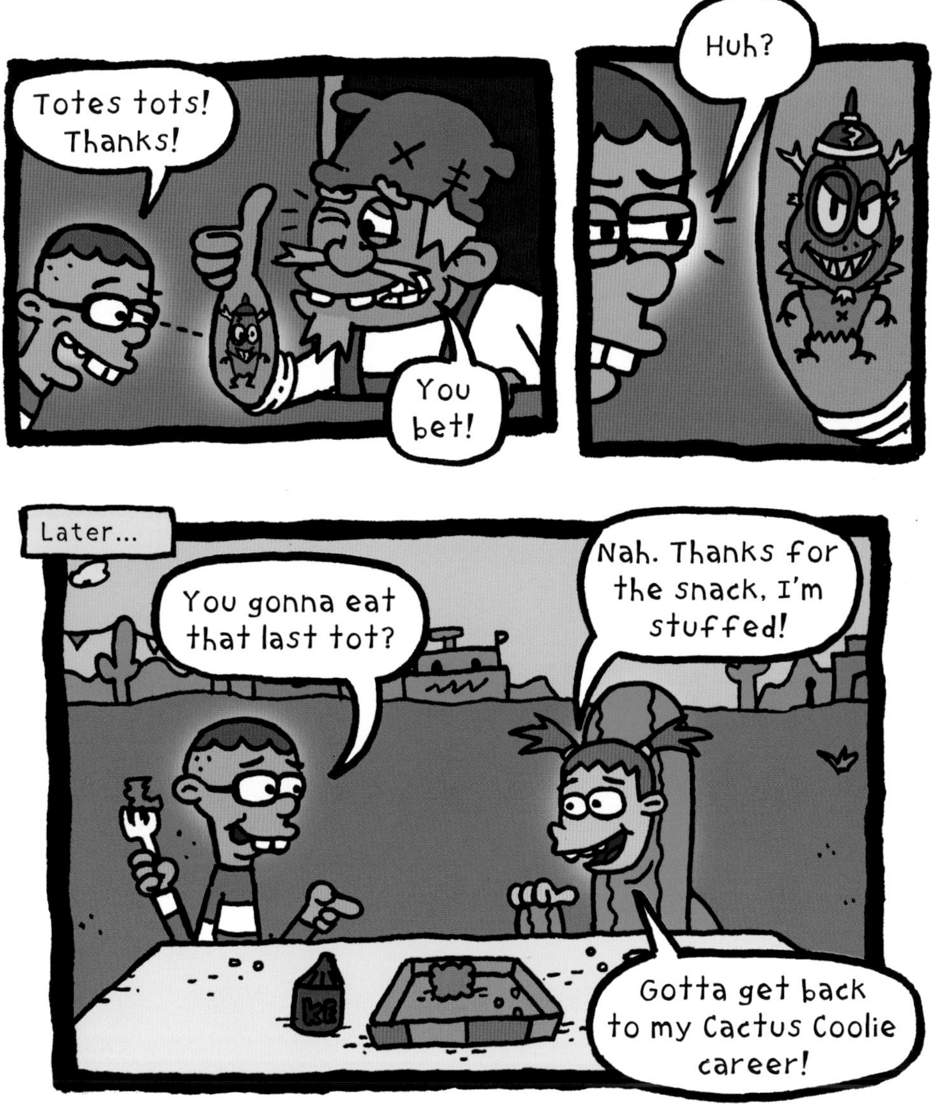
Totes tots! Thanks!
You bet!
Huh?
Later...
You gonna eat that last tot?
Nah. Thanks for the snack, I'm stuffed!
Gotta get back to my Cactus Coolie career!

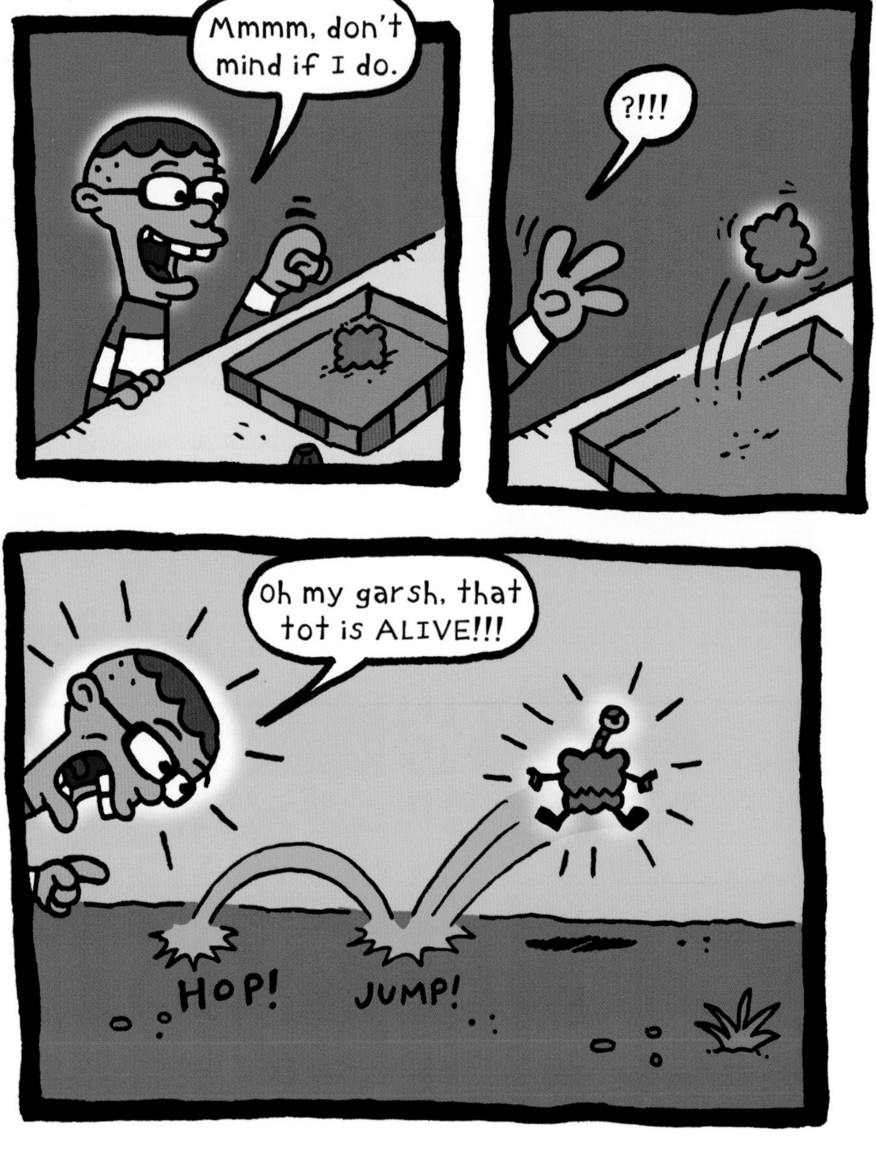
Mmmm, don't mind if I do.
?!!!
Oh my garsh, that tot is ALIVE!!!
HOP!
JUMP!

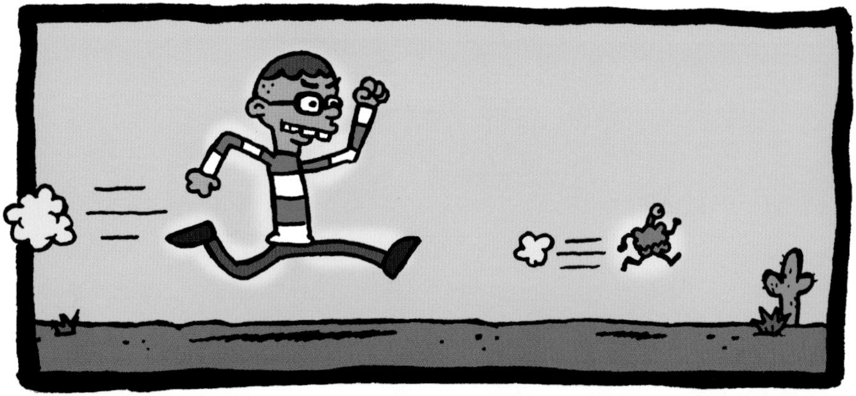

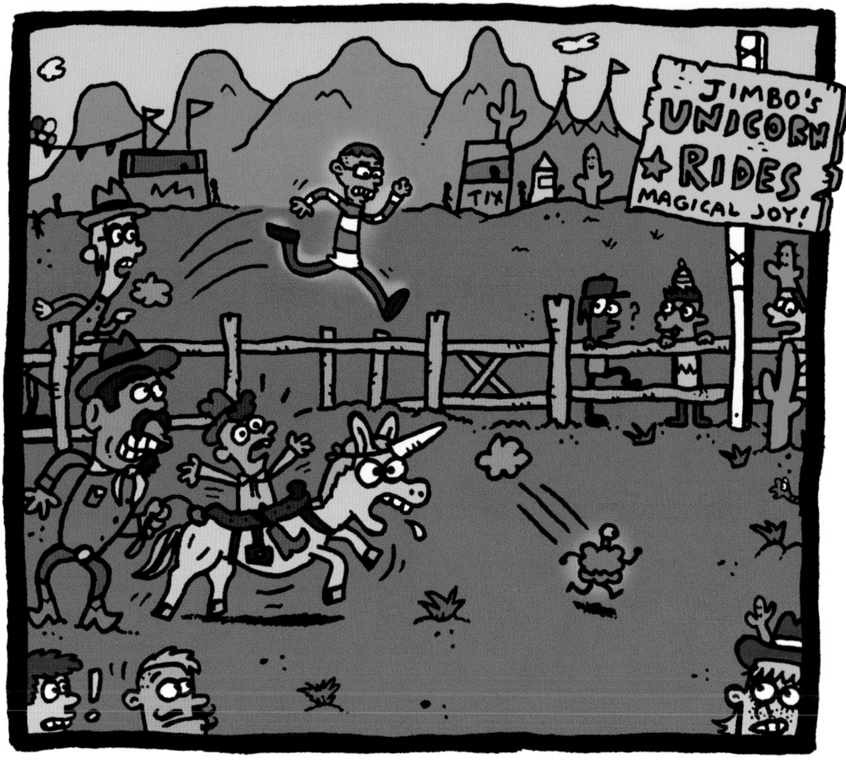
JIMBO'S UNICORN RIDES
MAGICAL JOY!
TIX
?
!

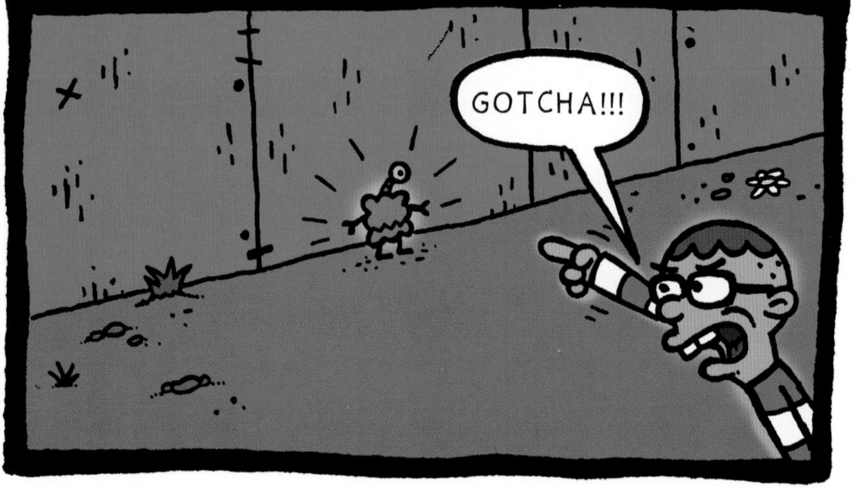
GOTCHA!!!

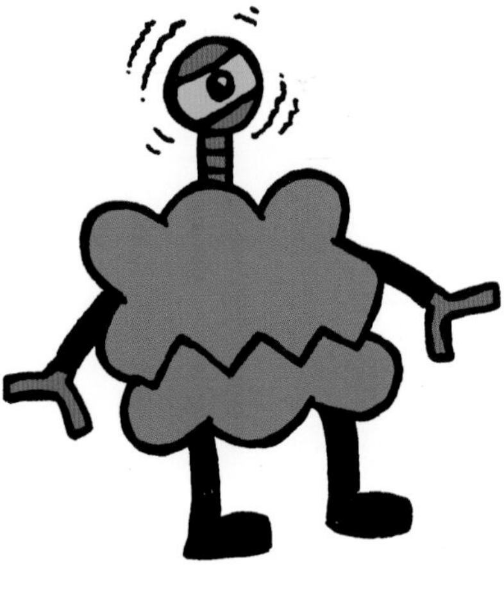

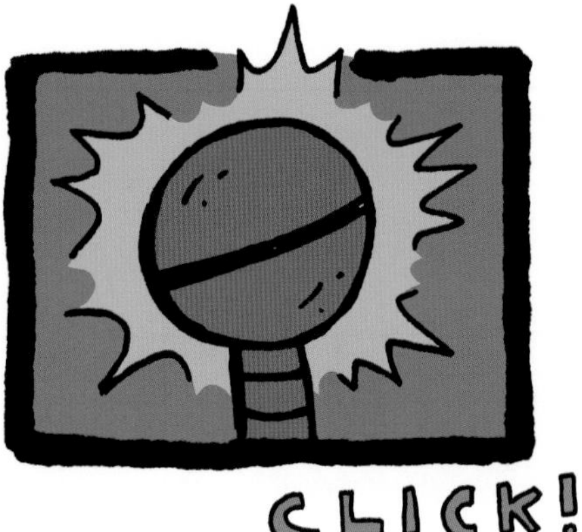
CLICK!

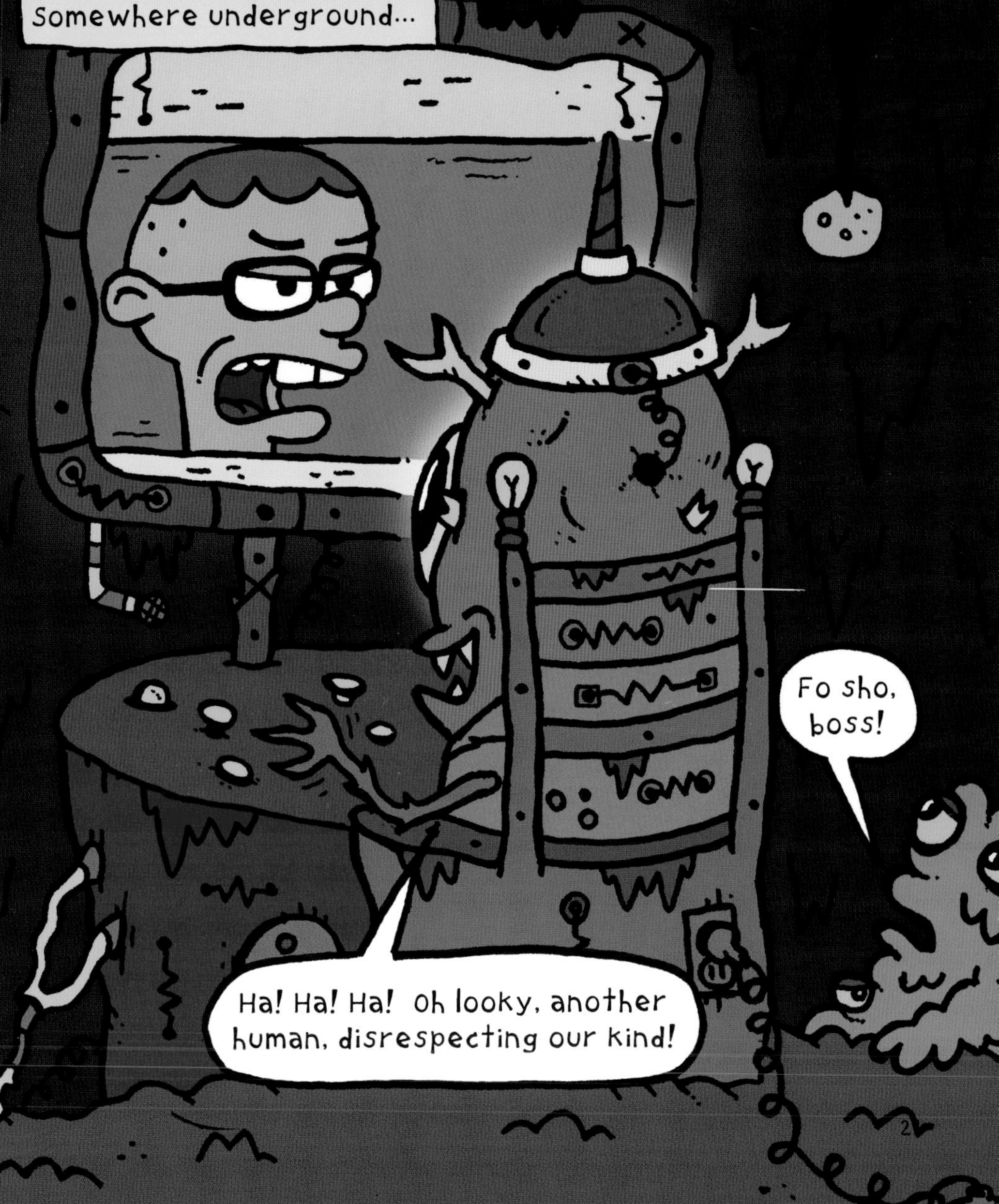
Somewhere underground...
Ha! Ha! Ha! Oh looky, another human, disrespecting our kind!
Fo sho, boss!

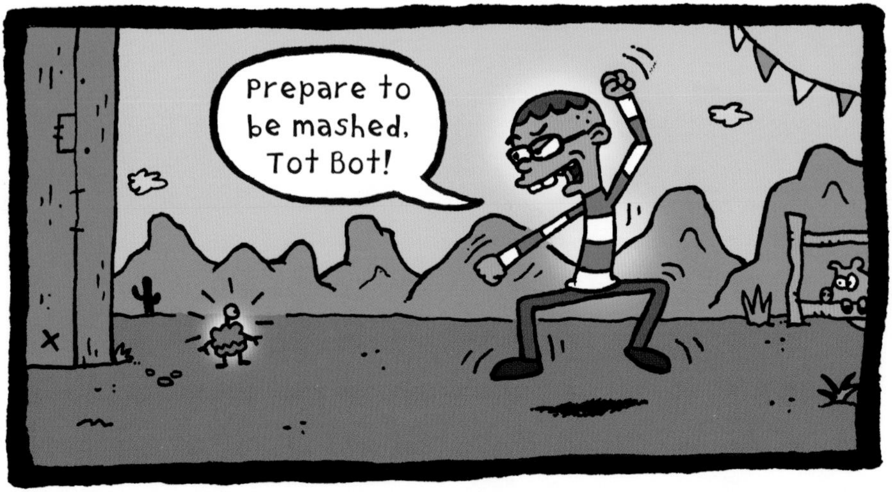
Prepare to be mashed, Tot Bot!

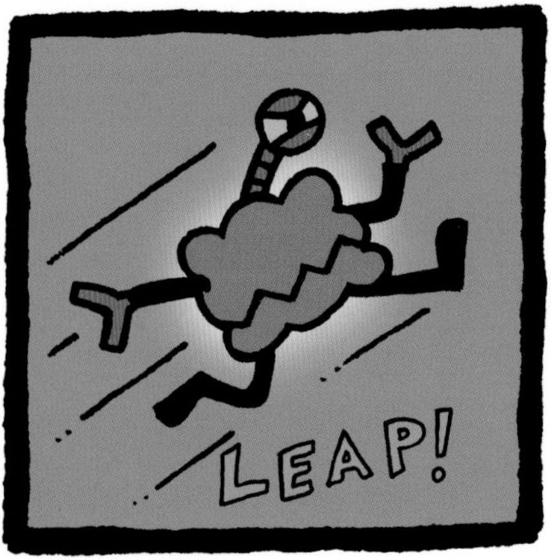
LEAP!

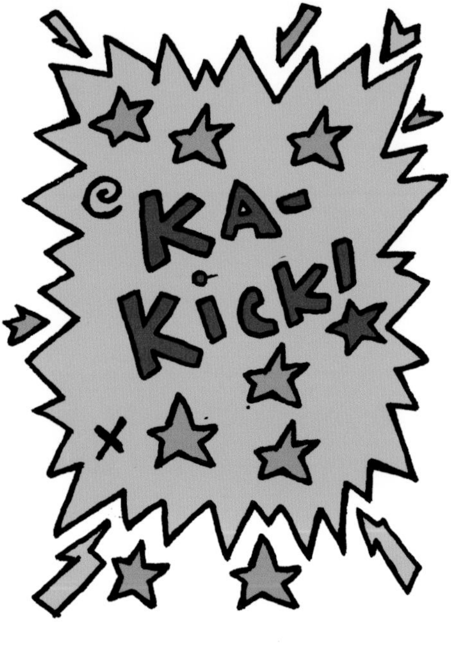
KA-KICK!

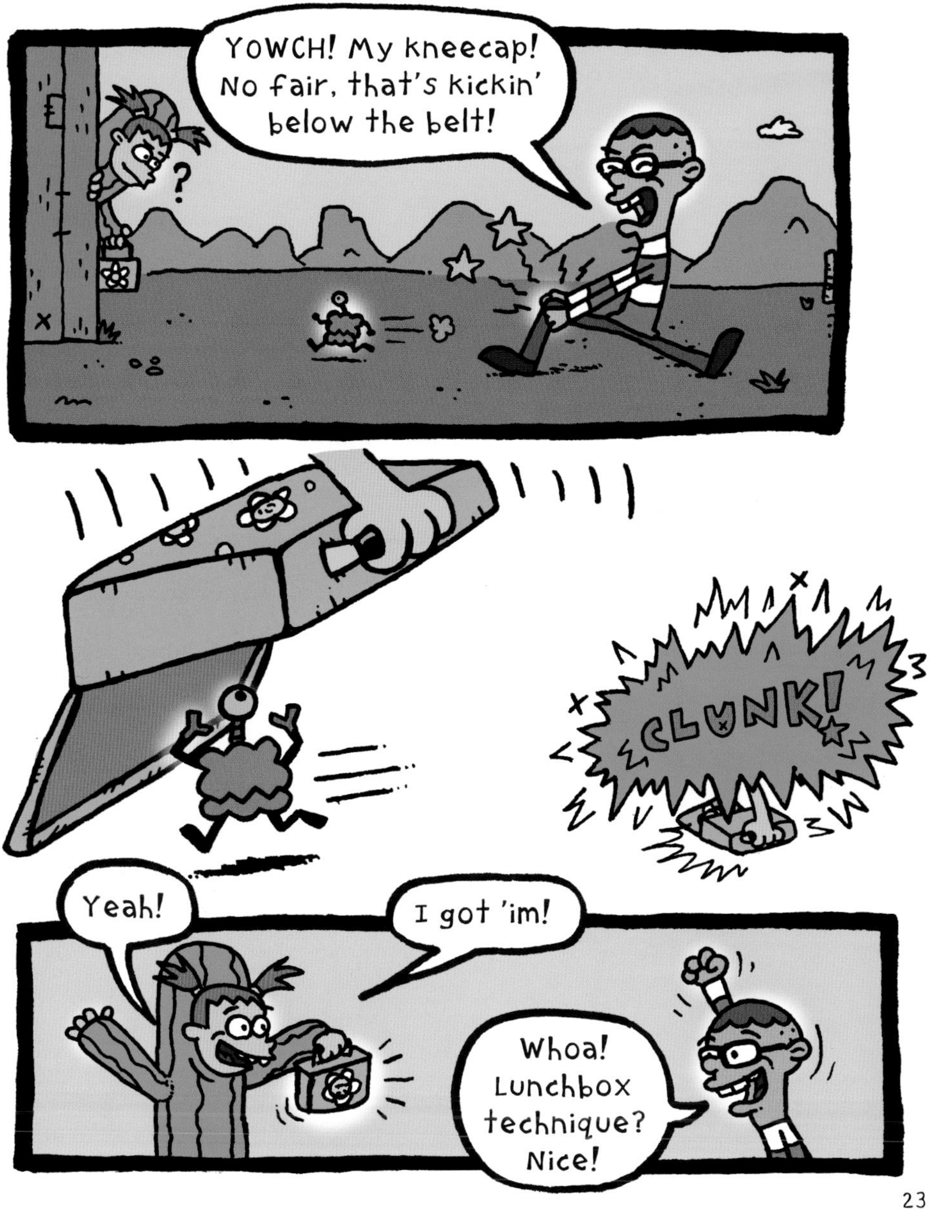
YOWCH! My kneecap! No fair, that's kickin' below the belt!
?
CLUNK!
Yeah!
I got 'im!
Whoa! Lunchbox technique? Nice!

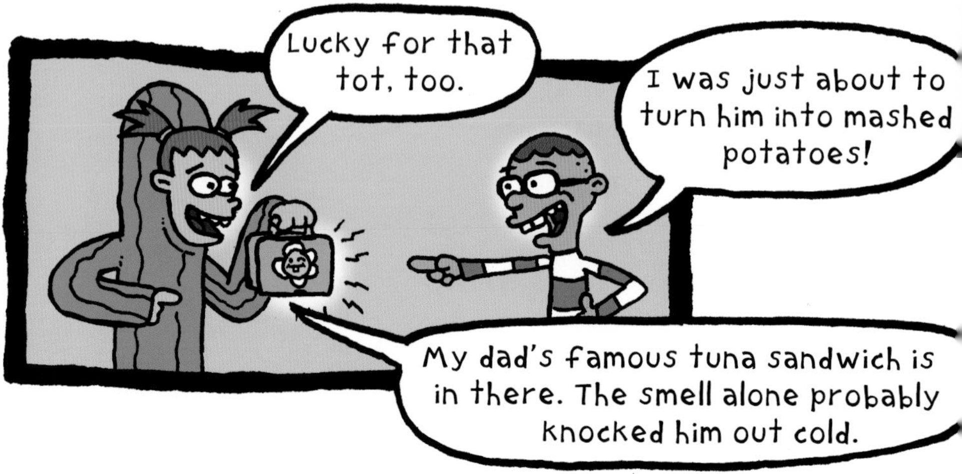
Lucky for that tot, too.
I was just about to turn him into mashed potatoes!
My dad's famous tuna sandwich is in there. The smell alone probably knocked him out cold.

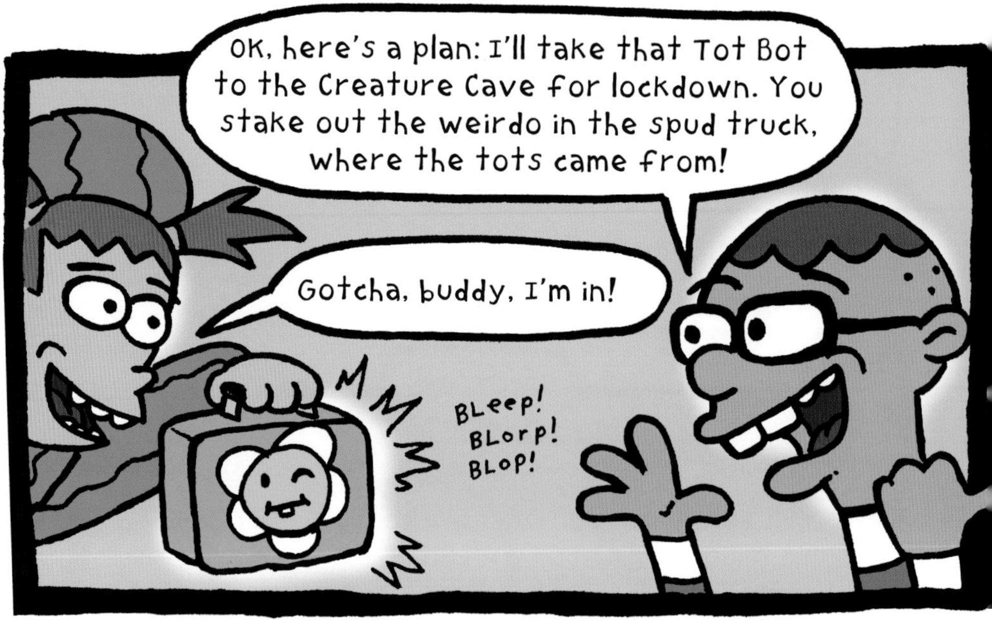
OK, here's a plan: I'll take that Tot Bot to the Creature Cave for lockdown. You stake out the weirdo in the spud truck, where the tots came from!
Gotcha, buddy, I'm in!
BLeep! BLorp! BLop!

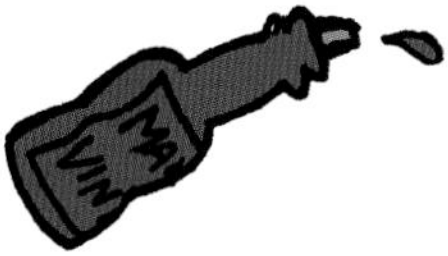

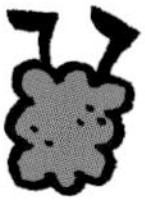

CHAPTER 3

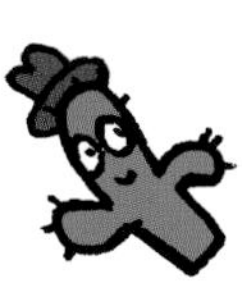

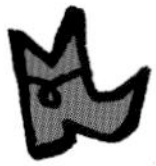

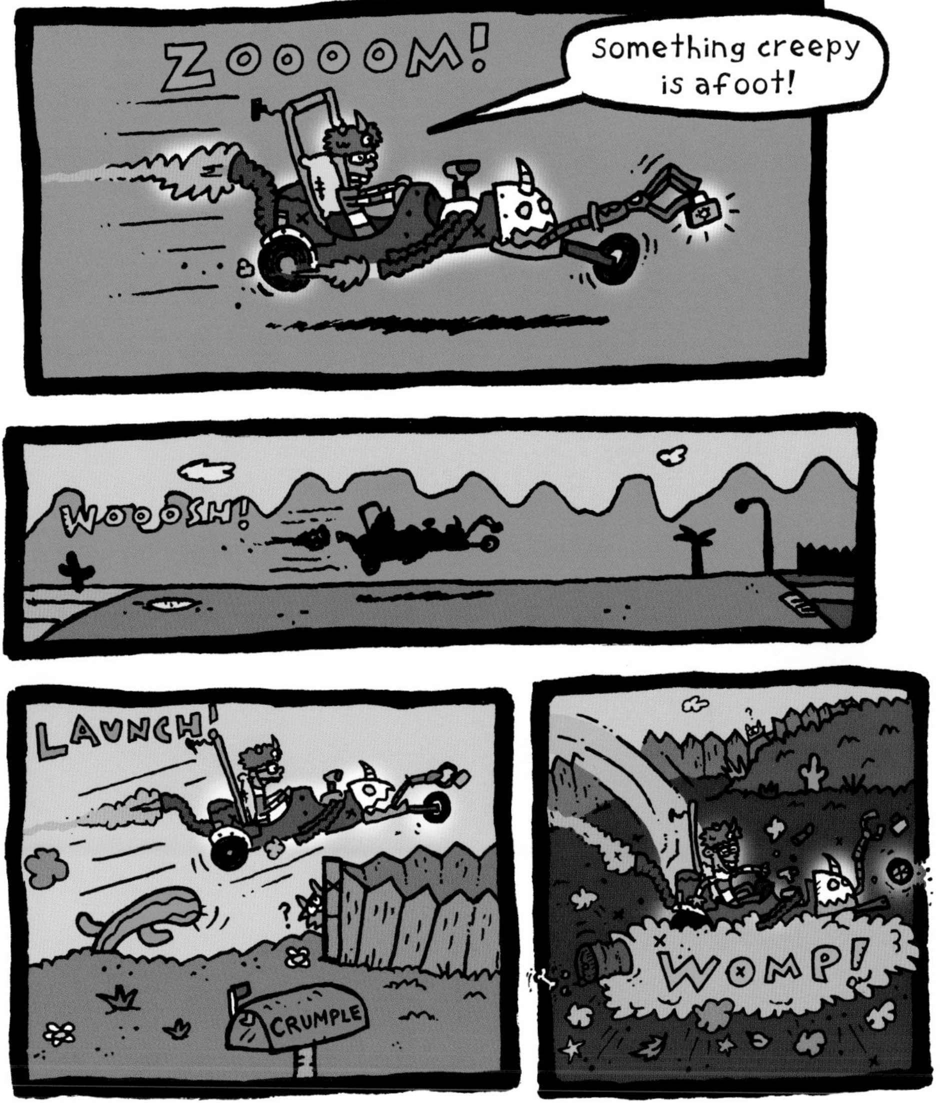
ZOOOOM!
Something creepy is afoot!
WOOOSH!
LAUNCH!
CRUMPLE
WOMP!

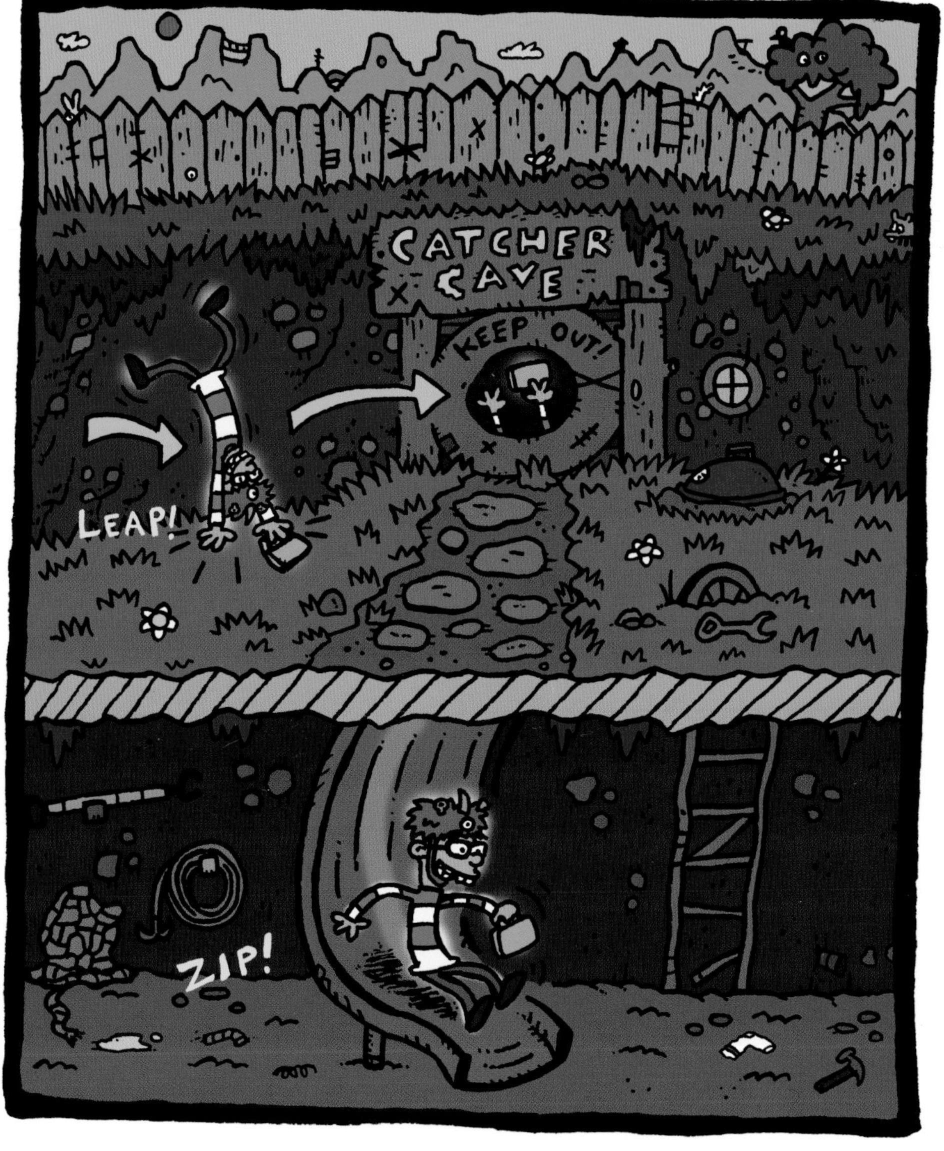
CATCHER CAVE
KEEP OUT!
LEAP!
ZIP!

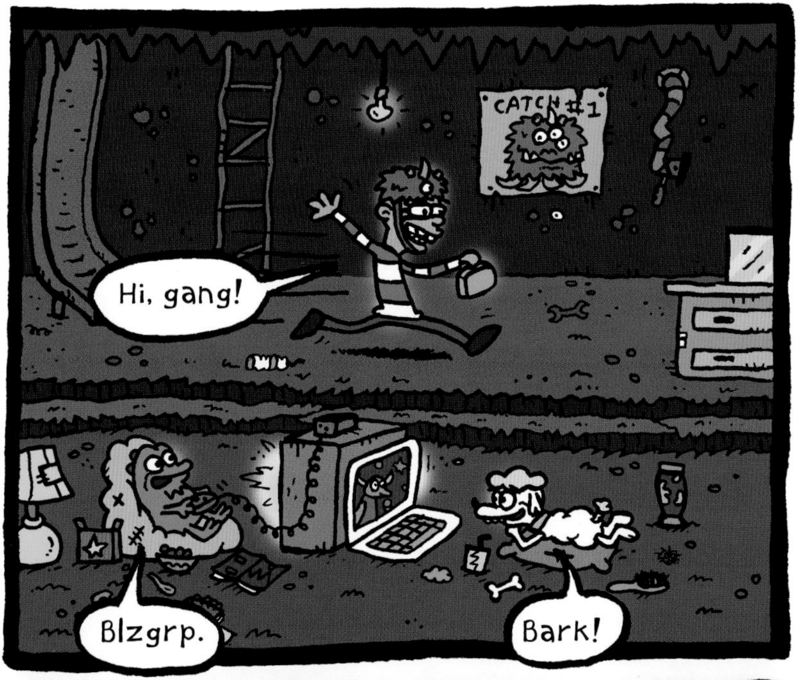
CATCH #1
Hi, gang!
Blzgrp.
Bark!

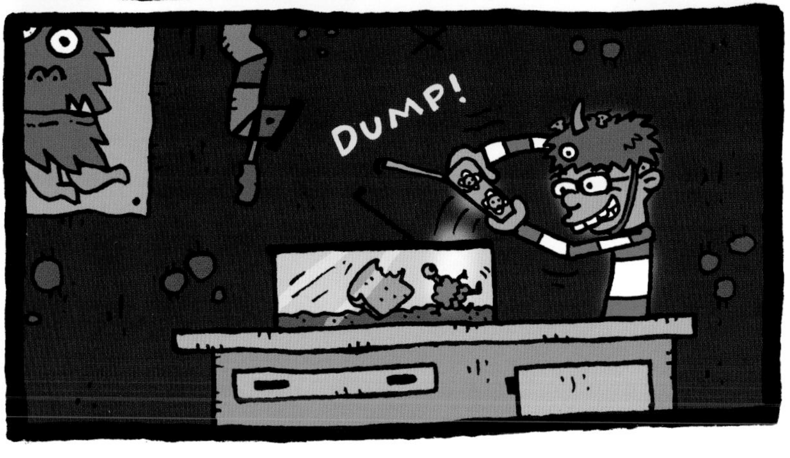
DUMP!

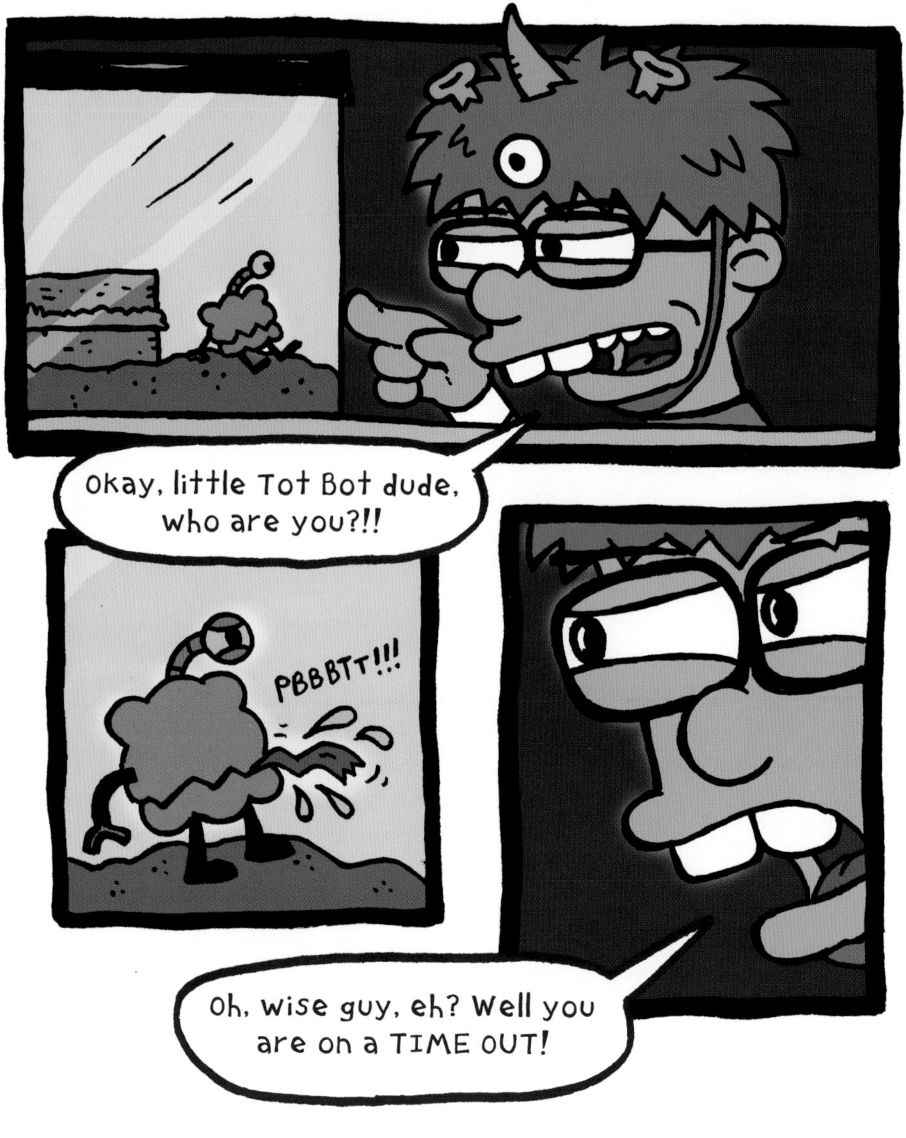
Okay, little Tot Bot dude, who are you?!!
PBBBTT!!!
Oh, wise guy, eh? Well you are on a TIME OUT!

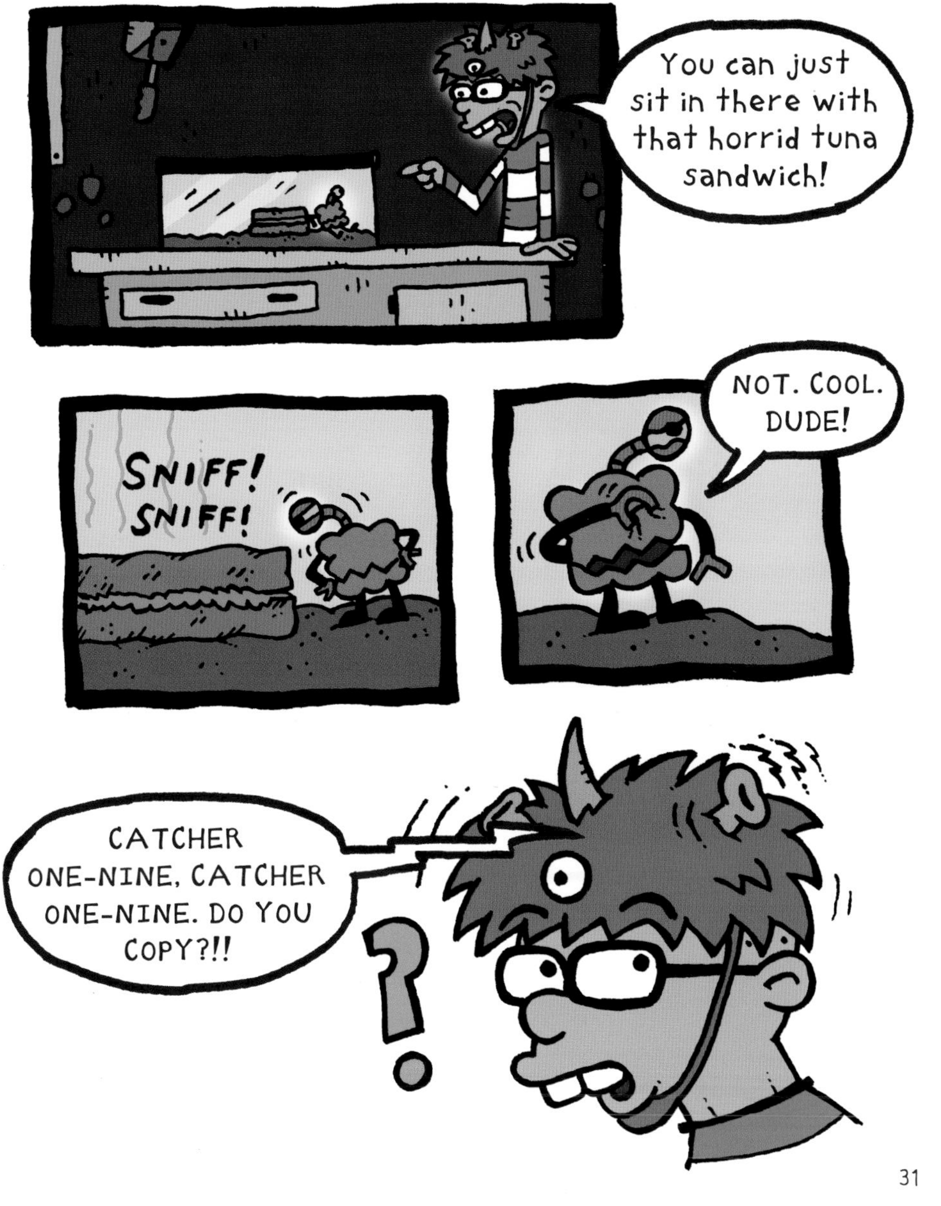
You can just sit in there with that horrid tuna sandwich!
SNIFF! SNIFF!
NOT. COOL. DUDE!
CATCHER ONE-NINE, CATCHER ONE-NINE. DO YOU COPY?!!

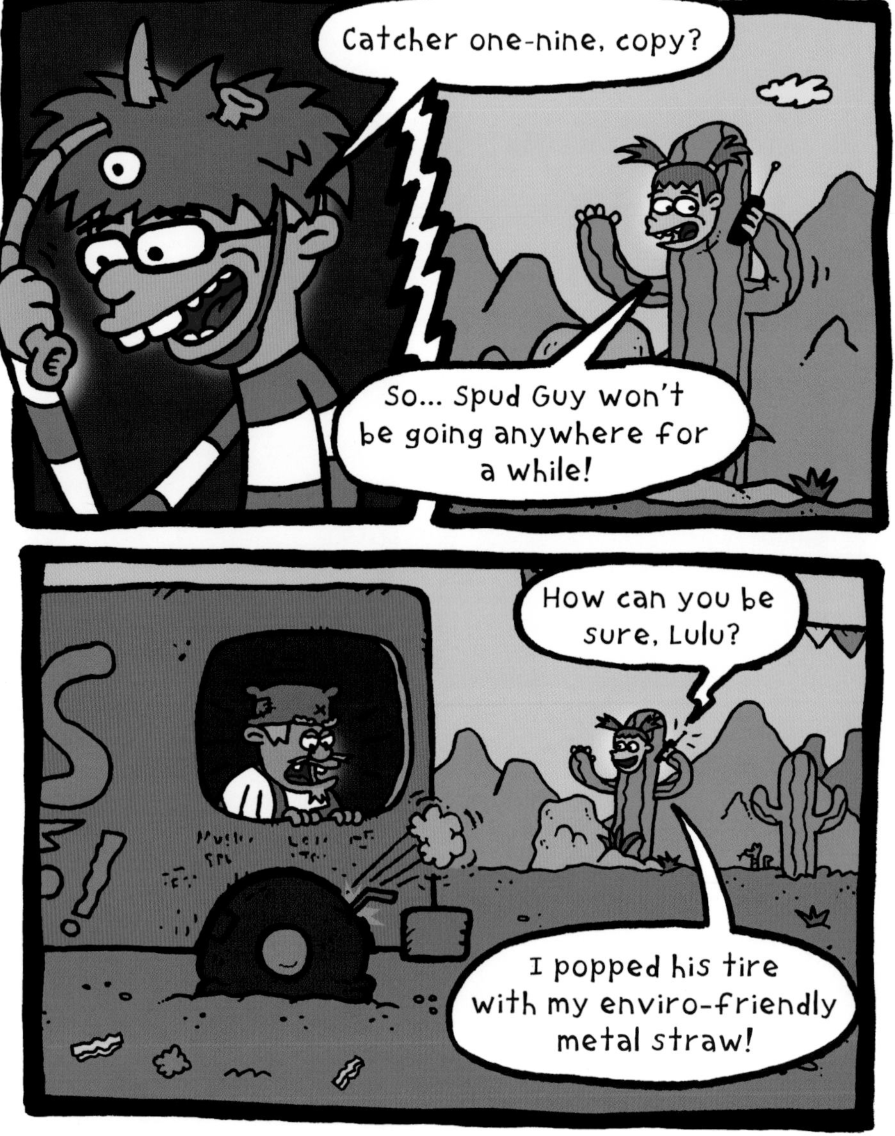
Catcher one-nine, copy?
So... Spud Guy won't be going anywhere for a while!
How can you be sure, Lulu?
I popped his tire with my enviro-friendly metal straw!

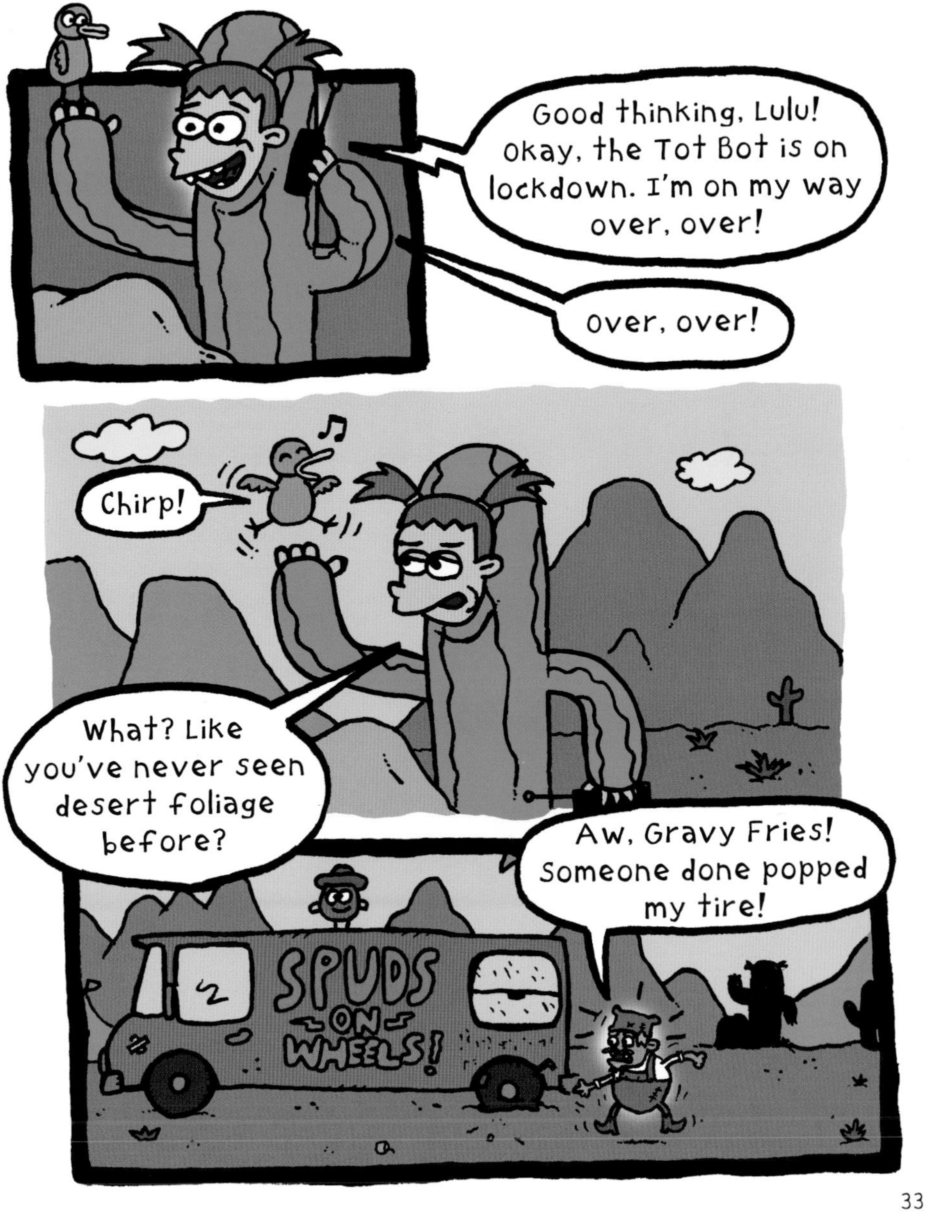
Good thinking, Lulu! Okay, the Tot Bot is on lockdown. I'm on my way over, over!
Over, over!
Chirp!
What? Like you've never seen desert foliage before?
Aw, Gravy Fries! Someone done popped my tire!
SPUDS ON WHEELS!

Okay, team. I gotta scram and go investigate that spud truck. Guard this cage.

And make sure this Tot Bot doesn't escape!

ZIP!

CATCHER CAVE

KEEP OUT

DASH!

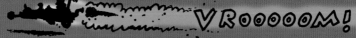

VROOOOOM!

34

CHAPTER 4

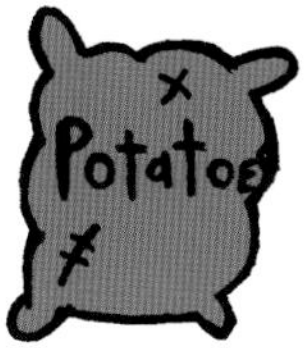
Potatoes

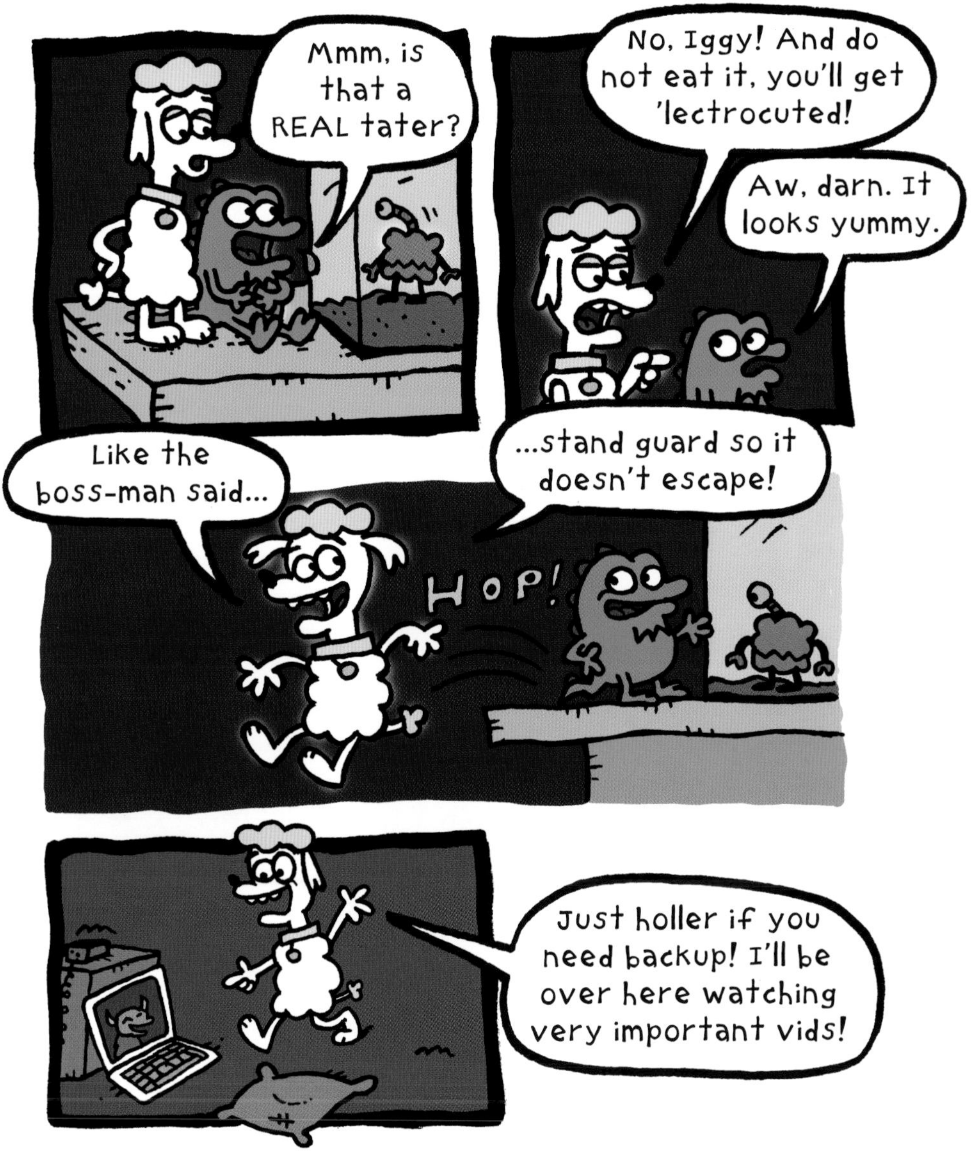
Mmm, is that a REAL tater?
No, Iggy! And do not eat it, you'll get 'lectrocuted!
Aw, darn. It looks yummy.
Like the boss-man said...
...stand guard so it doesn't escape!
HOP!
Just holler if you need backup! I'll be over here watching very important vids!

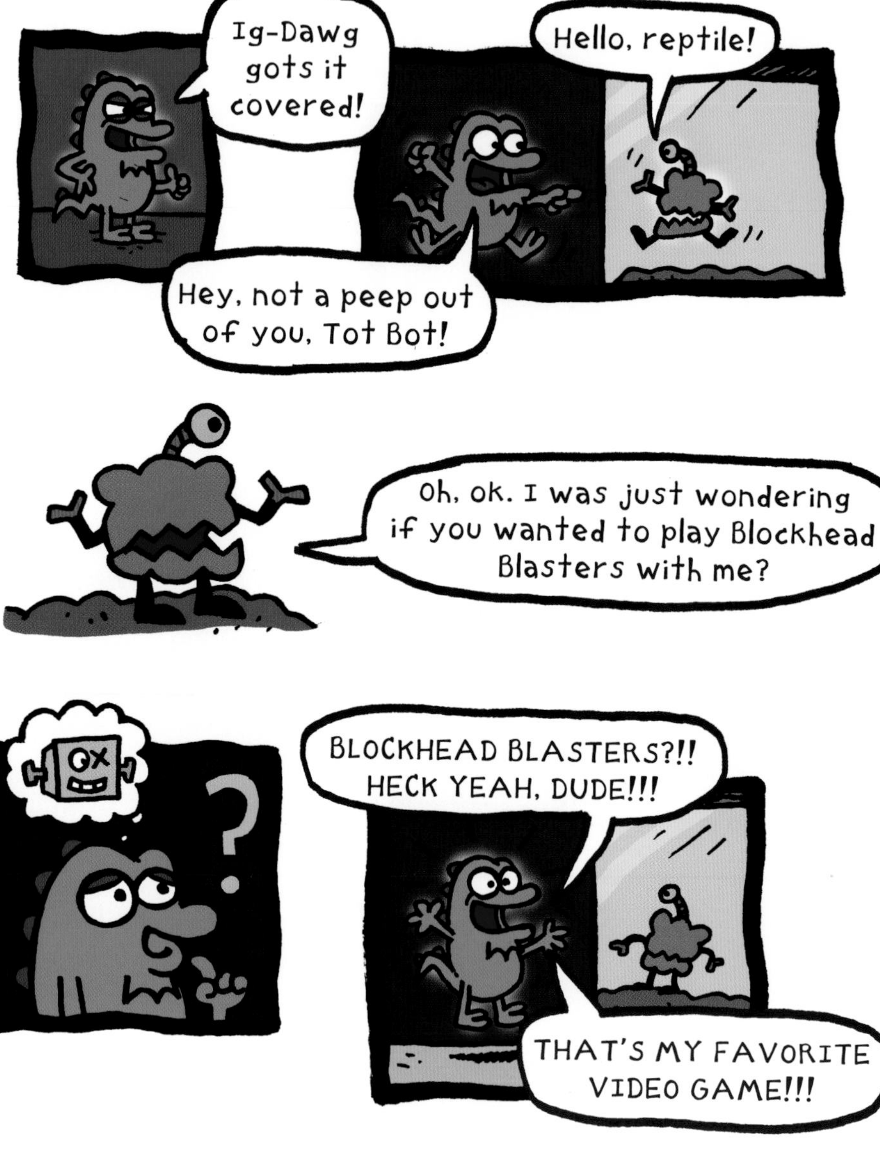
Ig-Dawg gots it covered!
Hello, reptile!
Hey, not a peep out of you, Tot Bot!
Oh, ok. I was just wondering if you wanted to play Blockhead Blasters with me?
BLOCKHEAD BLASTERS?!! HECK YEAH, DUDE!!!
THAT'S MY FAVORITE VIDEO GAME!!!

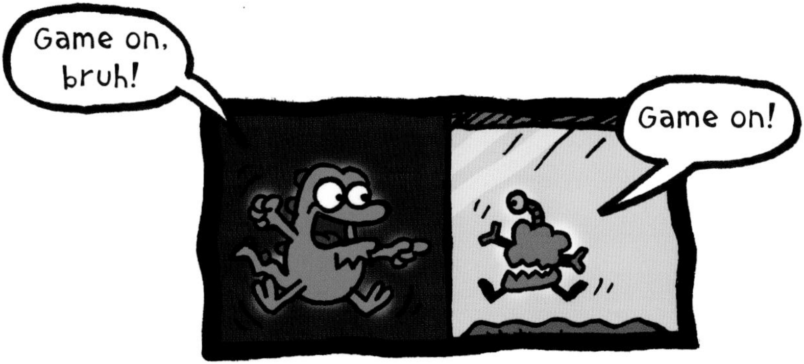
Game on, bruh!
Game on!

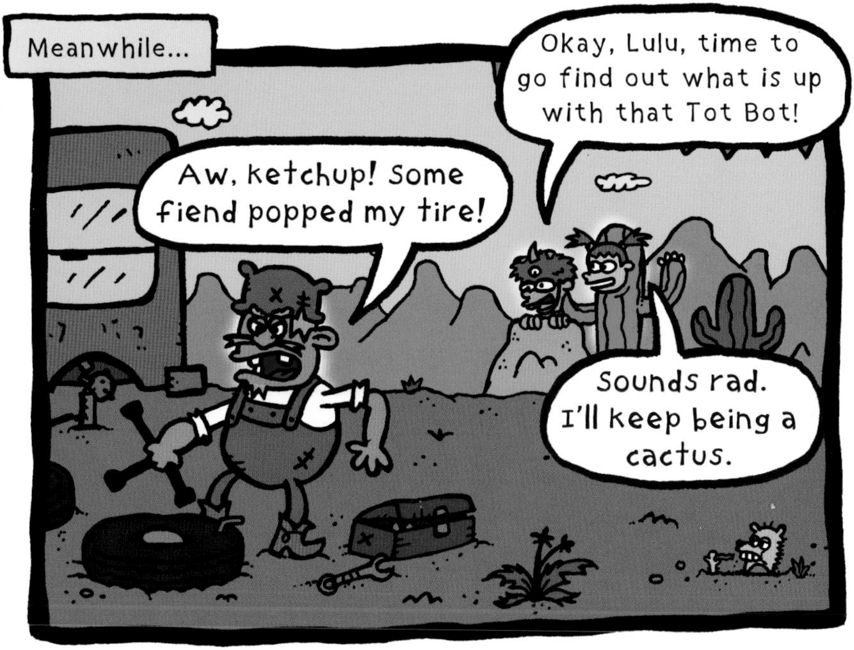
Meanwhile...
Aw, ketchup! Some fiend popped my tire!
Okay, Lulu, time to go find out what is up with that Tot Bot!
Sounds rad. I'll keep being a cactus.

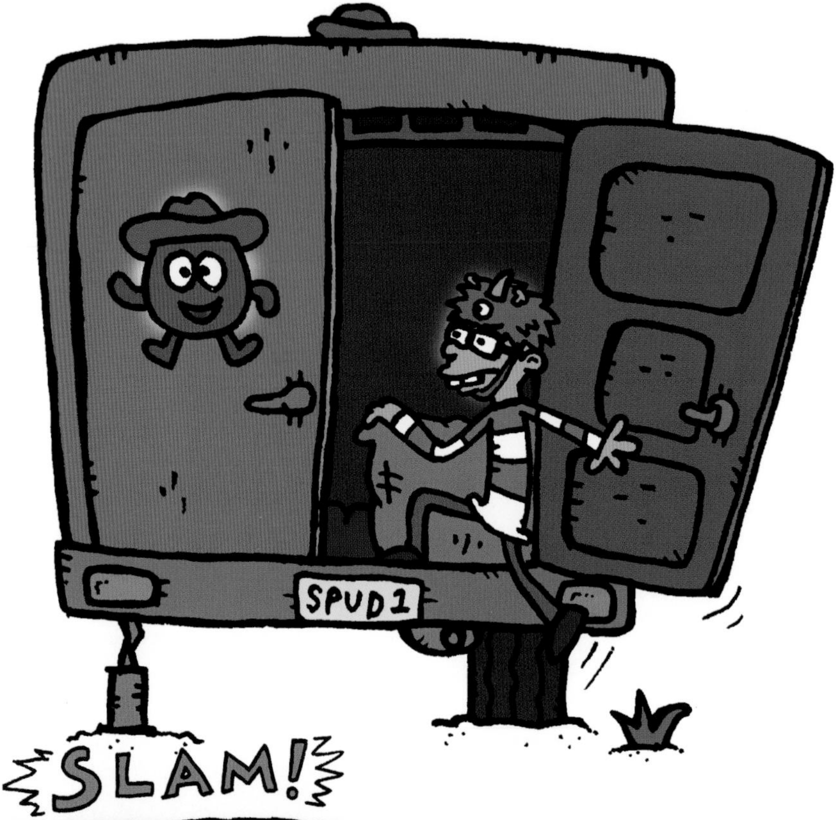
SPUD 1
SLAM!

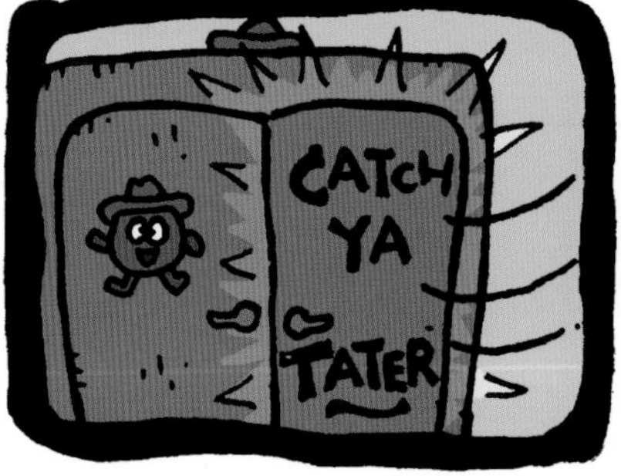
CATCH YA TATER

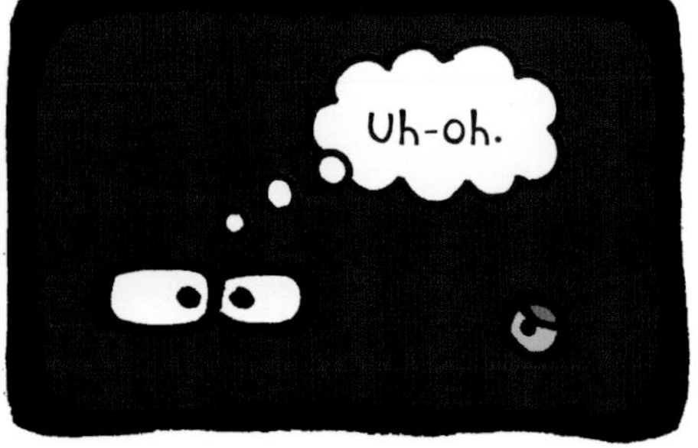
Uh-oh.

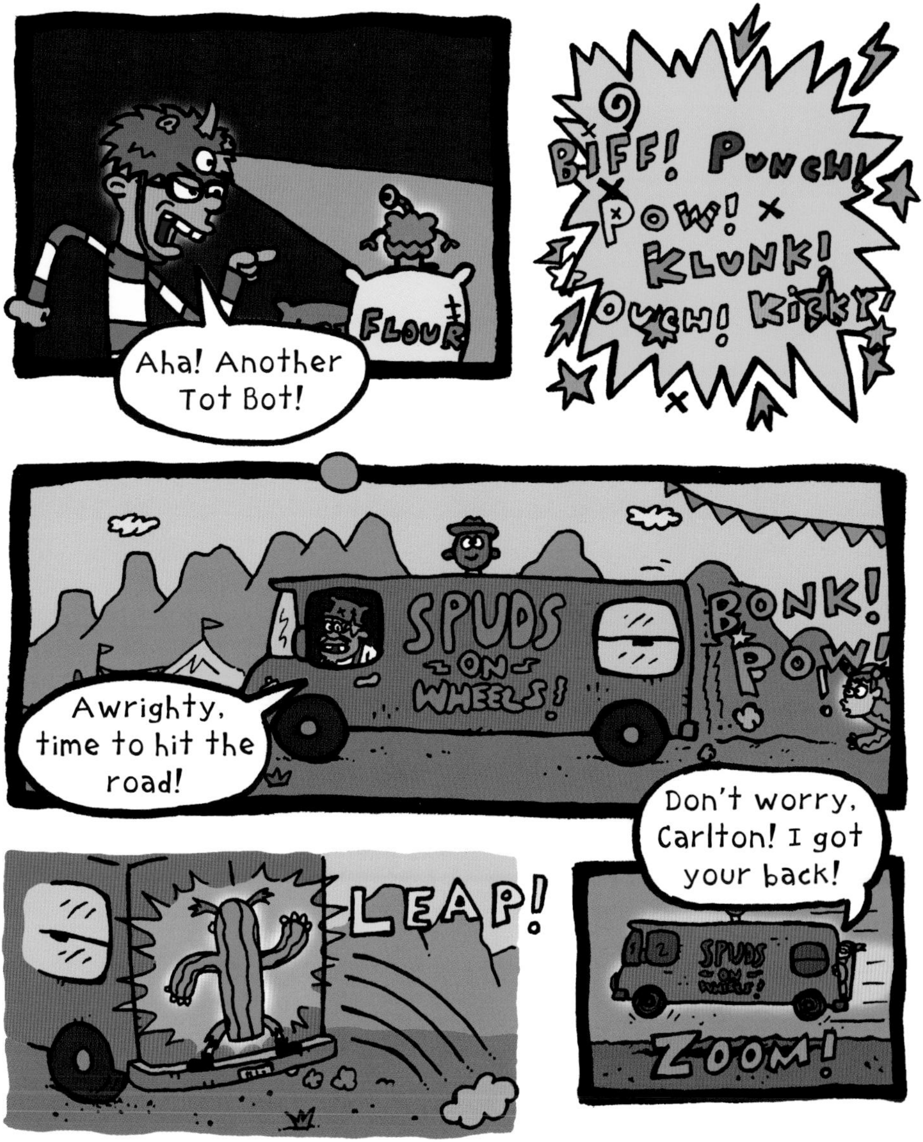

Aha! Another Tot Bot!
FLOUR
BIFF! PUNCH! POW! KLUNK! OUCH! KICK!
SPUDS -ON- WHEELS!
BONK! POW!
Awrighty, time to hit the road!
LEAP!
Don't worry, Carlton! I got your back!
ZOOM!

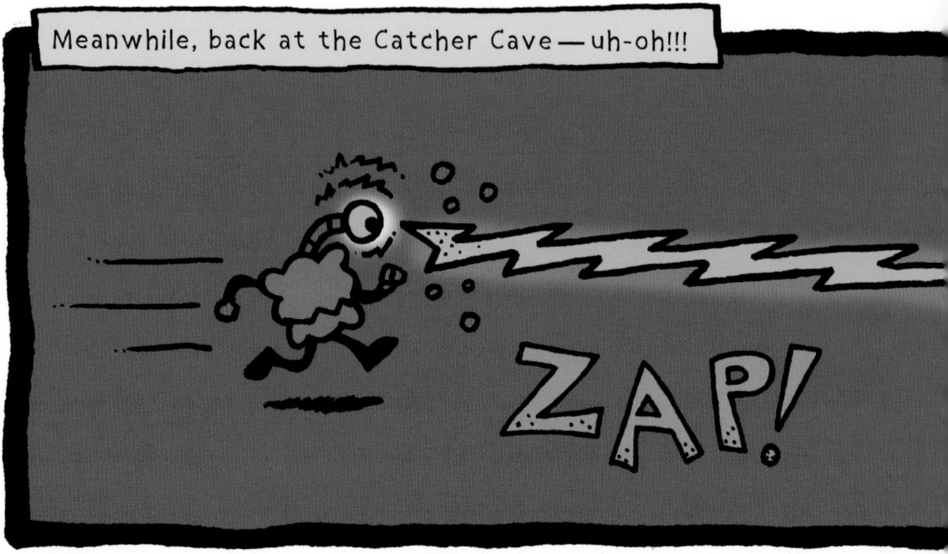
Meanwhile, back at the Catcher Cave—uh-oh!!!
ZAP!

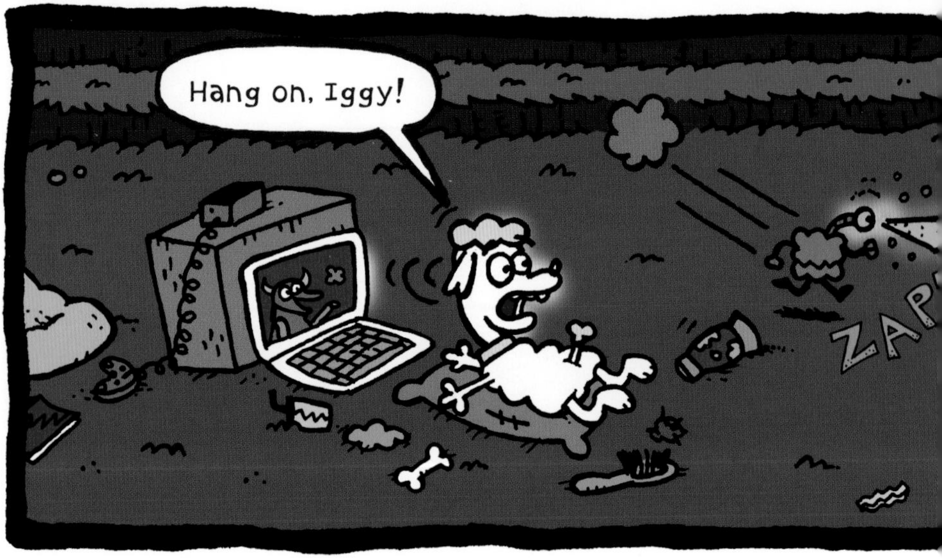
Hang on, Iggy!

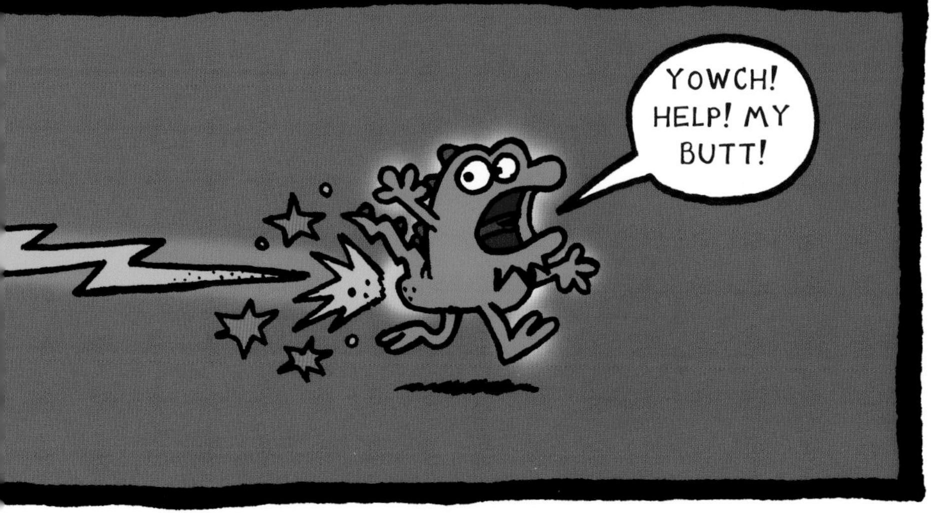
YOWCH! HELP! MY BUTT!

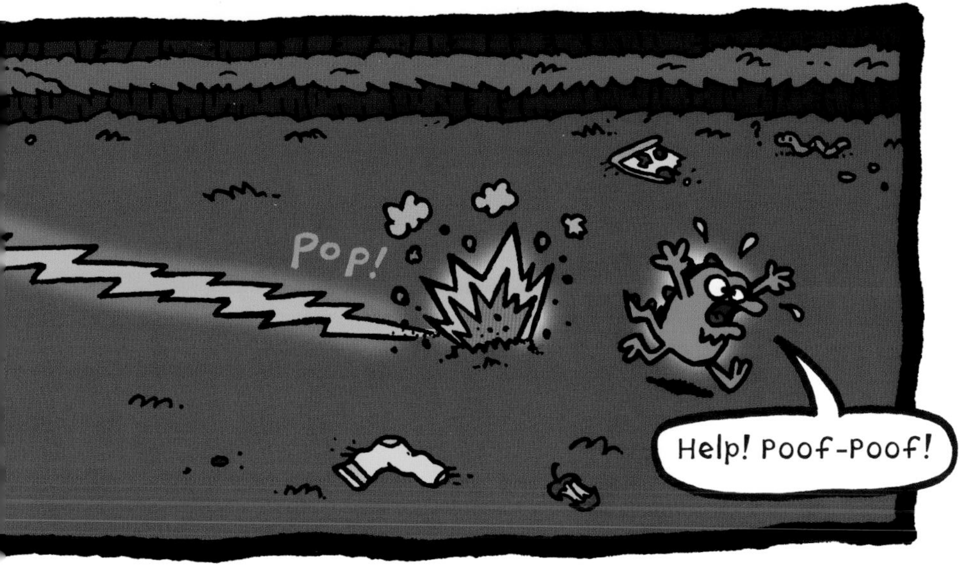
POP!
Help! Poof-Poof!

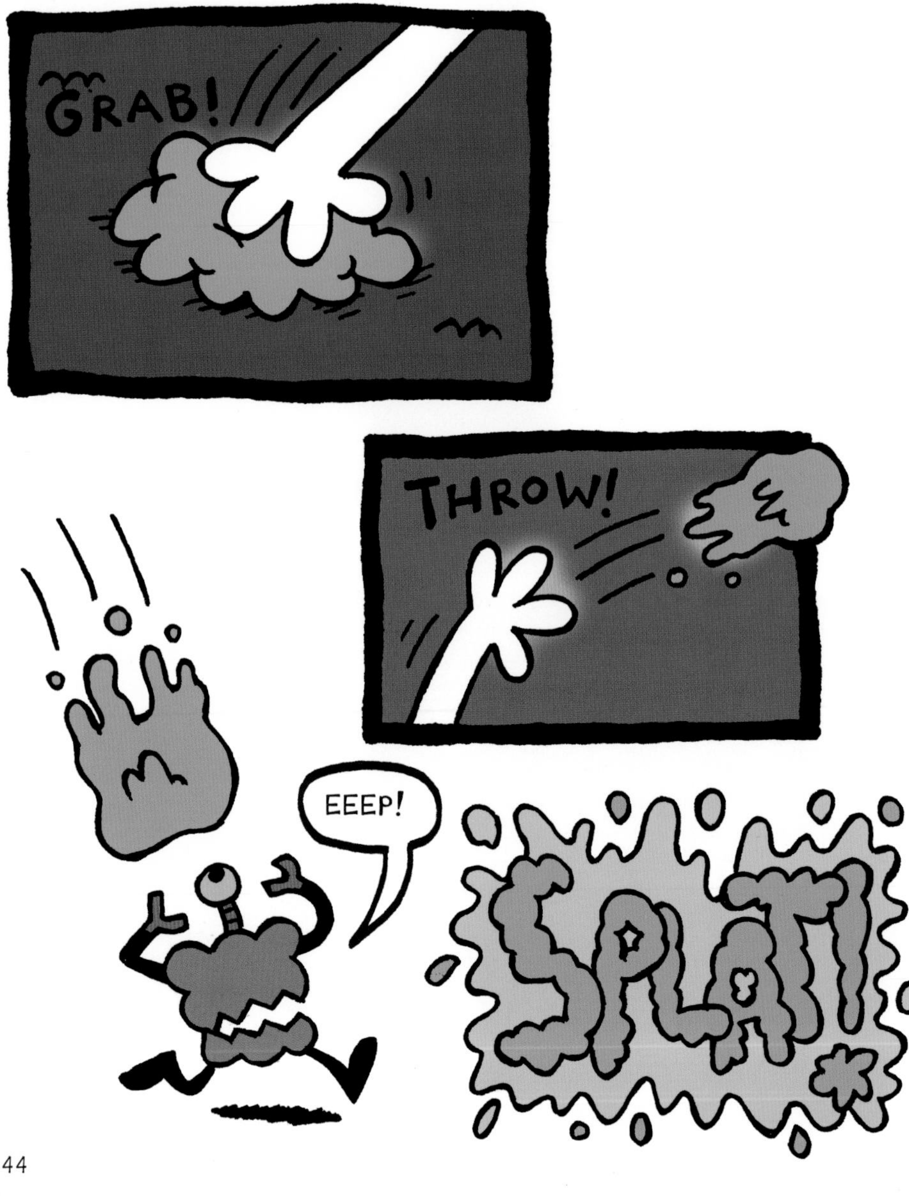
GRAB!
THROW!
EEEP!
SPLAT!

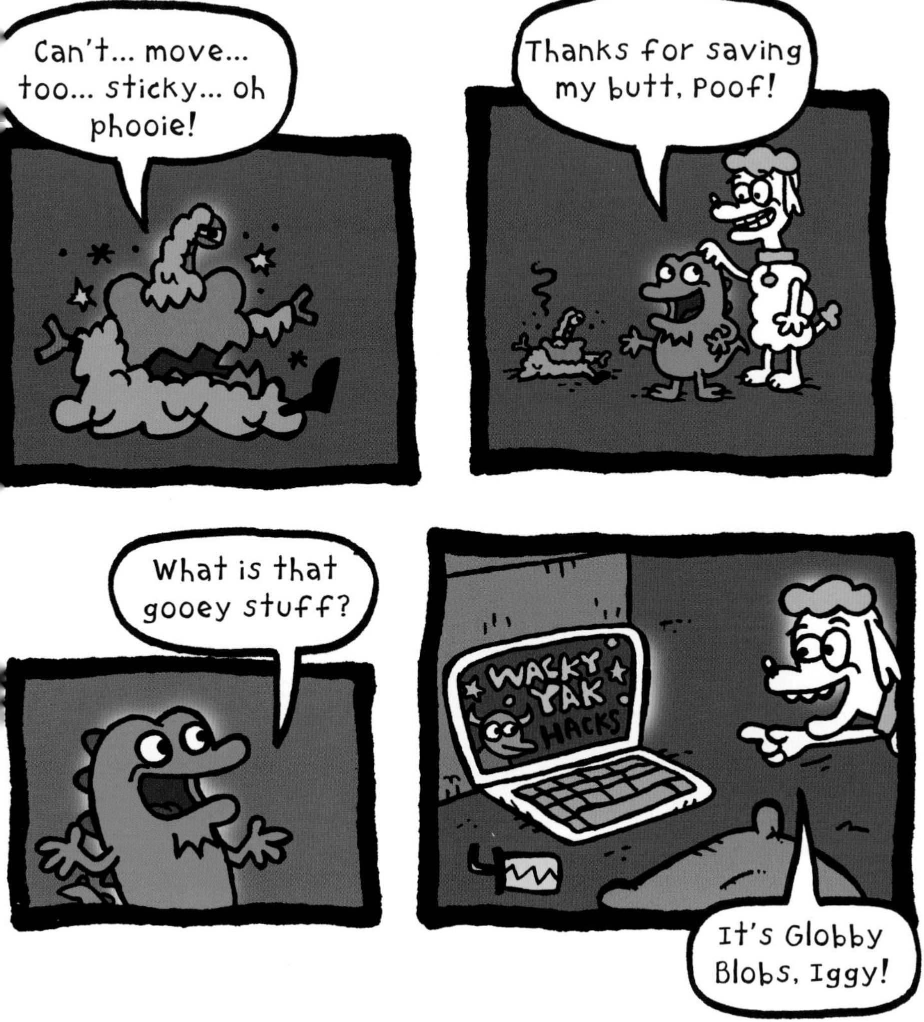
Can't... move... too... sticky... oh phooie!
Thanks for saving my butt, Poof!
What is that gooey stuff?
WACKY YAK HACKS
It's Globby Blobs, Iggy!

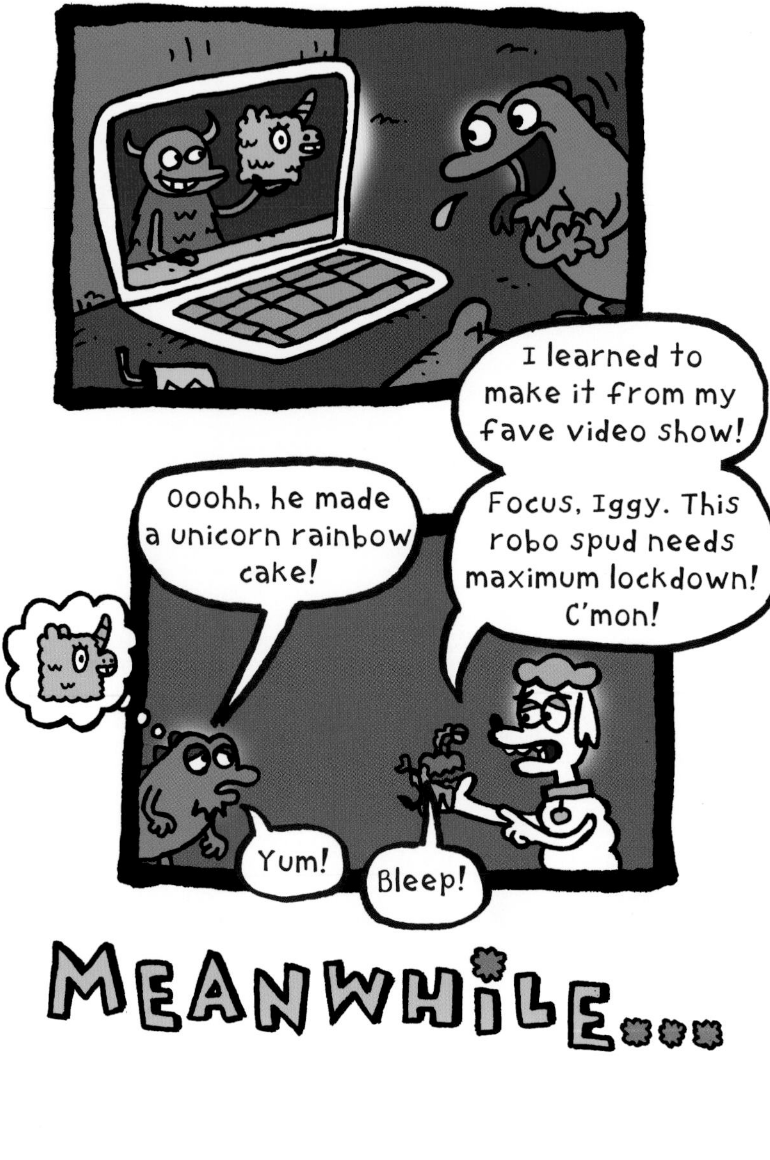
I learned to make it from my fave video show!
Ooohh, he made a unicorn rainbow cake!
Focus, Iggy. This robo spud needs maximum lockdown! C'mon!
Yum!
Bleep!

MEANWHILE...

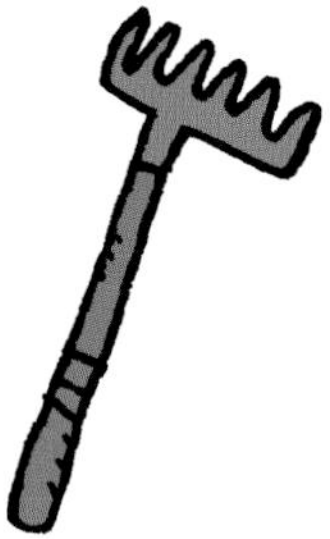

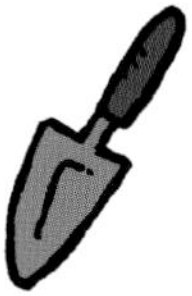

CHAPTER 5

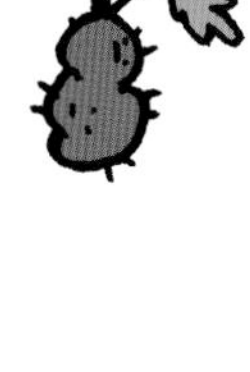

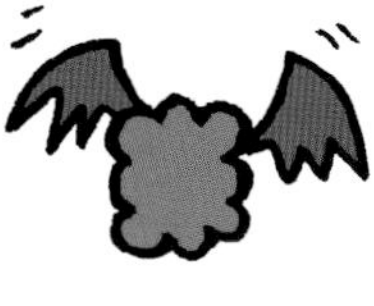

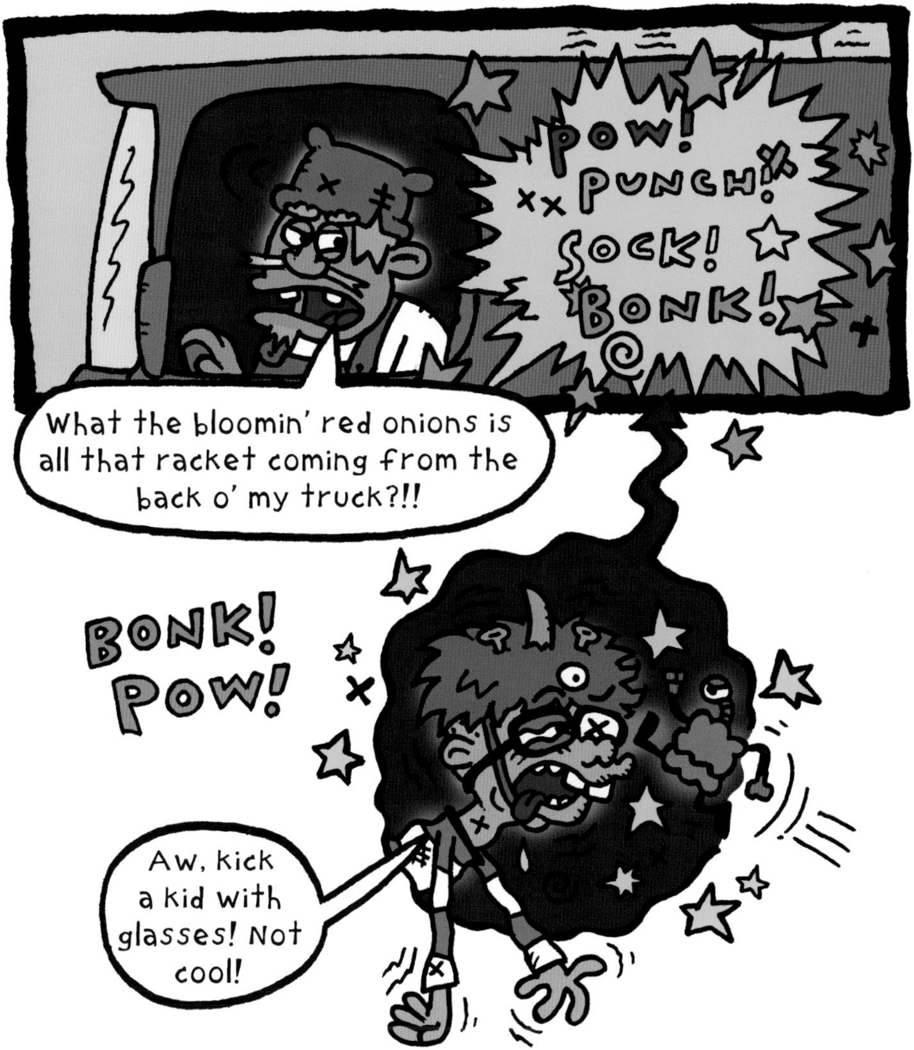
POW! PUNCH! SOCK! BONK!
What the bloomin' red onions is all that racket coming from the back o' my truck?!!
BONK! POW!
Aw, kick a kid with glasses! Not cool!

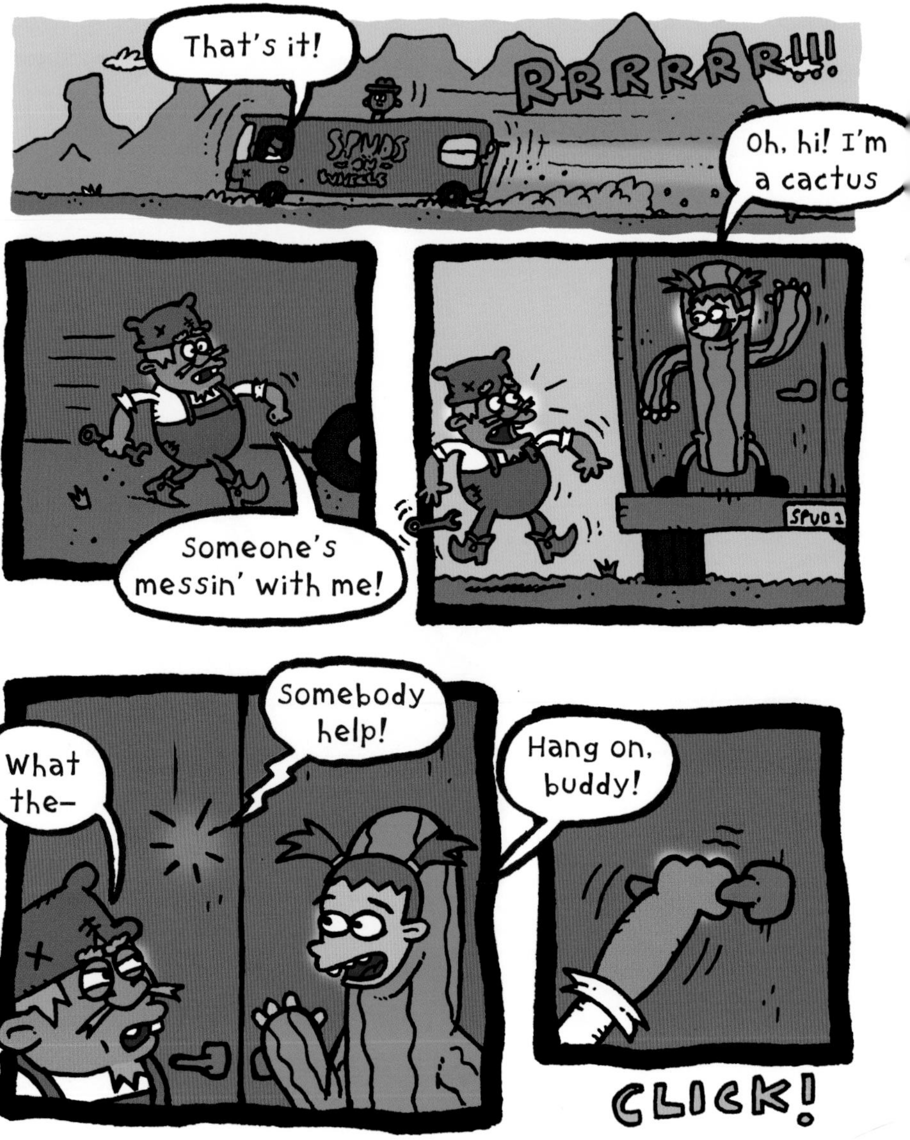
That's it!
RRRRRR!!!
Oh, hi! I'm a cactus
Someone's messin' with me!
What the-
Somebody help!
Hang on, buddy!
CLICK!

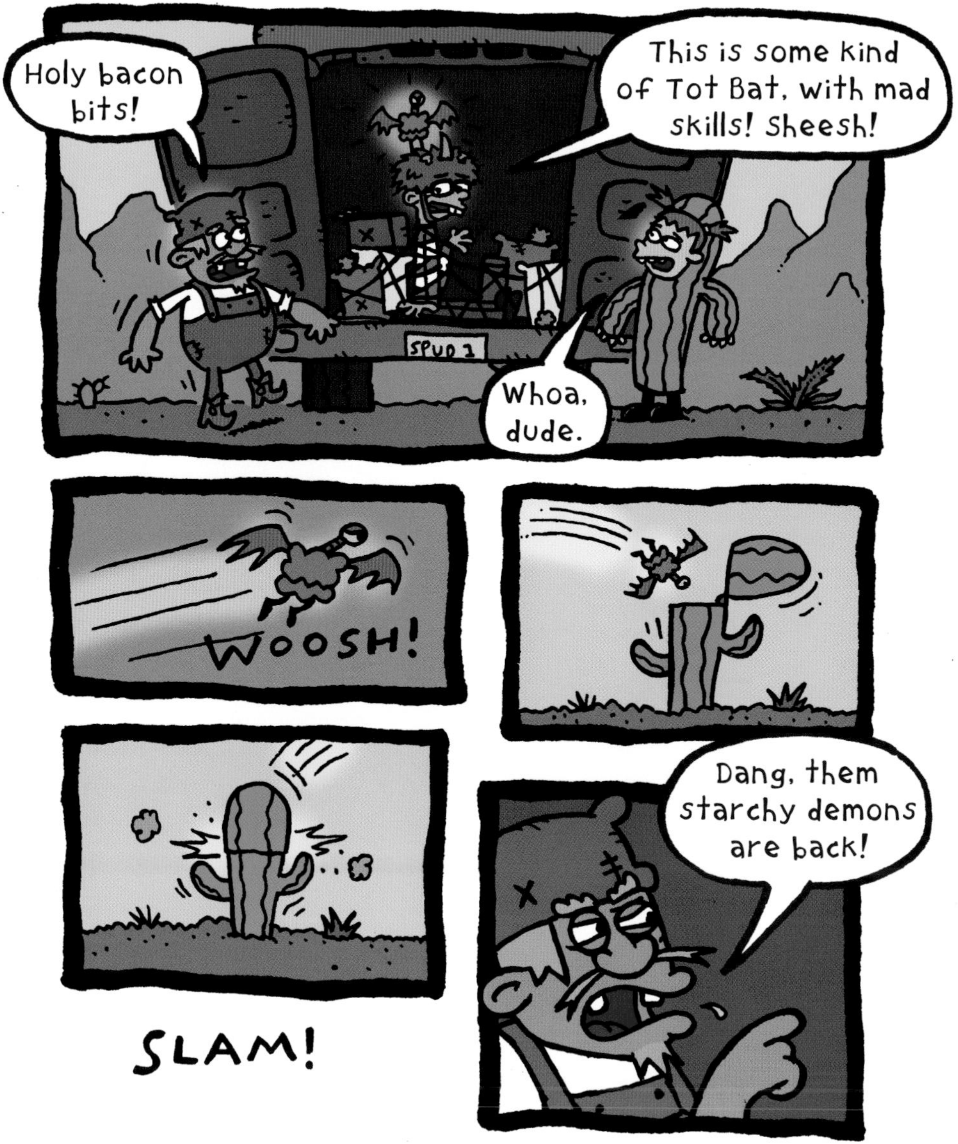
Holy bacon bits!
This is some kind of Tot Bat, with mad skills! Sheesh!
SPUD 1
Whoa, dude.
WOOSH!
SLAM!
Dang, them starchy demons are back!

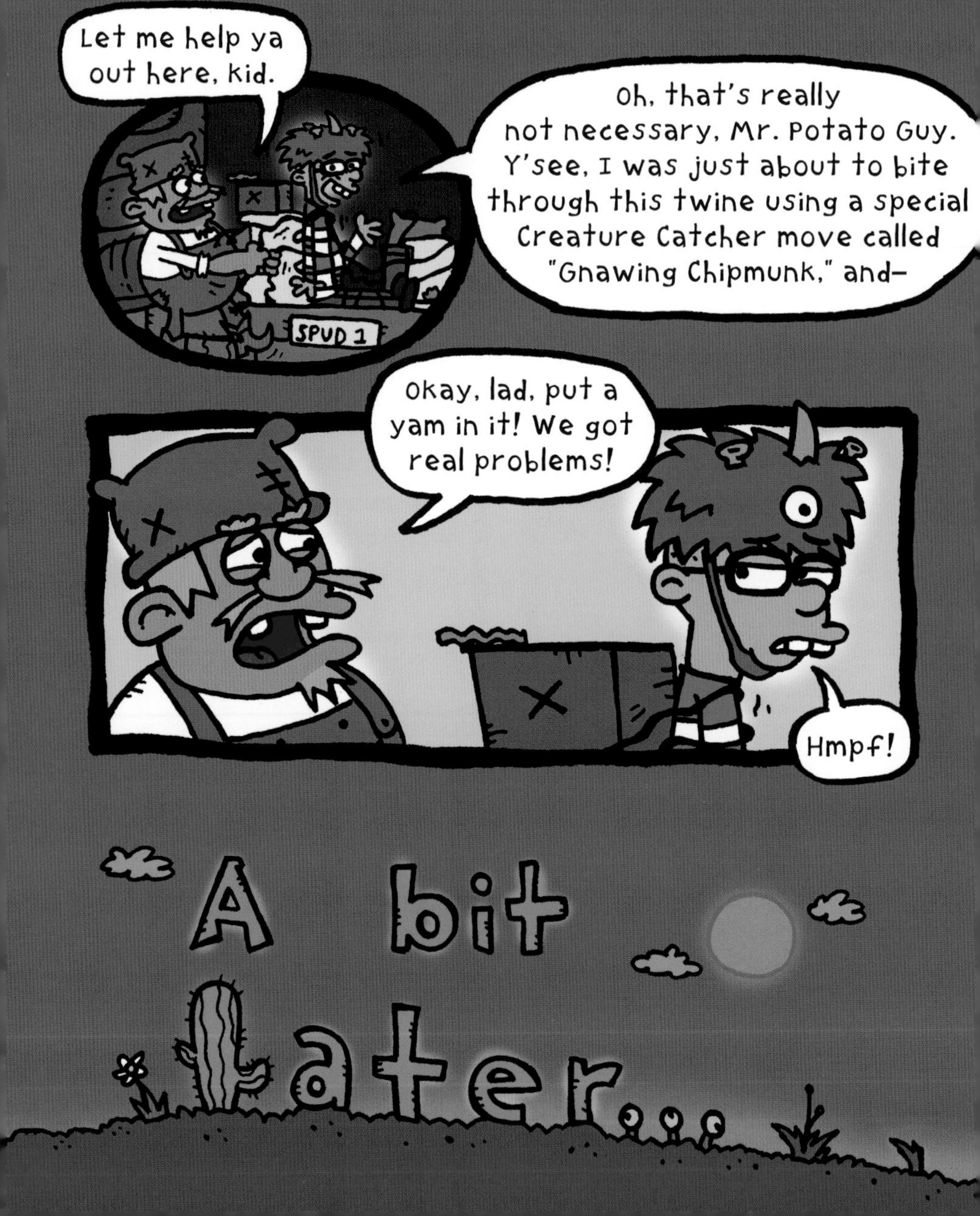
Let me help ya out here, kid.
Oh, that's really not necessary, Mr. Potato Guy. Y'see, I was just about to bite through this twine using a special Creature Catcher move called "Gnawing Chipmunk," and–
SPUD 1
Okay, lad, put a yam in it! We got real problems!
Hmpf!
A bit later...

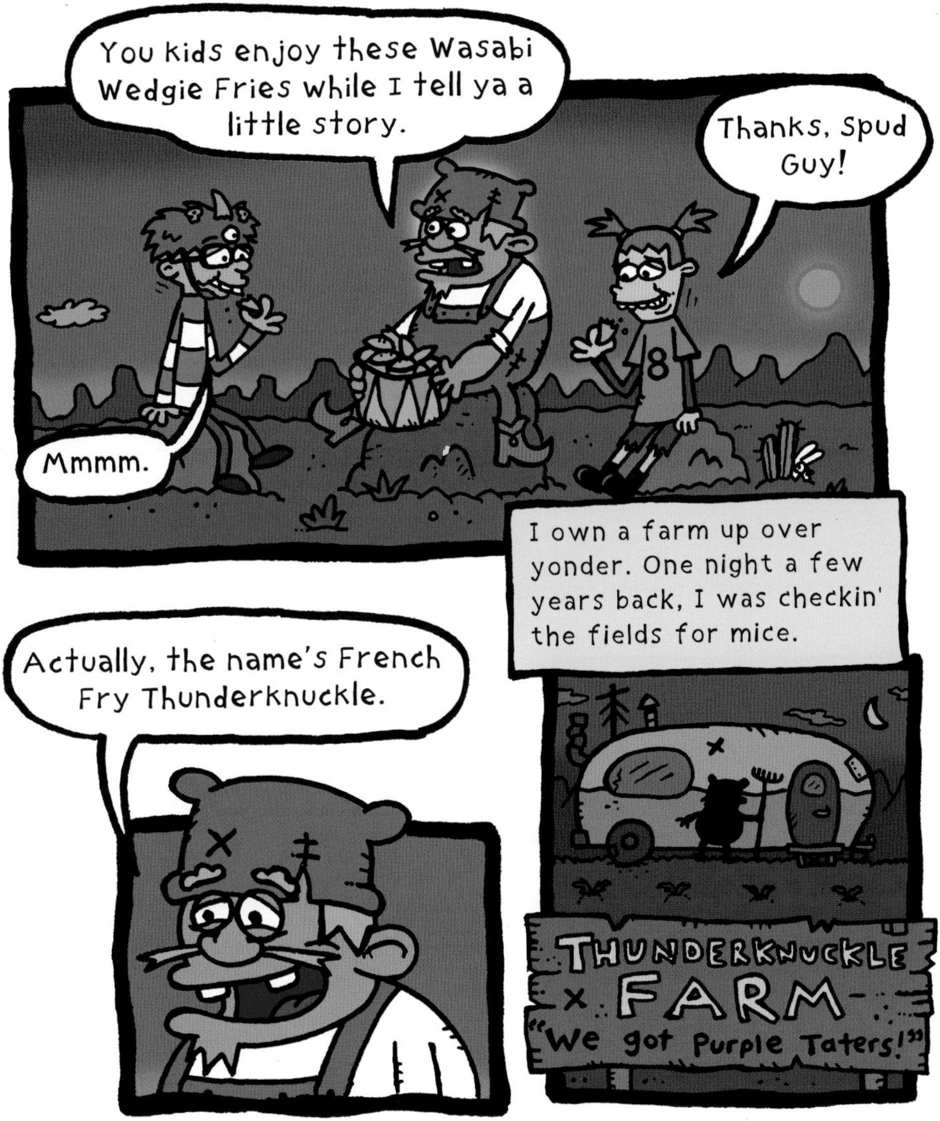
You kids enjoy these Wasabi Wedgie Fries while I tell ya a little story.
Thanks, Spud Guy!
Mmmm.
I own a farm up over yonder. One night a few years back, I was checkin' the fields for mice.
Actually, the name's French Fry Thunderknuckle.
THUNDERKNUCKLE FARM
"We got Purple Taters!"

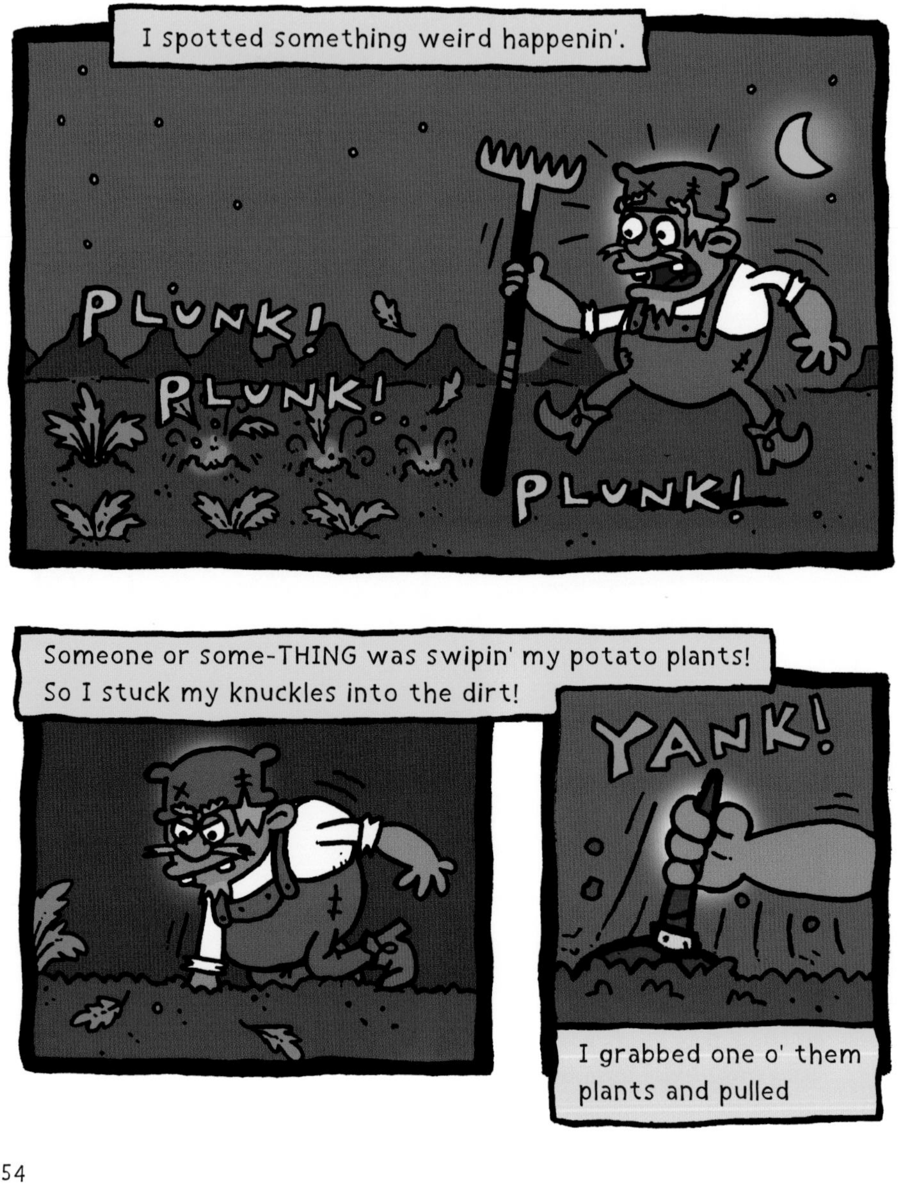
I spotted something weird happenin'.
PLUNK!
PLUNK!
PLUNK!
Someone or some-THING was swipin' my potato plants!
So I stuck my knuckles into the dirt!
YANK!
I grabbed one o' them plants and pulled

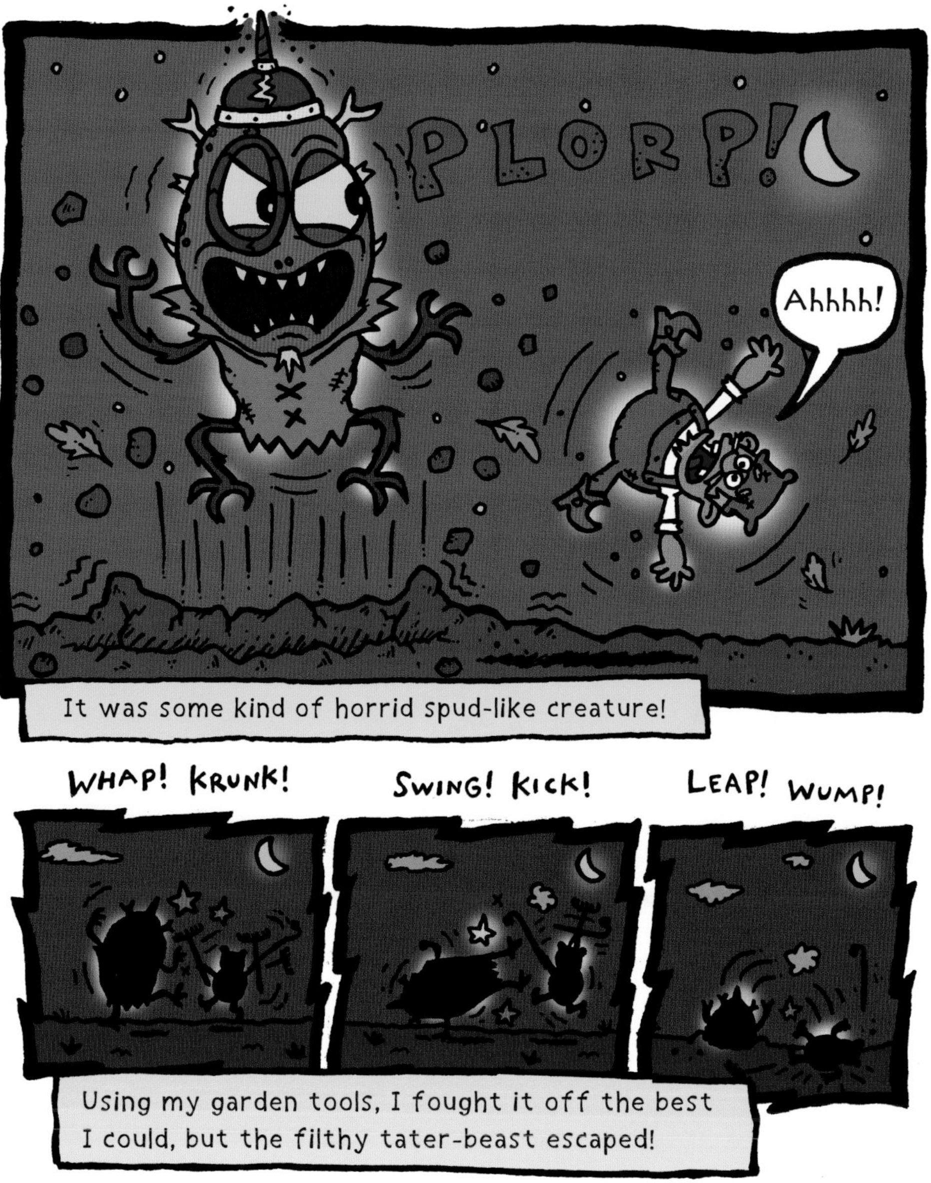
PLORP!
Ahhhh!
It was some kind of horrid spud-like creature!
WHAP! KRUNK!
SWING! KICK!
LEAP! WUMP!
Using my garden tools, I fought it off the best
I could, but the filthy tater-beast escaped!

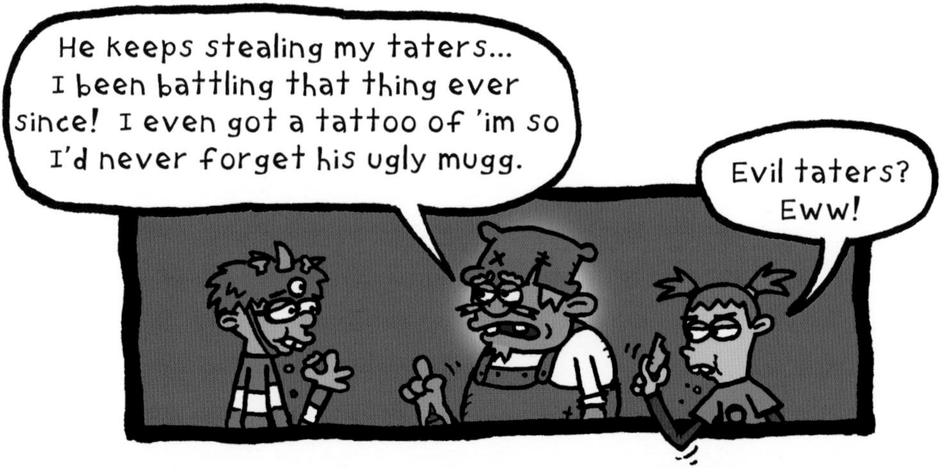
He keeps stealing my taters...
I been battling that thing ever
since! I even got a tattoo of 'im so
I'd never forget his ugly mugg.
Evil taters?
Eww!

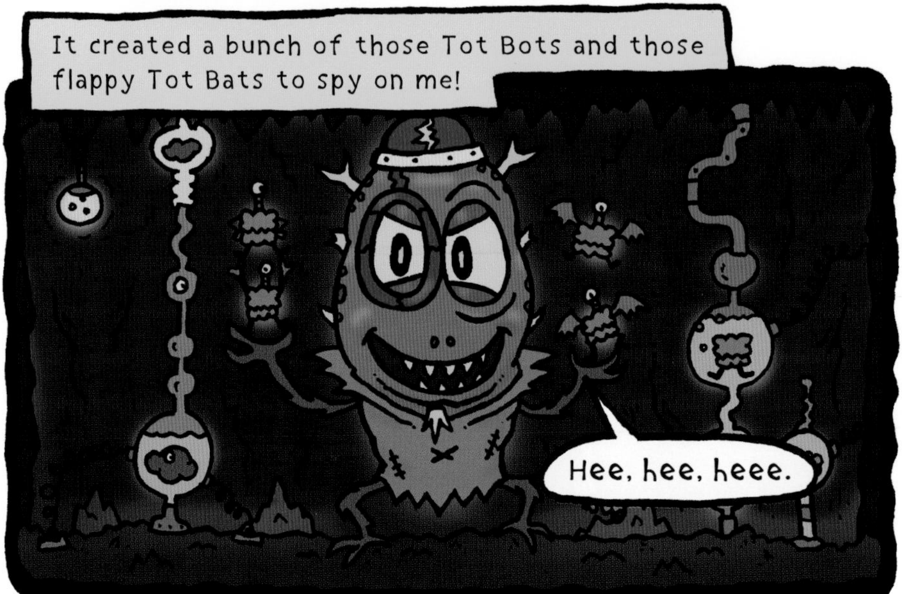
It created a bunch of those Tot Bots and those
flappy Tot Bats to spy on me!
Hee, hee, heee.

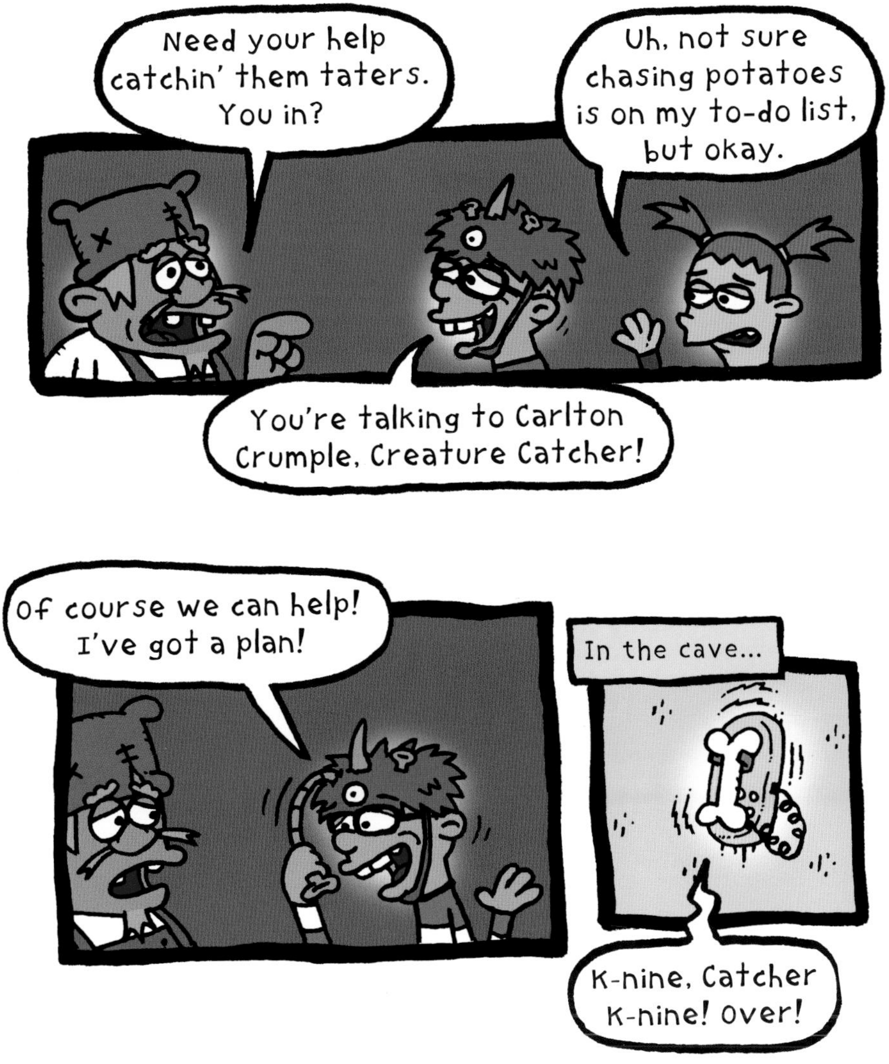
Need your help catchin' them taters. You in?
You're talking to Carlton Crumple, Creature Catcher!
Uh, not sure chasing potatoes is on my to-do list, but okay.
Of course we can help! I've got a plan!
In the cave...
K-nine, Catcher K-nine! Over!

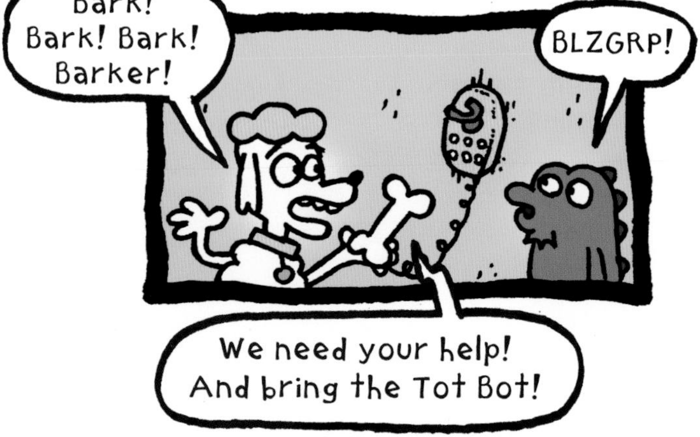
Bark!
Bark! Bark!
Barker!
BLZGRP!
We need your help!
And bring the Tot Bot!

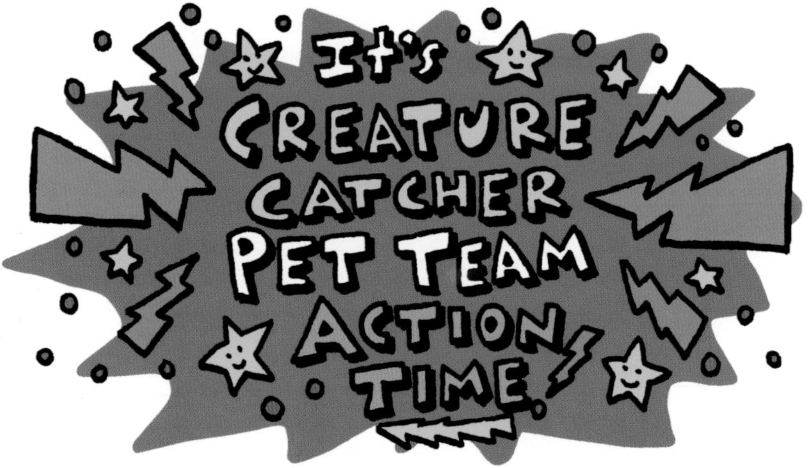
It's
CREATURE
CATCHER
PET TEAM
ACTION
TIME!

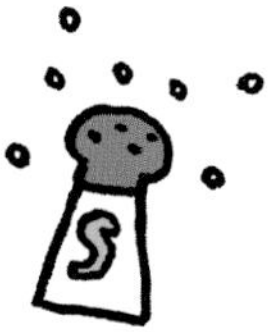

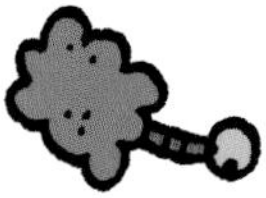

CHAPTER 6

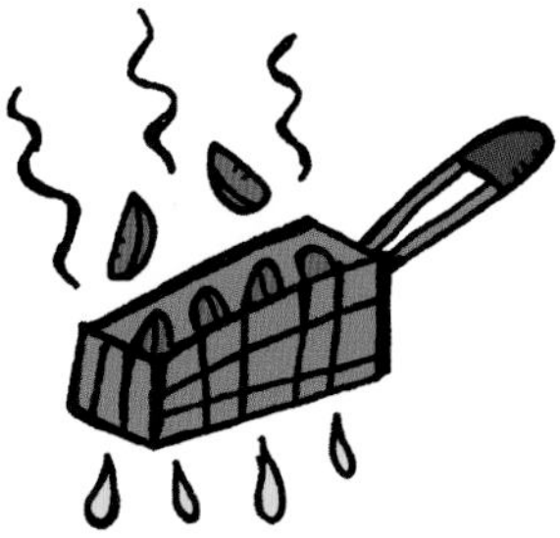

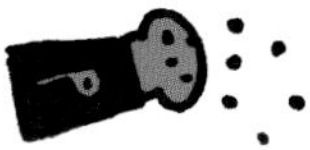

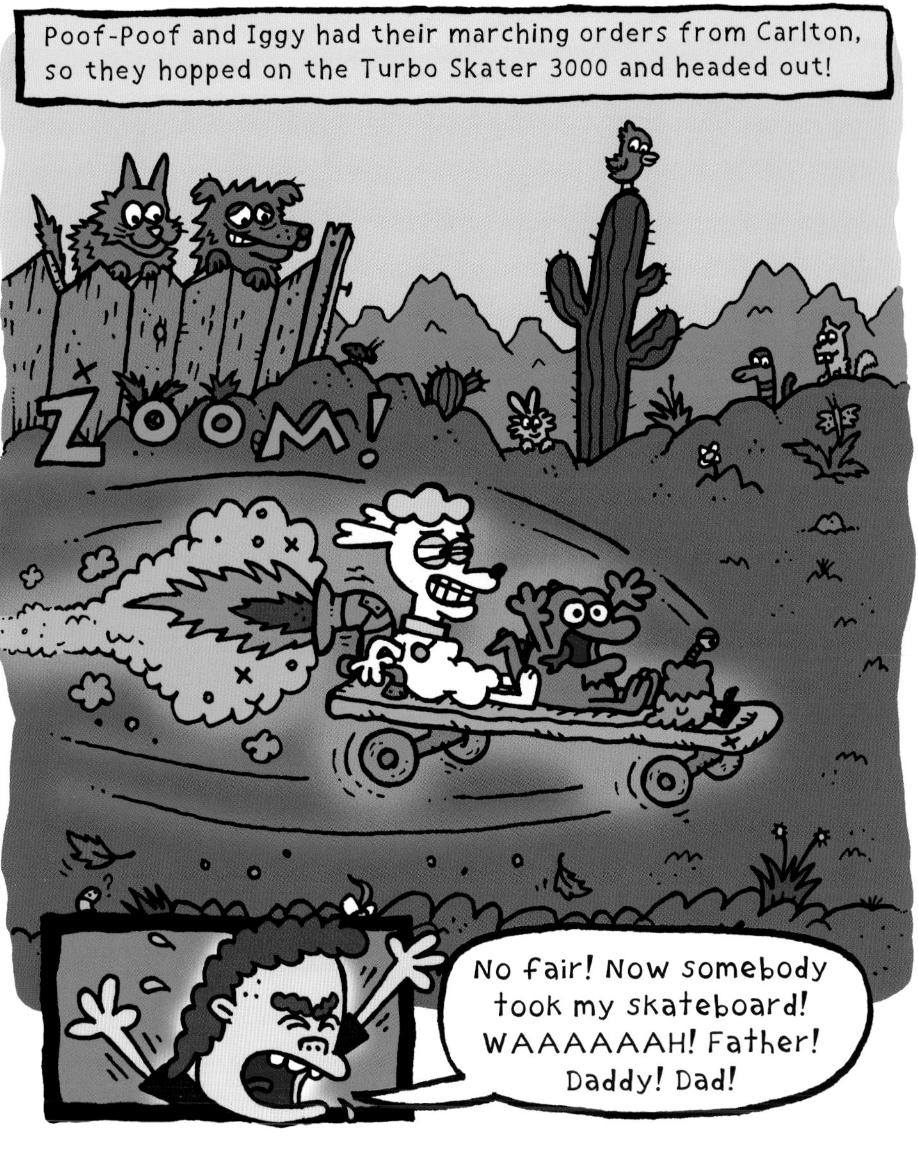
Poof-Poof and Iggy had their marching orders from Carlton, so they hopped on the Turbo Skater 3000 and headed out!
ZOOM!
No fair! Now somebody took my skateboard! WAAAAAAH! Father! Daddy! Dad!

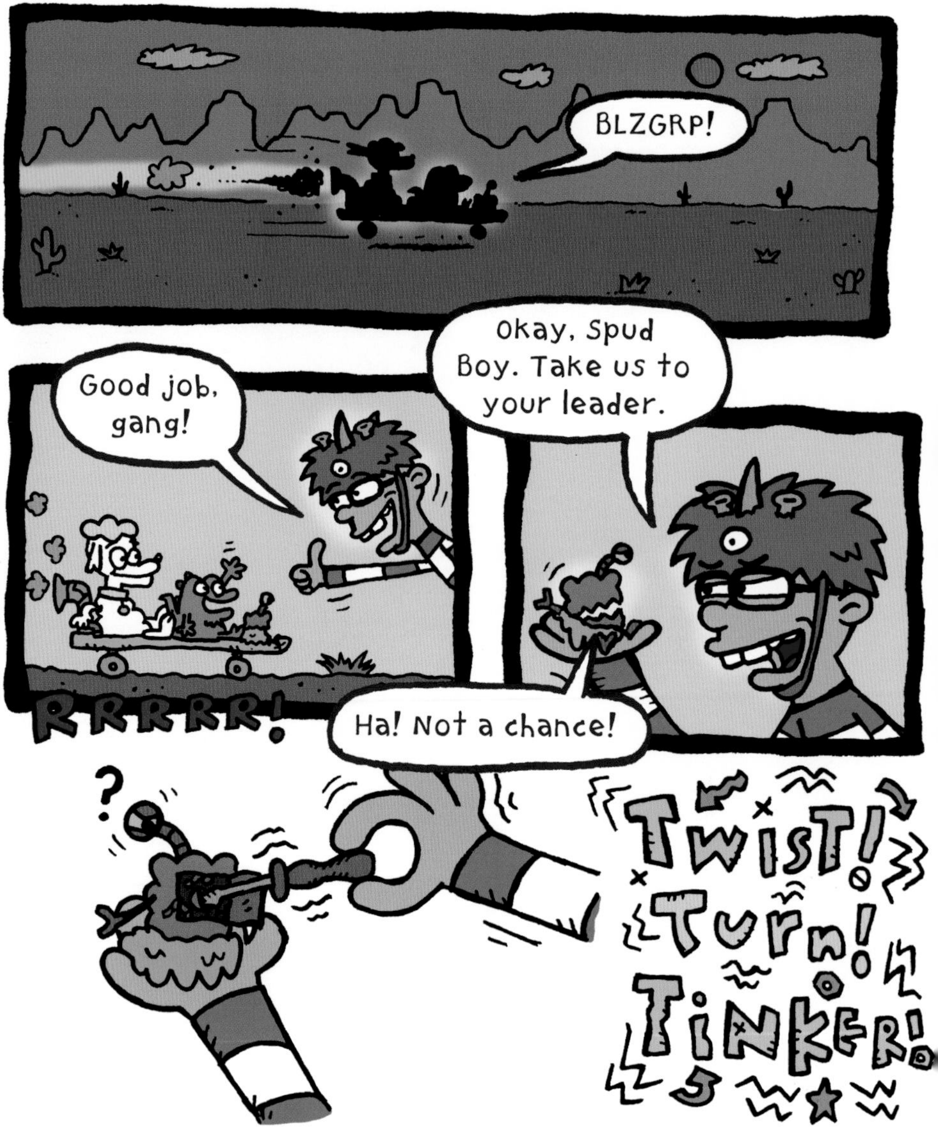
BLZGRP!
Good job, gang!
Okay, Spud Boy. Take us to your leader.
RRRRR!
Ha! Not a chance!
?
TWIST! TURN! TINKER!

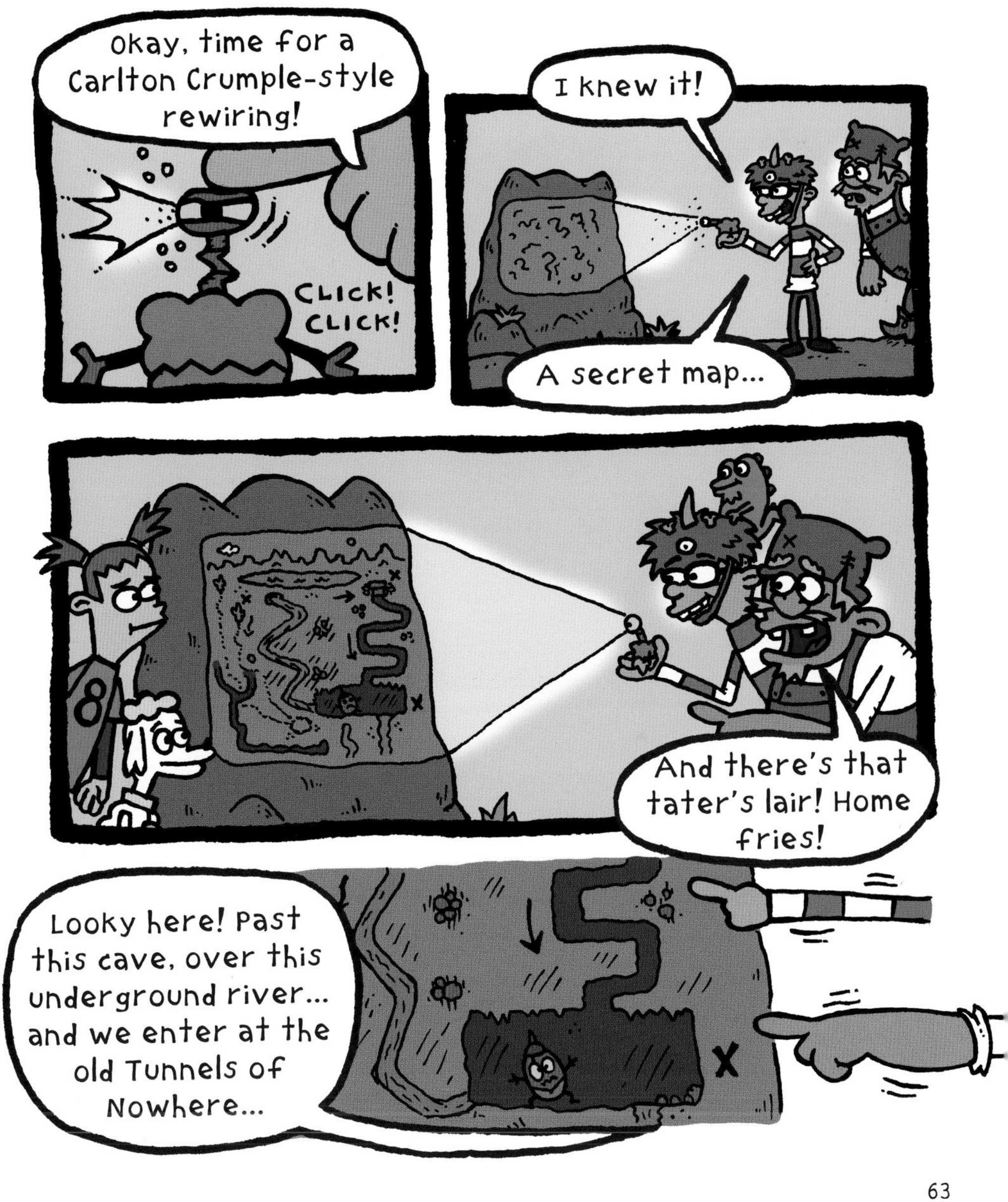
Okay, time for a Carlton Crumple-style rewiring!
CLICK! CLICK!
I knew it!
A secret map...
And there's that tater's lair! Home fries!
Looky here! Past this cave, over this underground river... and we enter at the old Tunnels of Nowhere...

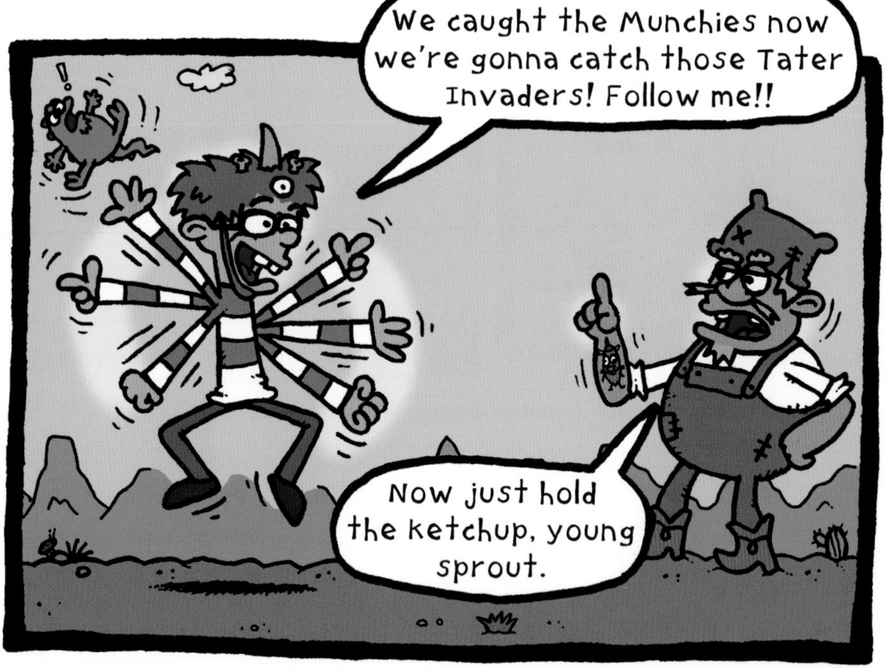
We caught the Munchies now we're gonna catch those Tater Invaders! Follow me!!
Now just hold the ketchup, young sprout.

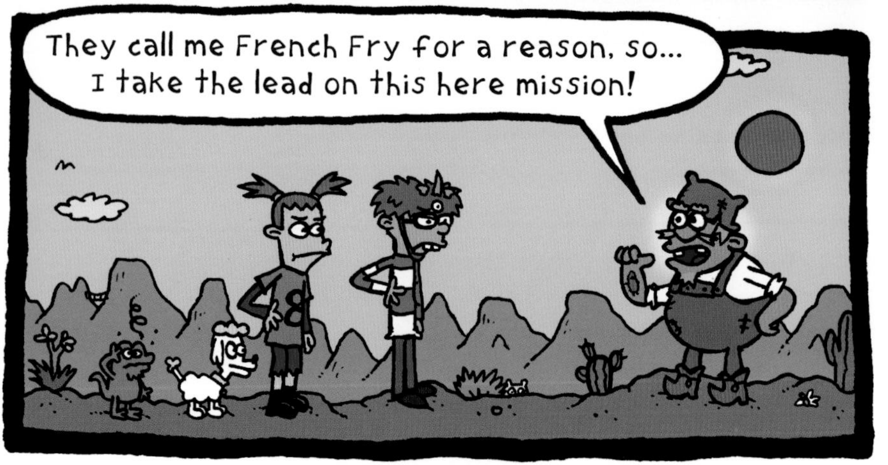
They call me French Fry for a reason, so... I take the lead on this here mission!

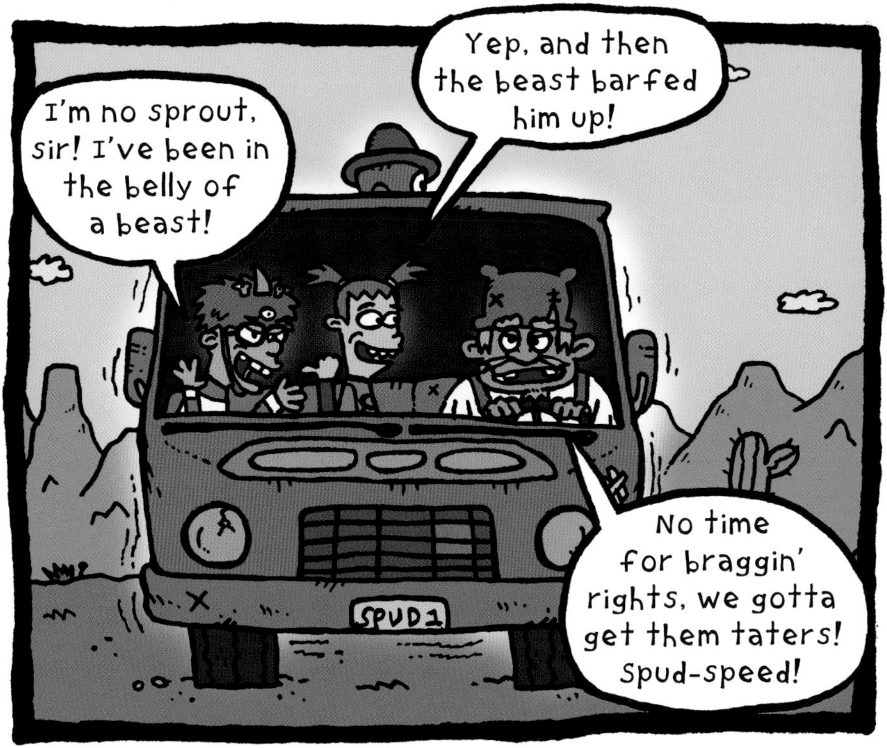
I'm no sprout, sir! I've been in the belly of a beast!
Yep, and then the beast barfed him up!
No time for braggin' rights, we gotta get them taters! Spud-speed!
SPUD 1

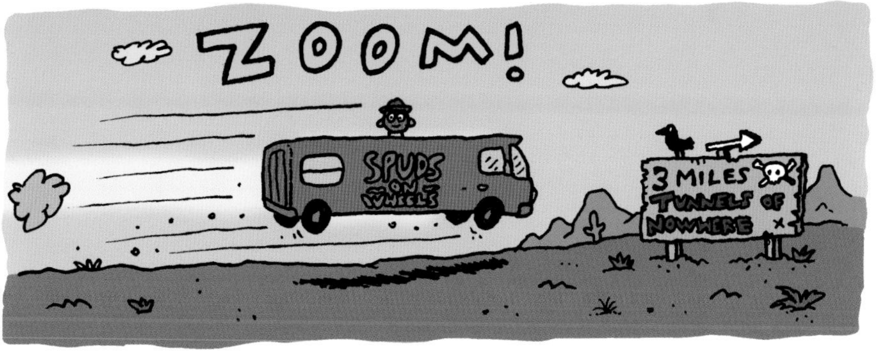
ZOOM!
SPUDS ON WHEELS
3 MILES TUNNELS OF NOWHERE

CHAPTER V

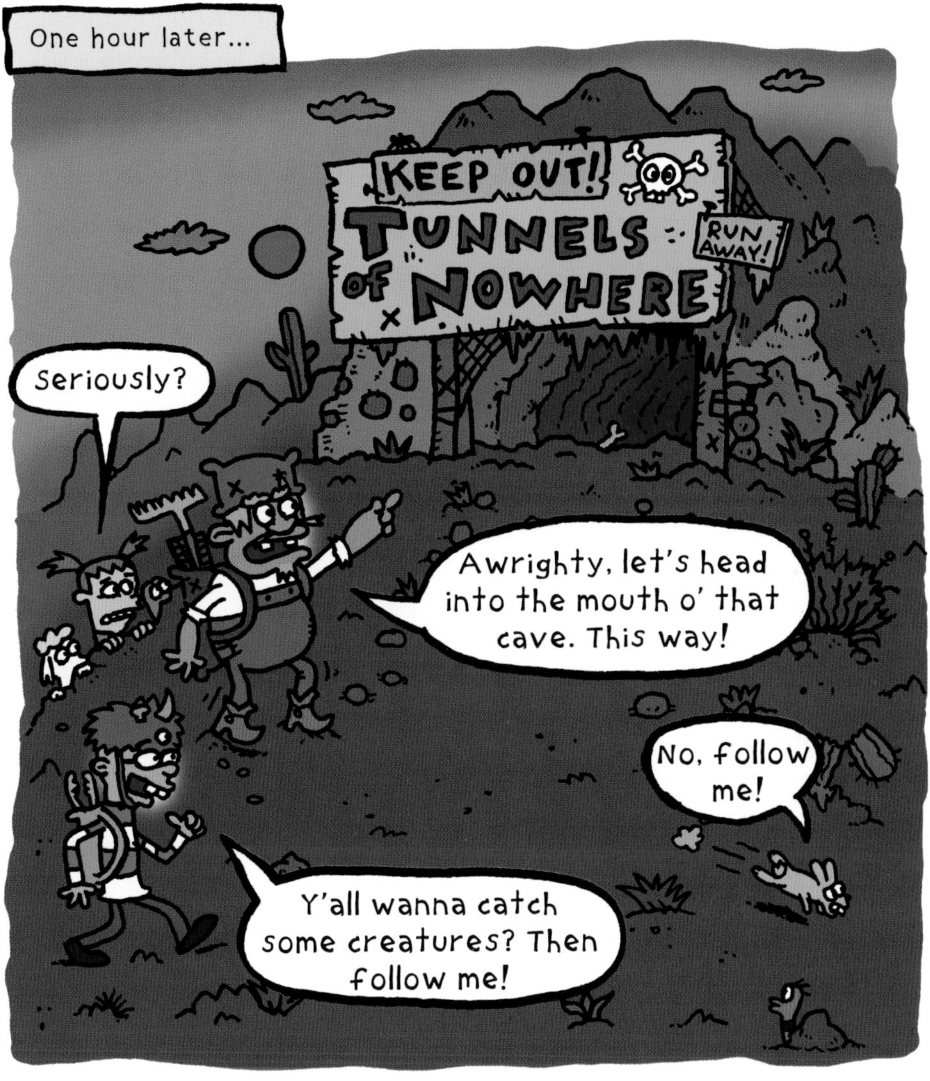
One hour later...
KEEP OUT!
TUNNELS OF NOWHERE
RUN AWAY!
Seriously?
Awrighty, let's head into the mouth o' that cave. This way!
Y'all wanna catch some creatures? Then follow me!
No, follow me!

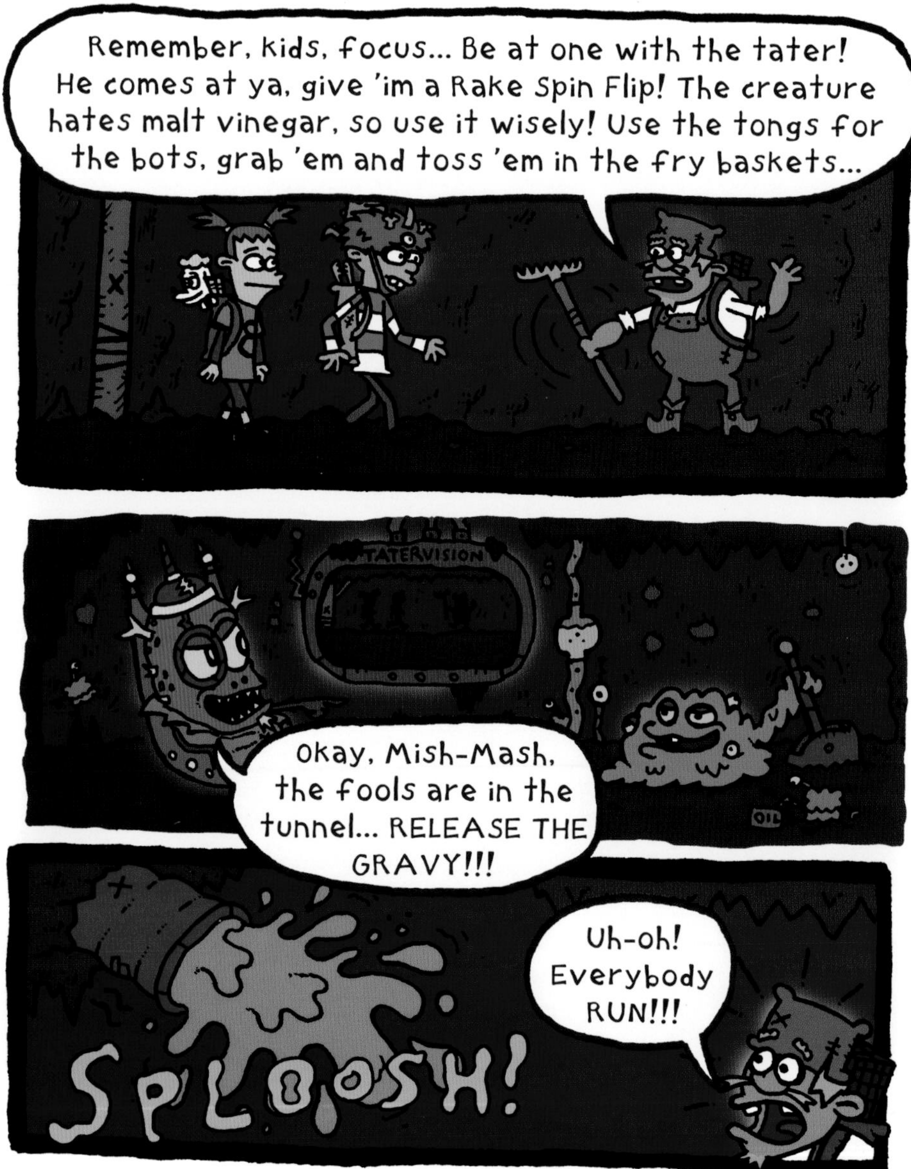
Remember, kids, focus... Be at one with the tater! He comes at ya, give 'im a Rake Spin Flip! The creature hates malt vinegar, so use it wisely! Use the tongs for the bots, grab 'em and toss 'em in the fry baskets...
TATERVISION
Okay, Mish-Mash, the fools are in the tunnel... RELEASE THE GRAVY!!!
OIL
SPLOOSH!
Uh-oh! Everybody RUN!!!

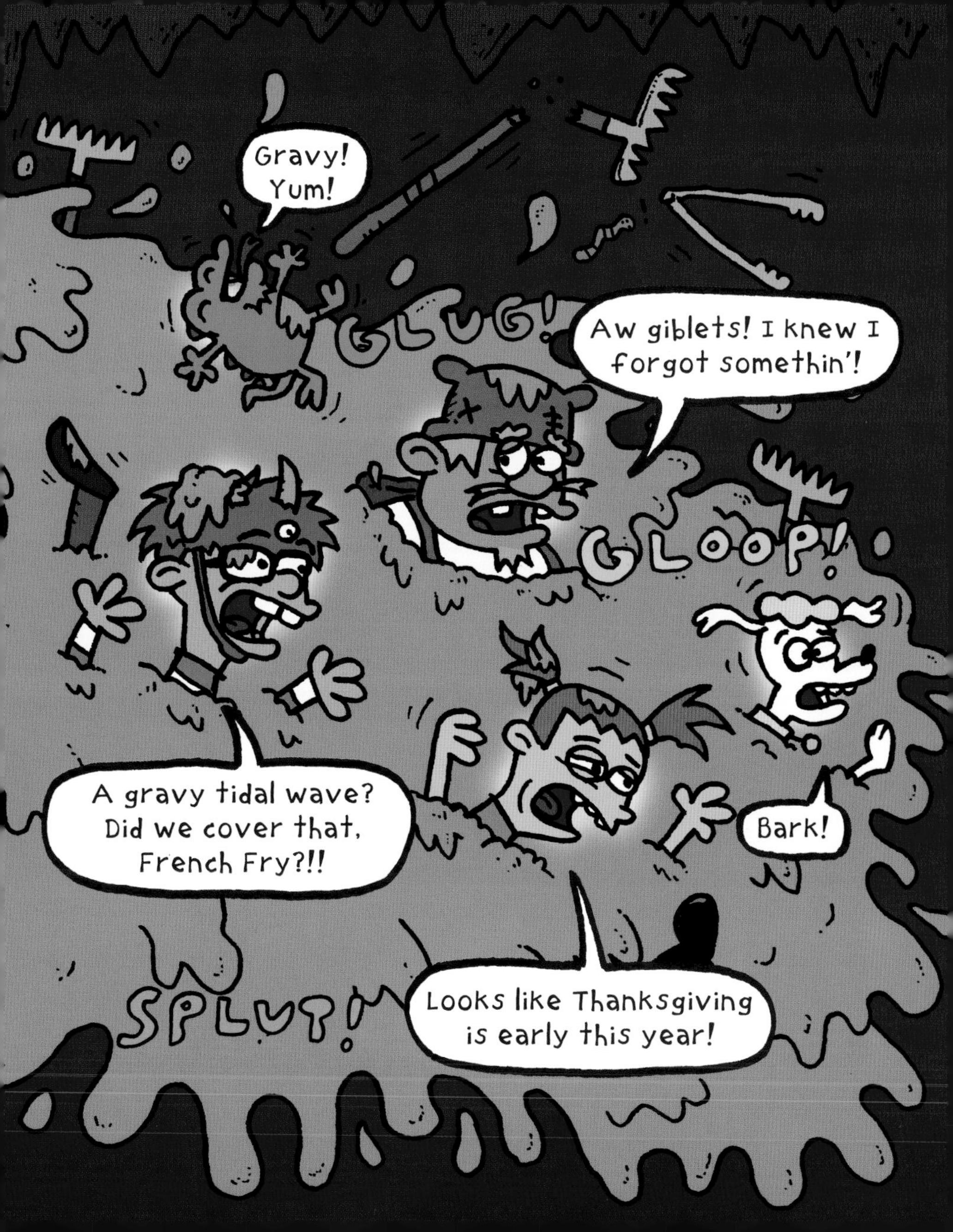
Gravy! Yum!
GLUG!
Aw giblets! I knew I forgot somethin'!
GLOOP!
A gravy tidal wave? Did we cover that, French Fry?!!
Bark!
SPLUT!
Looks like Thanksgiving is early this year!

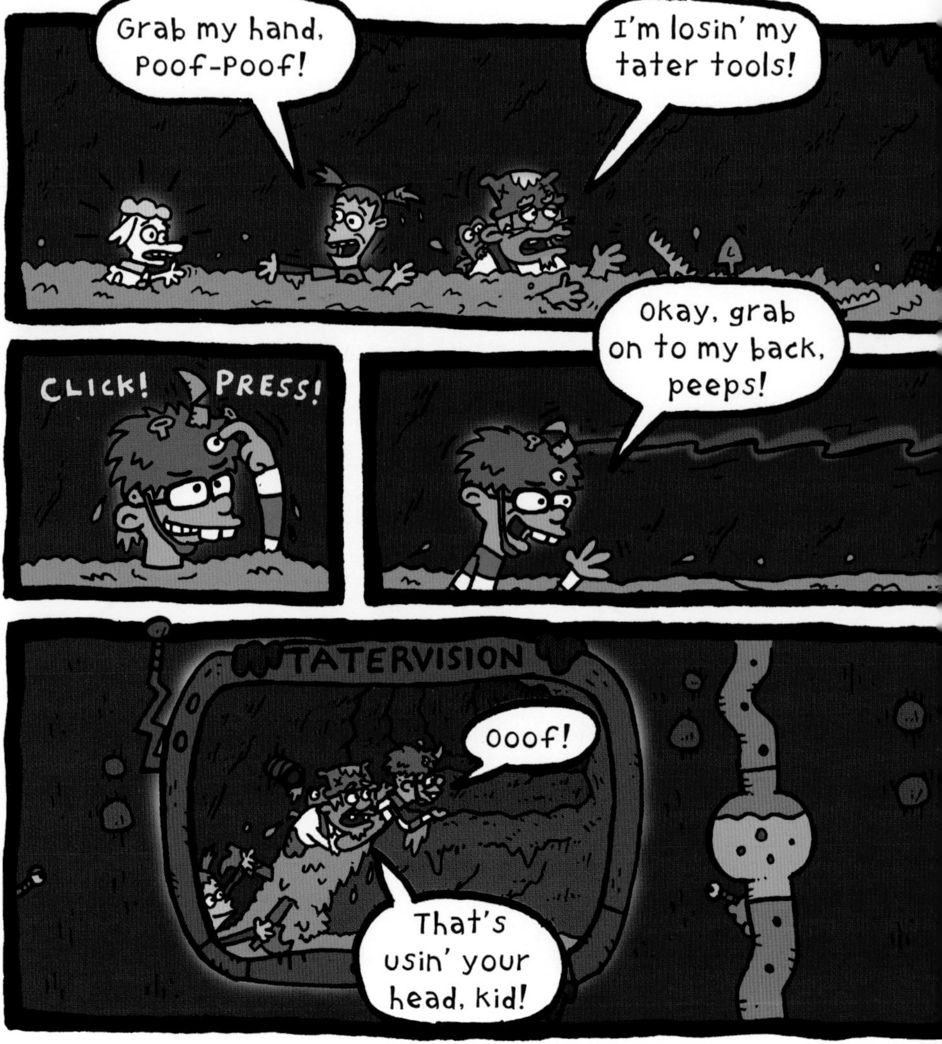

Grab my hand, Poof-Poof!
I'm losin' my tater tools!
CLICK!
PRESS!
Okay, grab on to my back, peeps!
TATERVISION
Ooof!
That's usin' your head, kid!

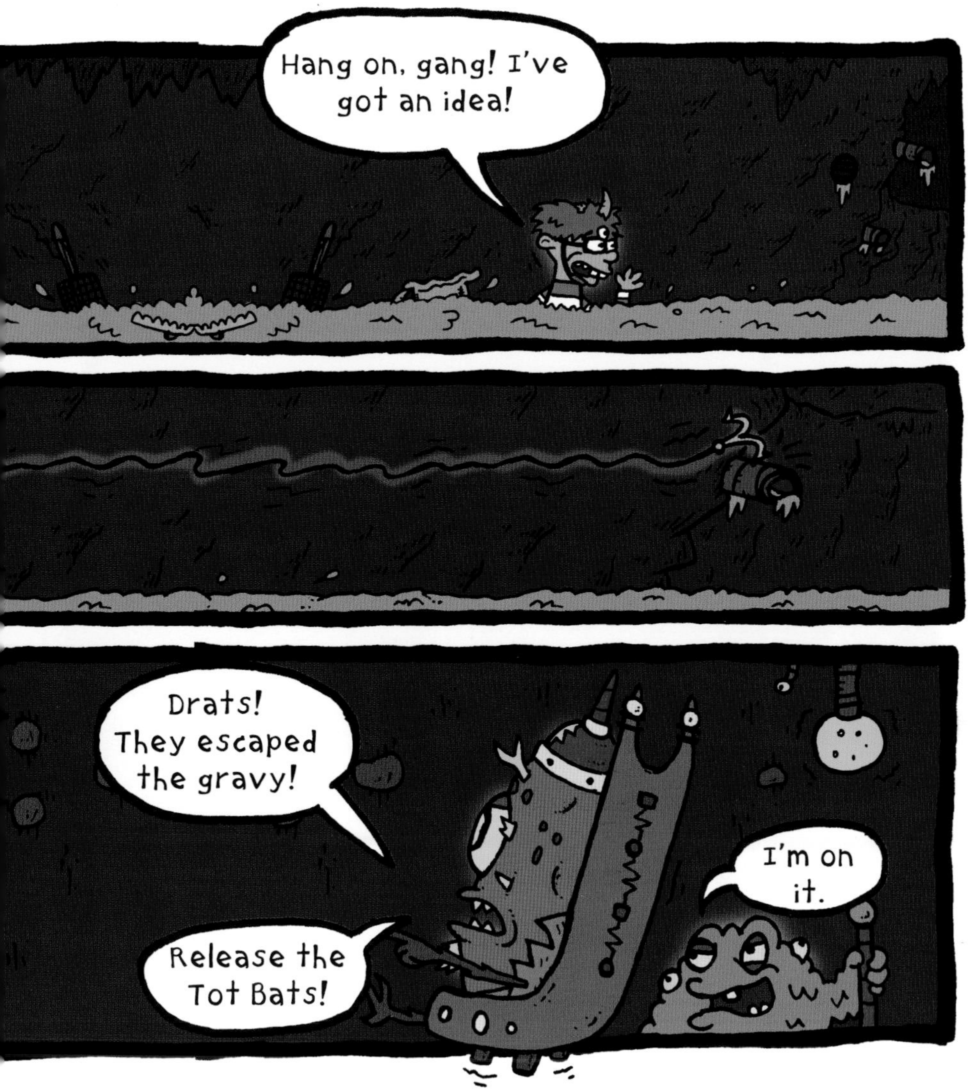
Hang on, gang! I've got an idea!
Drats! They escaped the gravy!
Release the Tot Bats!
I'm on it.

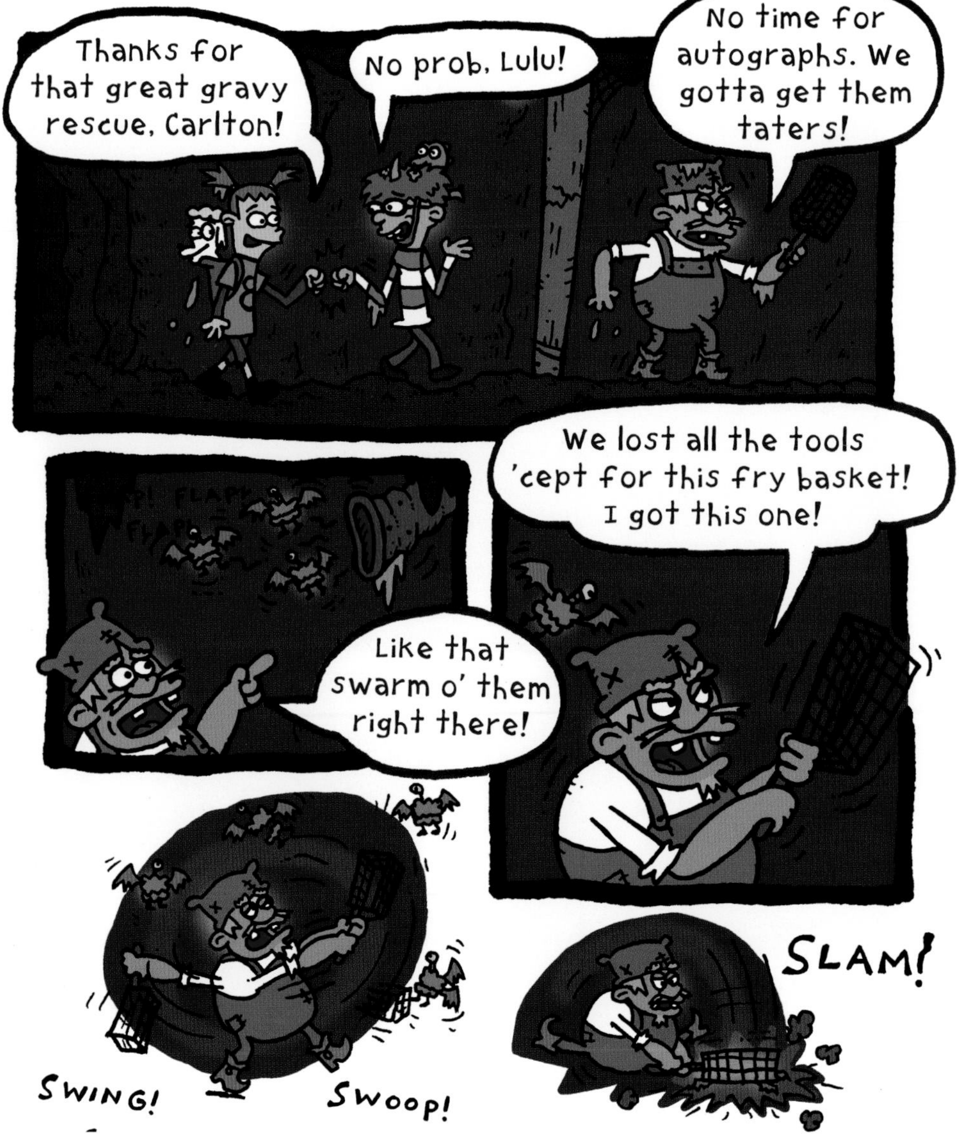

Thanks for that great gravy rescue, Carlton!
No prob, Lulu!
No time for autographs. We gotta get them taters!
Like that swarm o' them right there!
We lost all the tools 'cept for this fry basket! I got this one!
SWING!
SWOOP!
SLAM!

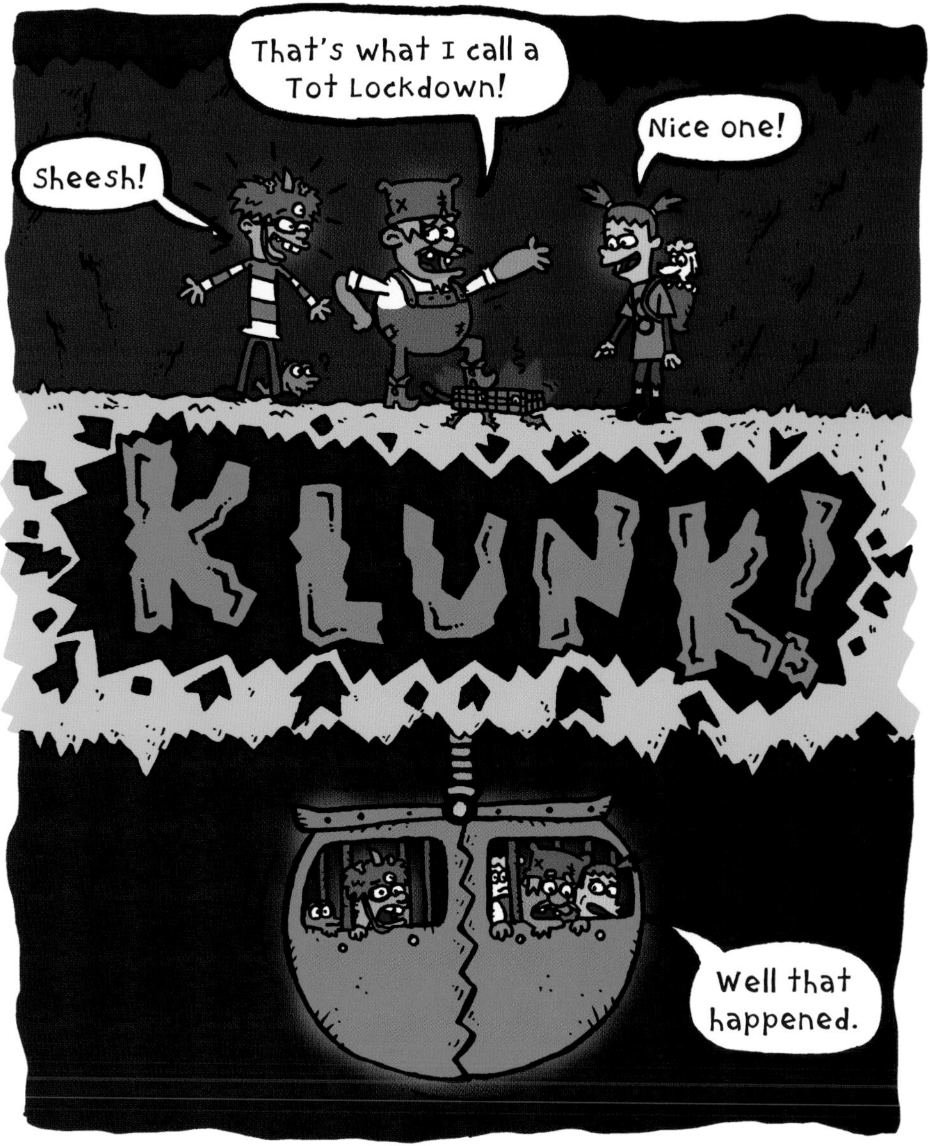
Sheesh!
That's what I call a Tot Lockdown!
Nice one!
KLUNK!
Well that happened.

CHAPTER 8

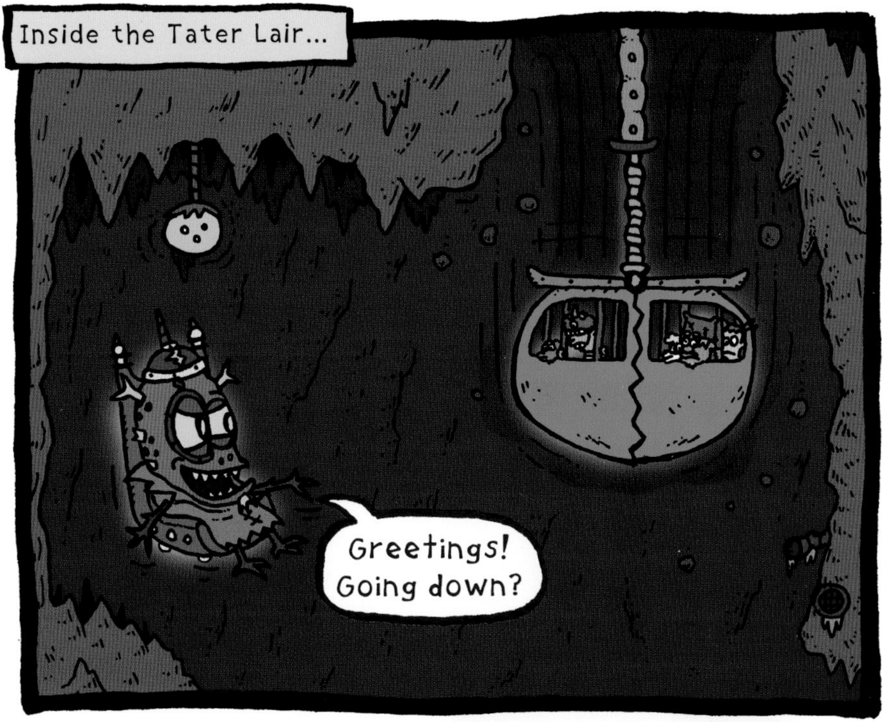
Inside the Tater Lair...
Greetings! Going down?

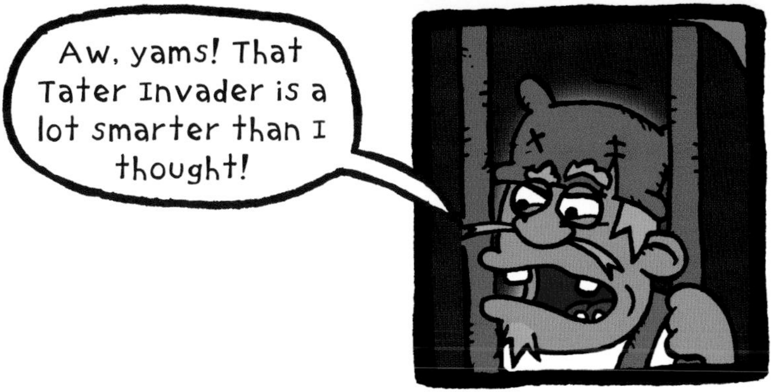
Aw, yams! That Tater Invader is a lot smarter than I thought!

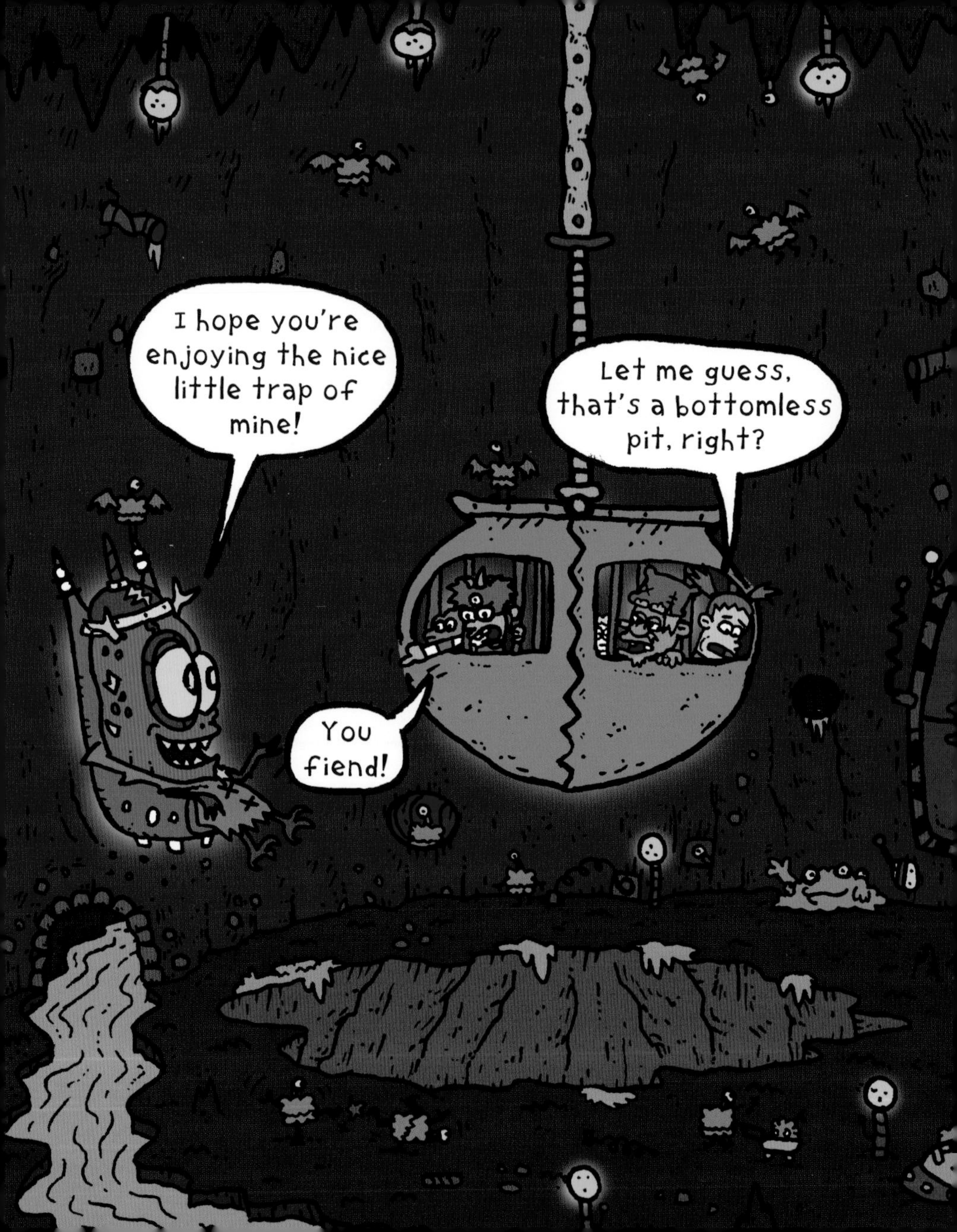
I hope you're enjoying the nice little trap of mine!
Let me guess, that's a bottomless pit, right?
You fiend!

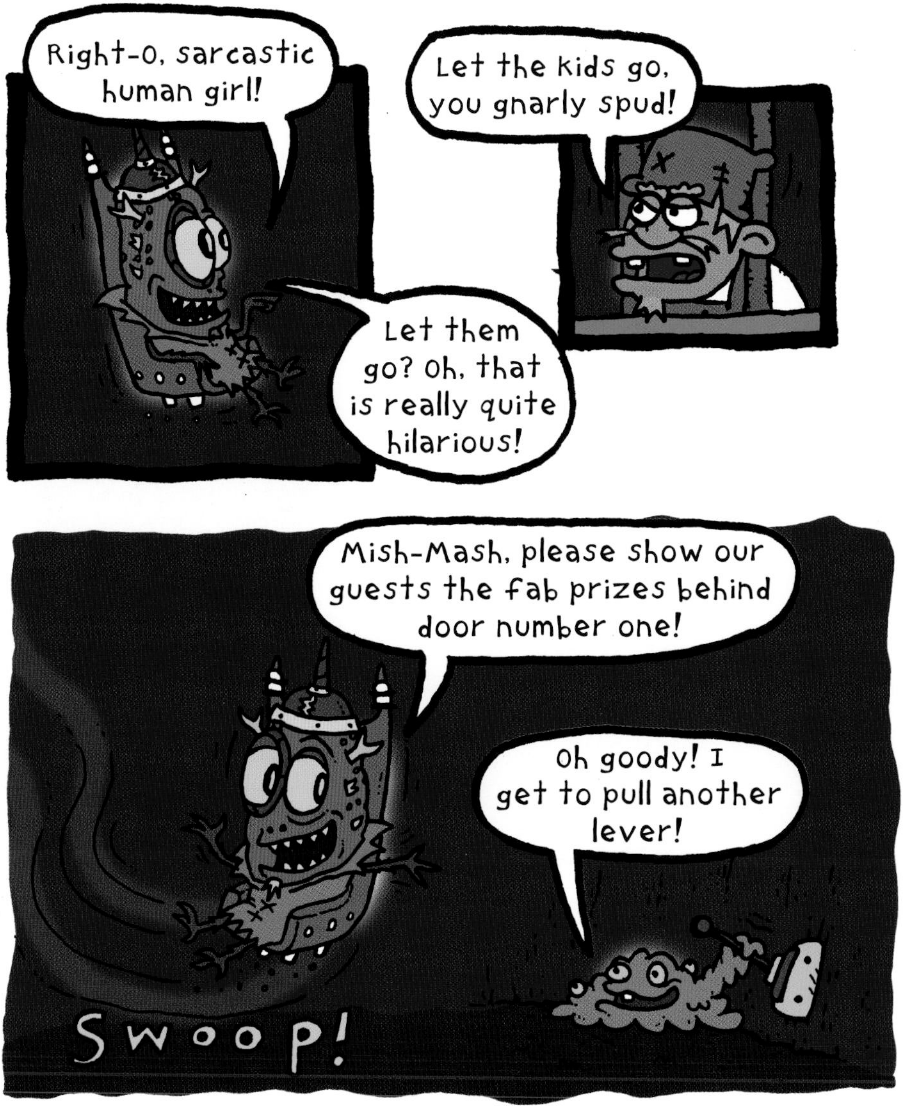
Right-o, sarcastic human girl!
Let the kids go, you gnarly spud!
Let them go? Oh, that is really quite hilarious!
Mish-Mash, please show our guests the fab prizes behind door number one!
Oh goody! I get to pull another lever!
SWOOP!

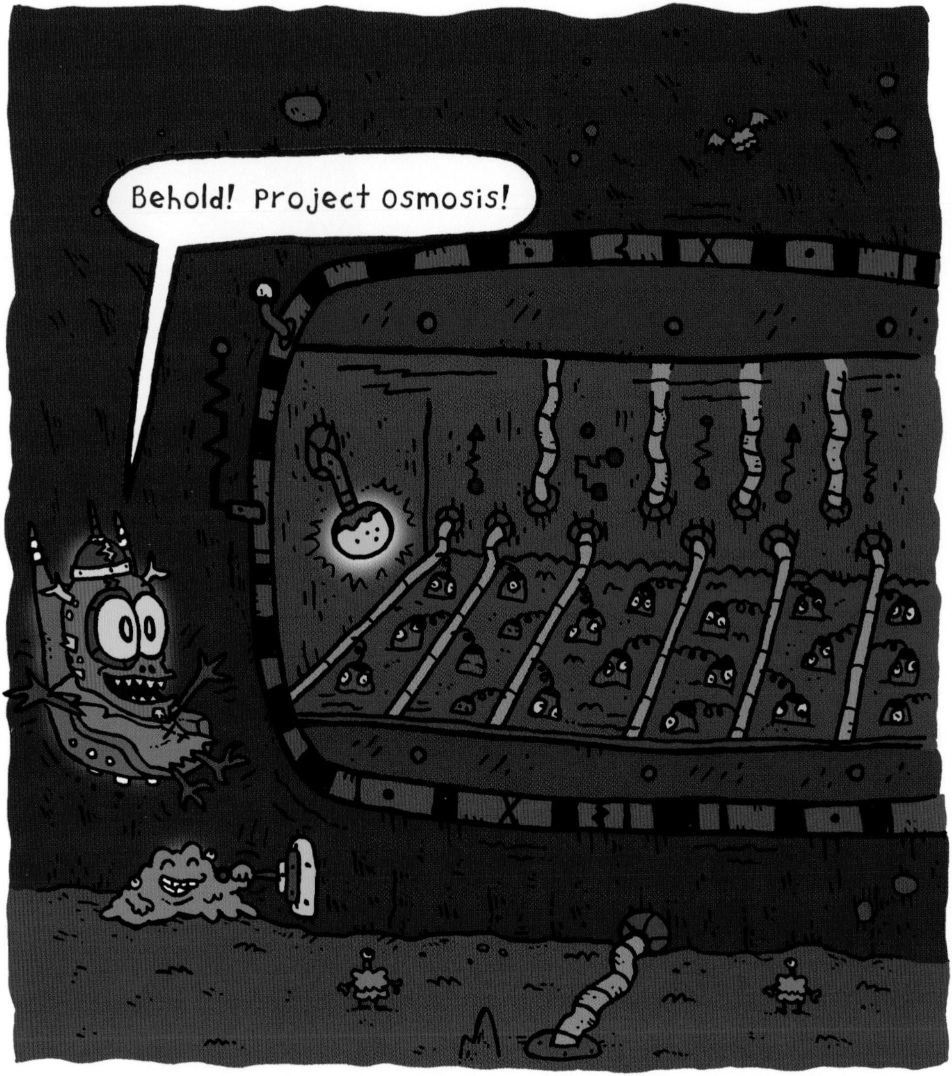
Behold! Project Osmosis!

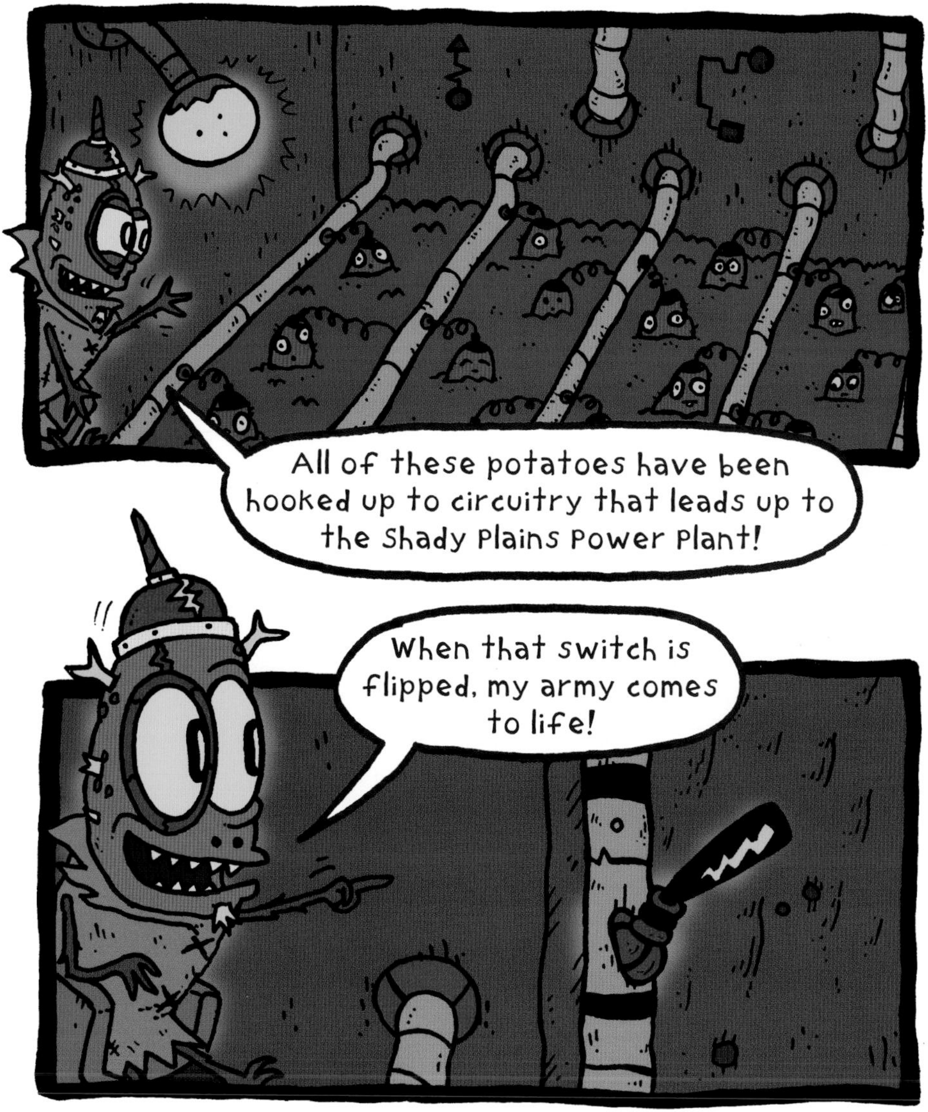
All of these potatoes have been hooked up to circuitry that leads up to the Shady Plains Power Plant!
When that switch is flipped, my army comes to life!

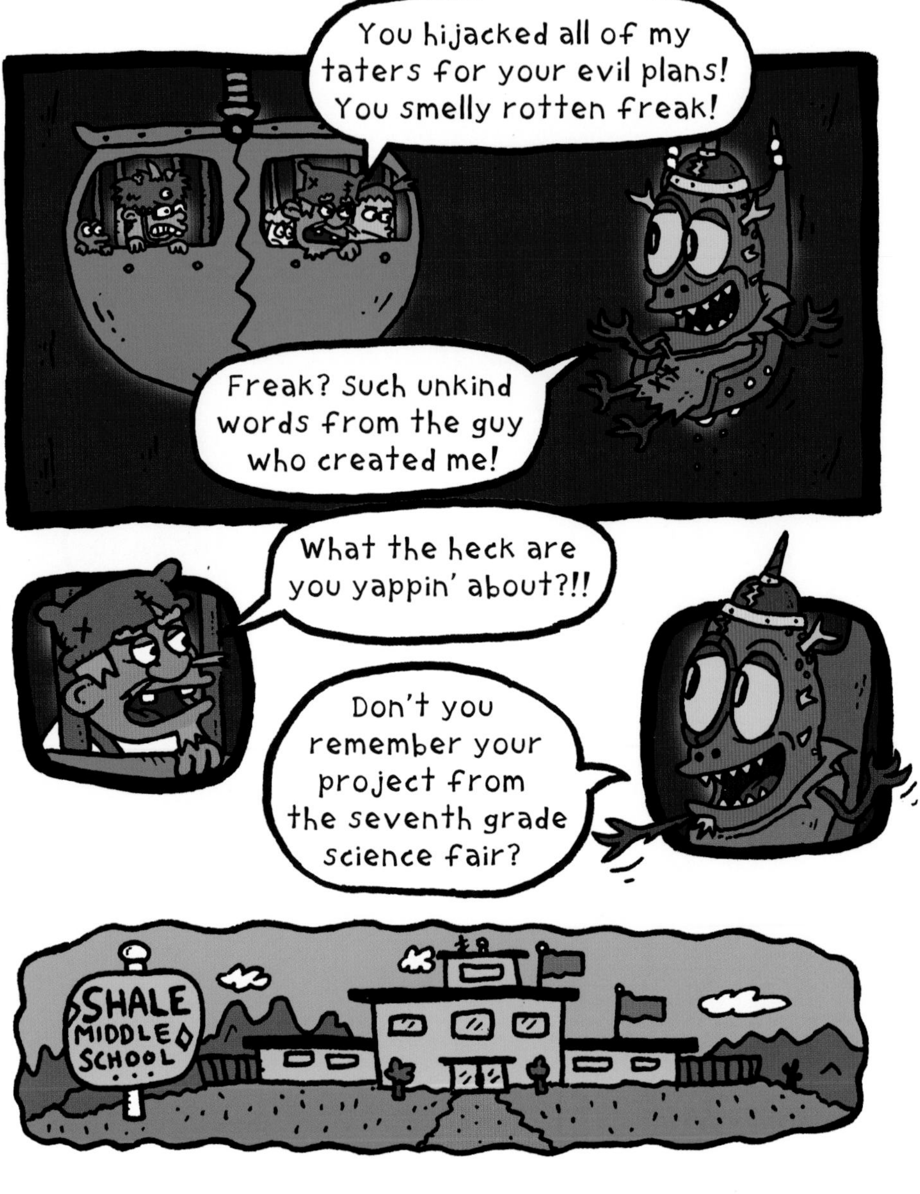
You hijacked all of my taters for your evil plans! You smelly rotten freak!
Freak? Such unkind words from the guy who created me!
What the heck are you yappin' about?!!
Don't you remember your project from the seventh grade science fair?
SHALE MIDDLE SCHOOL

You tried to prove that a potato can generate electricity through osmosis, but you got carried away.

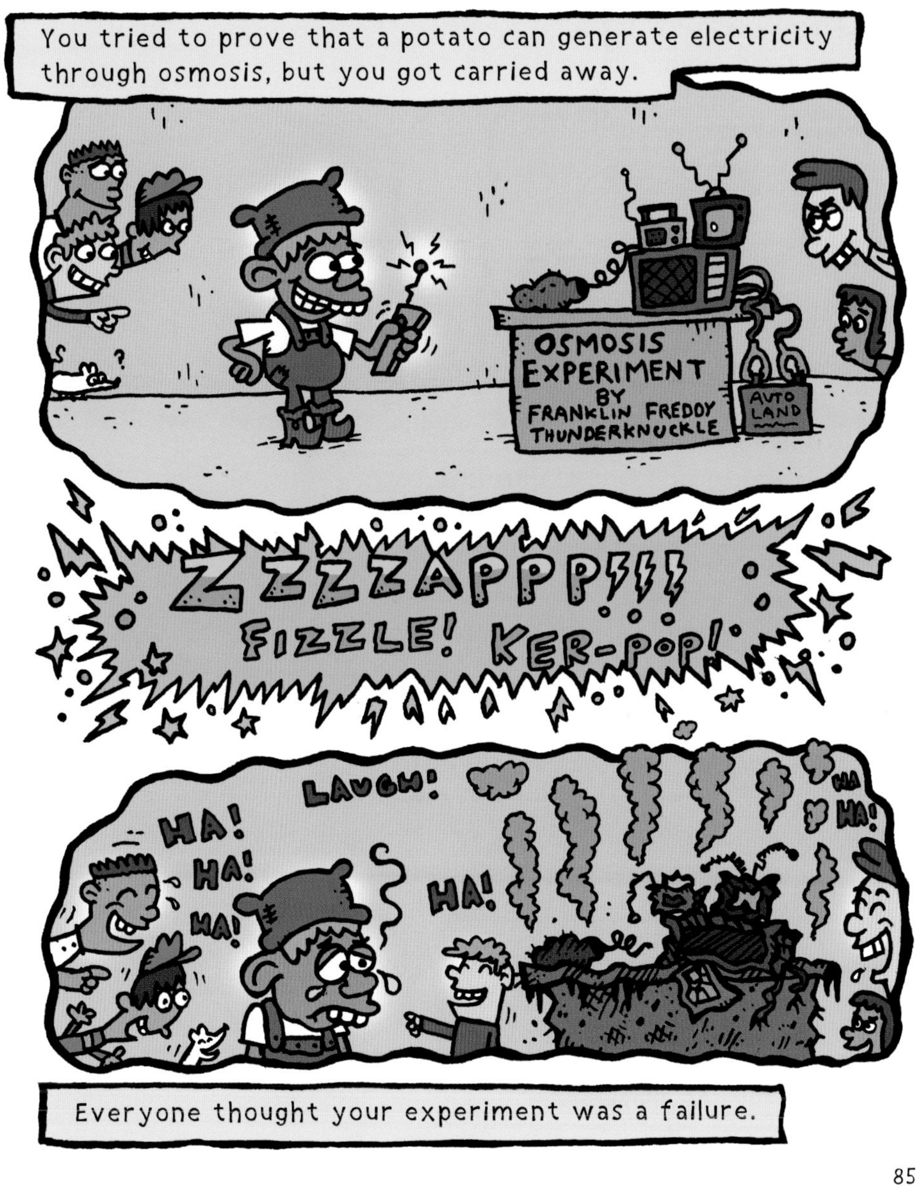
OSMOSIS EXPERIMENT BY FRANKLIN FREDDY THUNDERKNUCKLE
AUTO LAND
ZZZZAPPP!!!
FIZZLE! KER-POP!
LAUGH!
HA!
HA!
HA!
HA!
HA HA!

Everyone thought your experiment was a failure.

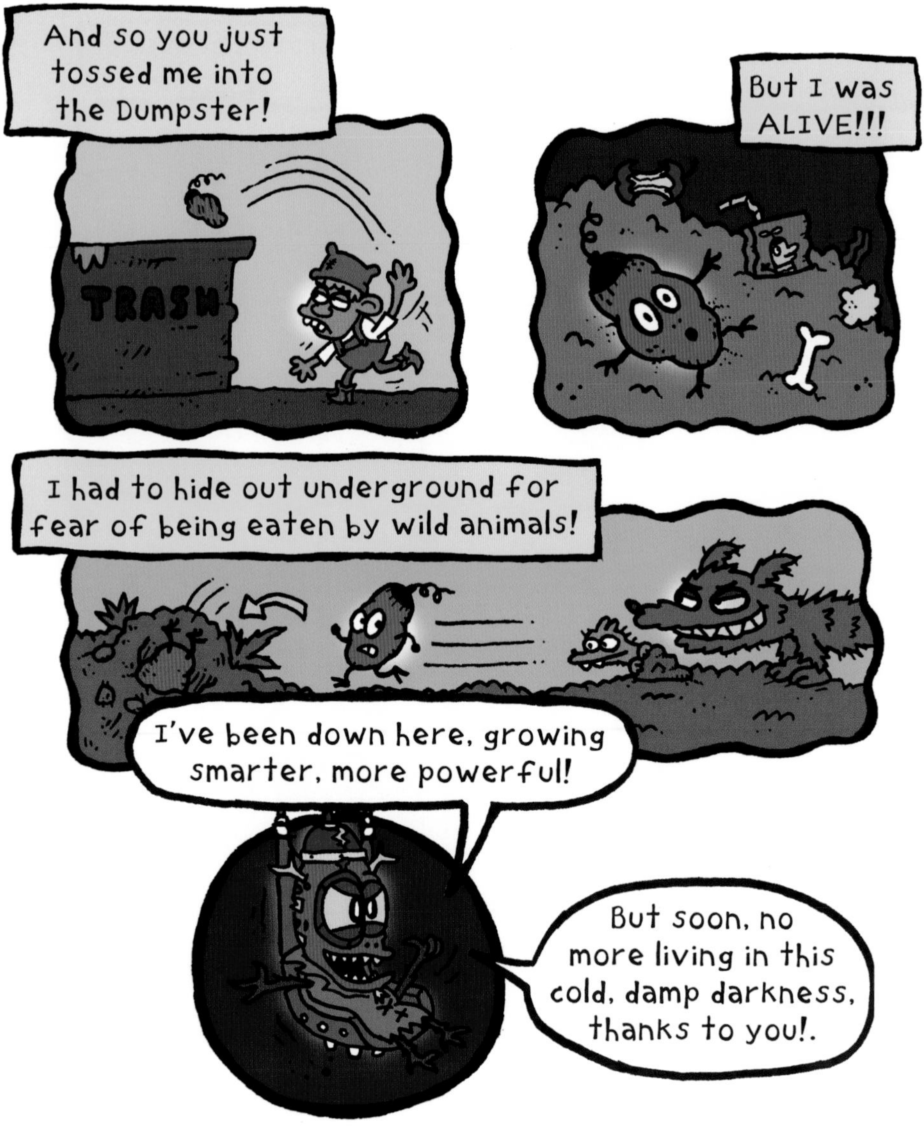

And so you just tossed me into the Dumpster!
TRASH
But I was ALIVE!!!
I had to hide out underground for fear of being eaten by wild animals!
I've been down here, growing smarter, more powerful!
But soon, no more living in this cold, damp darkness, thanks to you!.

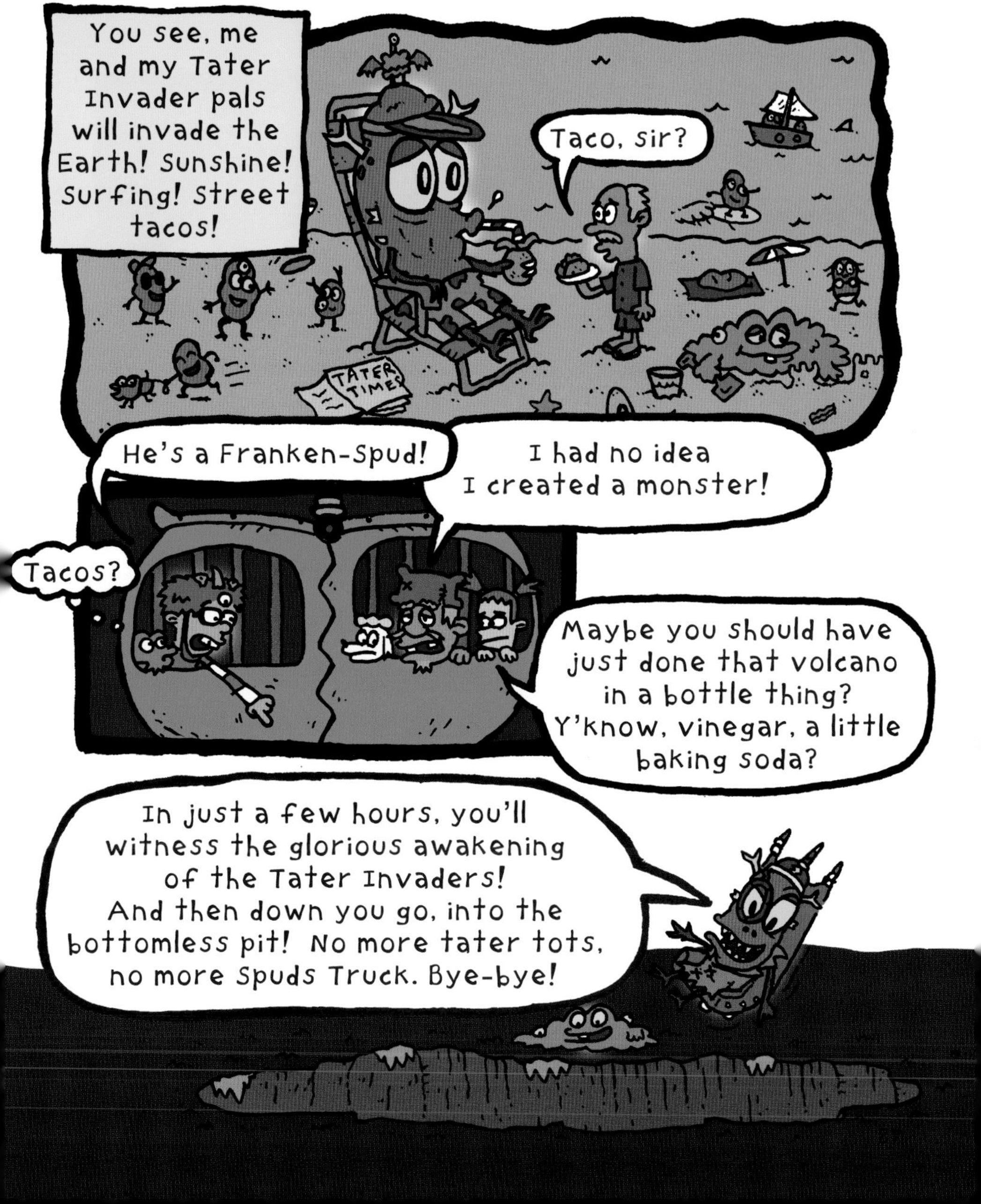
You see, me and my Tater Invader pals will invade the Earth! Sunshine! Surfing! Street tacos!
Taco, sir?
TATER TIMES
He's a Franken-Spud!
I had no idea I created a monster!
Tacos?
Maybe you should have just done that volcano in a bottle thing? Y'know, vinegar, a little baking soda?
In just a few hours, you'll witness the glorious awakening of the Tater Invaders! And then down you go, into the bottomless pit! No more tater tots, no more Spuds Truck. Bye-bye!

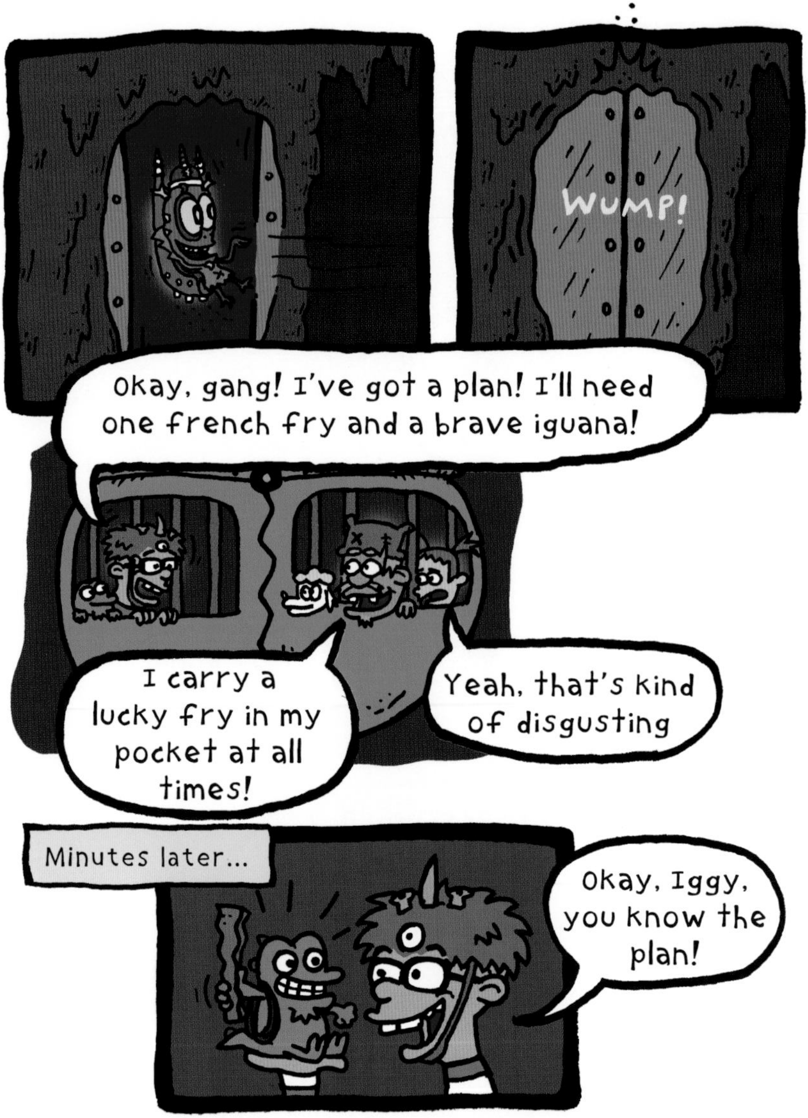
WUMP!
Okay, gang! I've got a plan! I'll need one french fry and a brave iguana!
I carry a lucky fry in my pocket at all times!
Yeah, that's kind of disgusting
Minutes later...
Okay, Iggy, you know the plan!

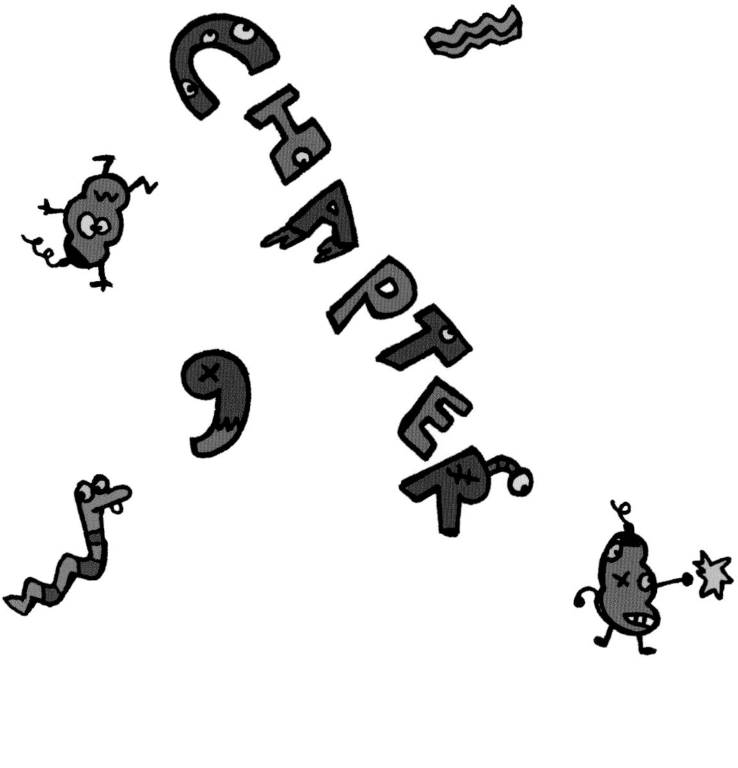
CHAPTER
9

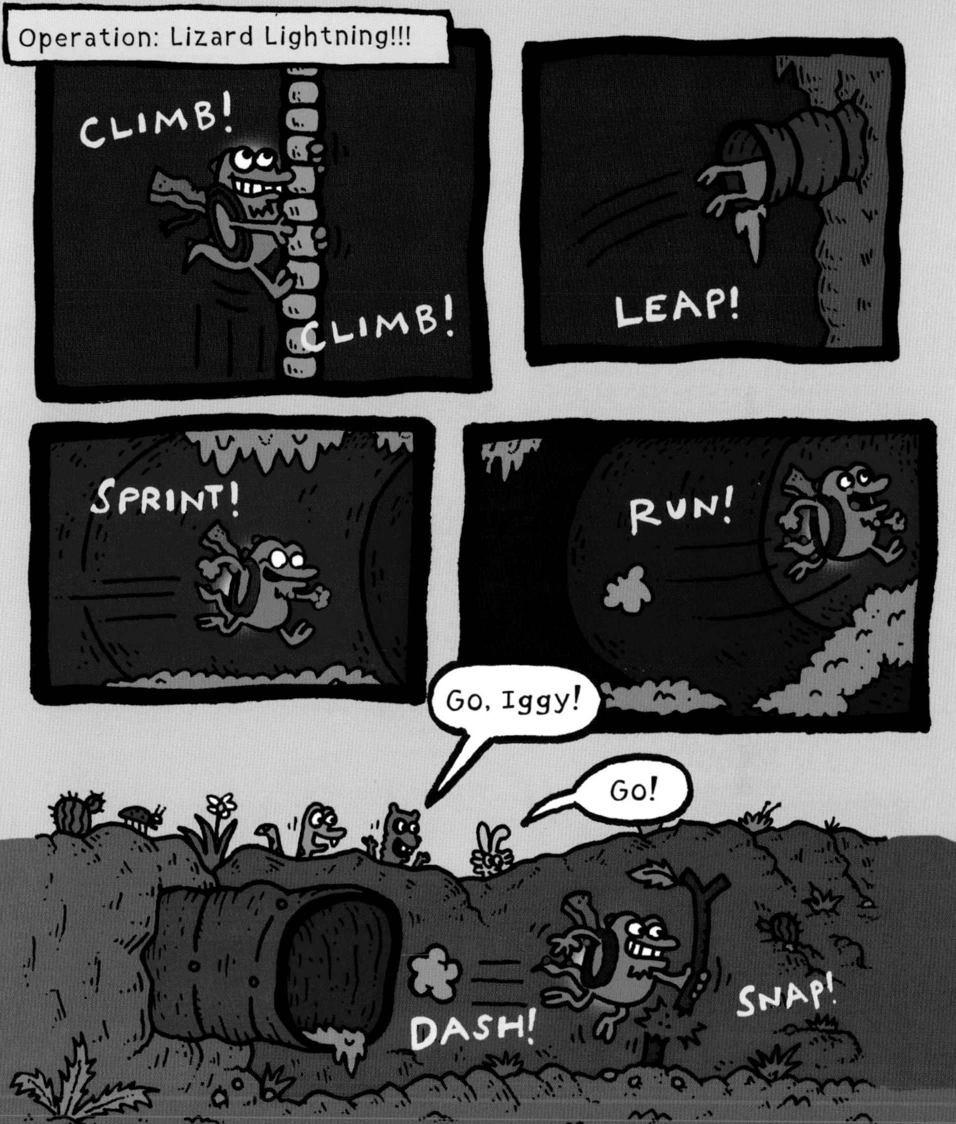
Operation: Lizard Lightning!!!
CLIMB!
CLIMB!
LEAP!
SPRINT!
RUN!
Go, Iggy!
Go!
DASH!
SNAP!

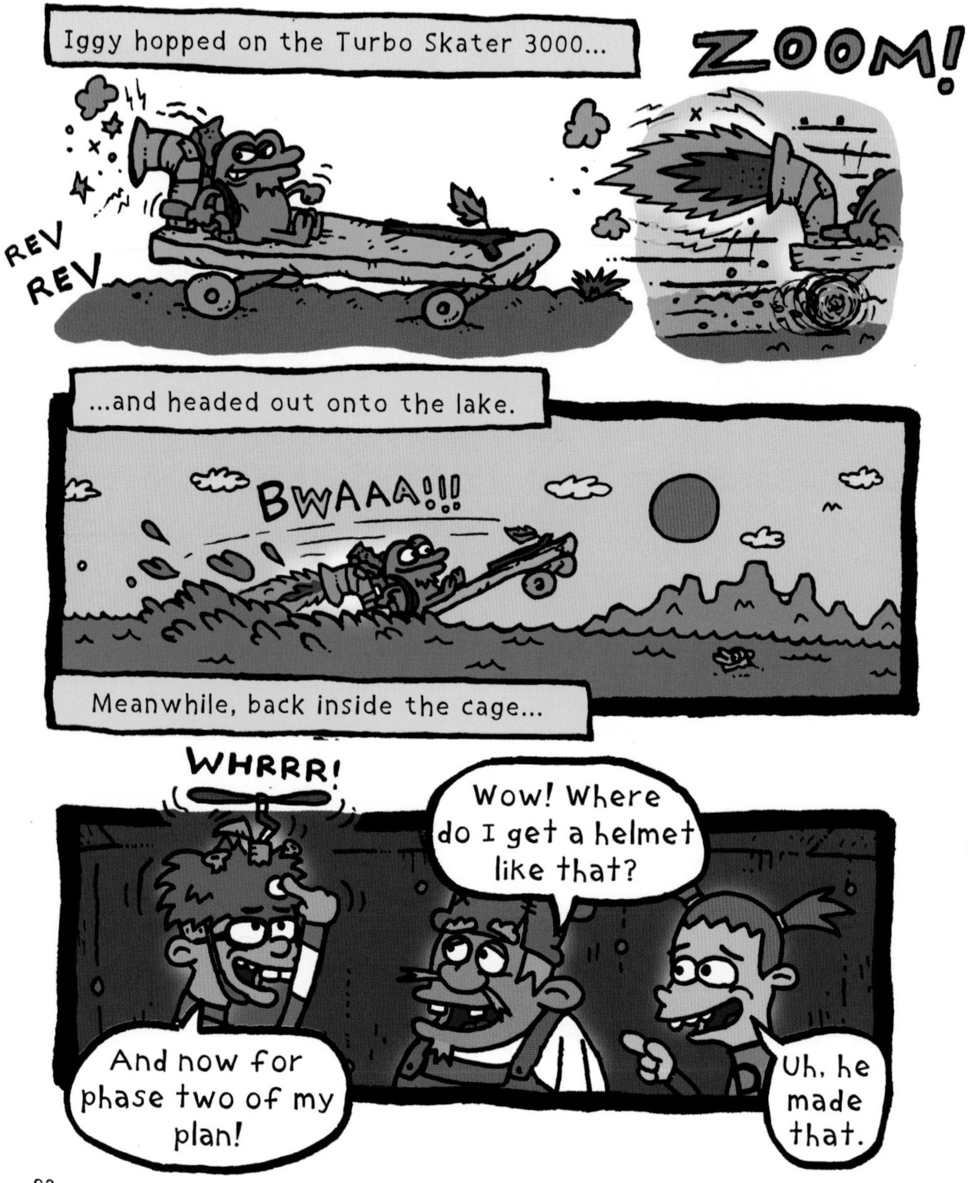
Iggy hopped on the Turbo Skater 3000...
REV REV
ZOOM!
...and headed out onto the lake.
BWAAA!!!
Meanwhile, back inside the cage...
WHRRR!
Wow! Where do I get a helmet like that?
And now for phase two of my plan!
Uh, he made that.

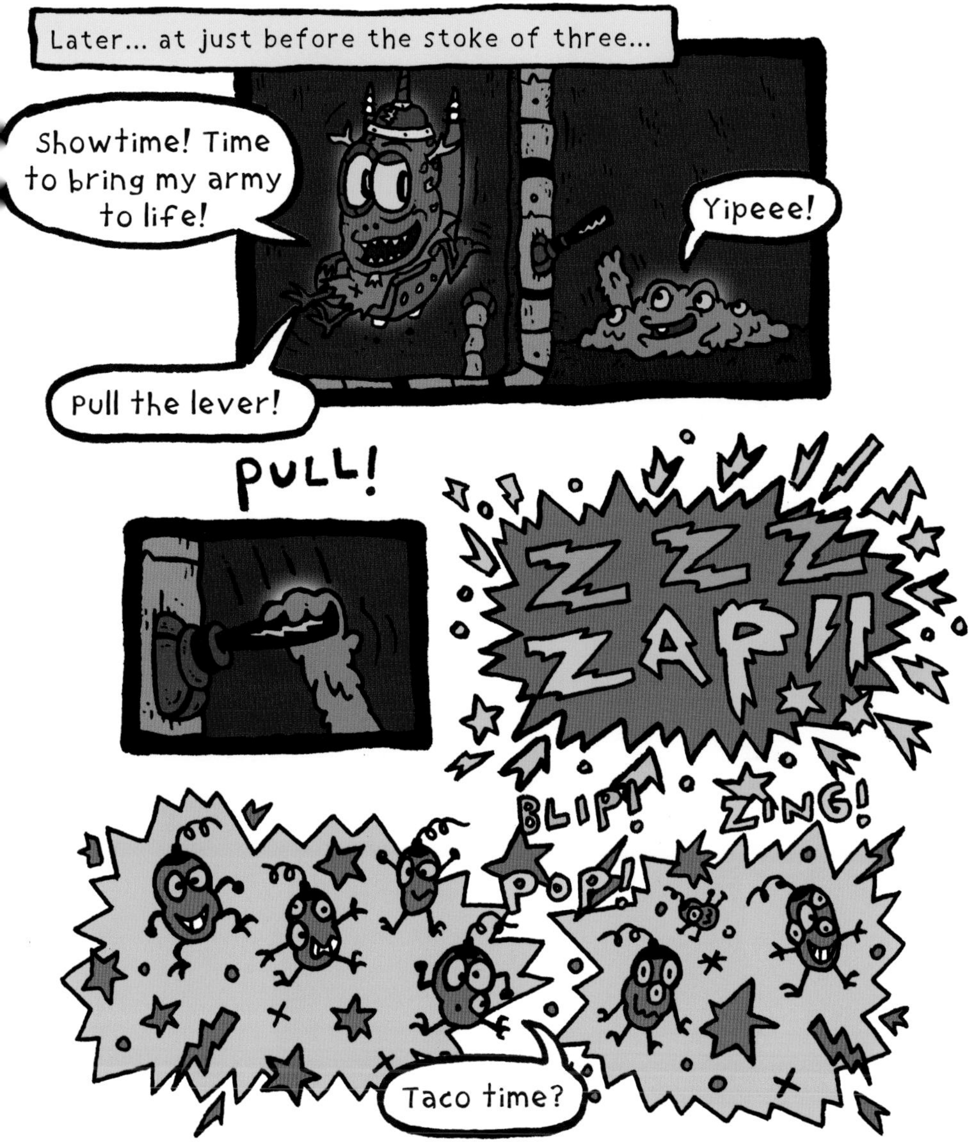

Later... at just before the stoke of three...
Showtime! Time to bring my army to life!
Yipeee!
Pull the lever!
PULL!
ZZZZAP!!
BLIP!
ZING!
POP!
Taco time?

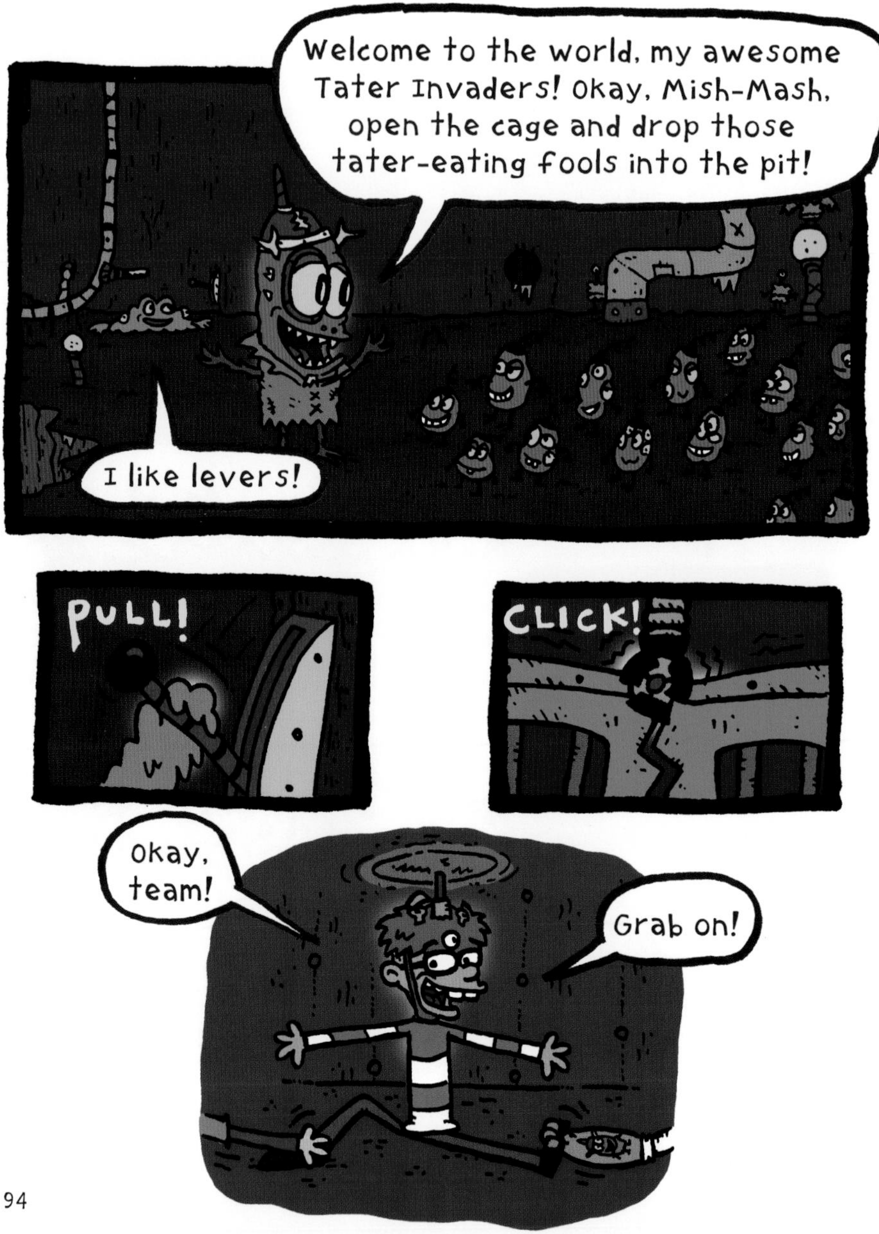
Welcome to the world, my awesome Tater Invaders! Okay, Mish-Mash, open the cage and drop those tater-eating fools into the pit!
I like levers!
PULL!
CLICK!
Okay, team!
Grab on!

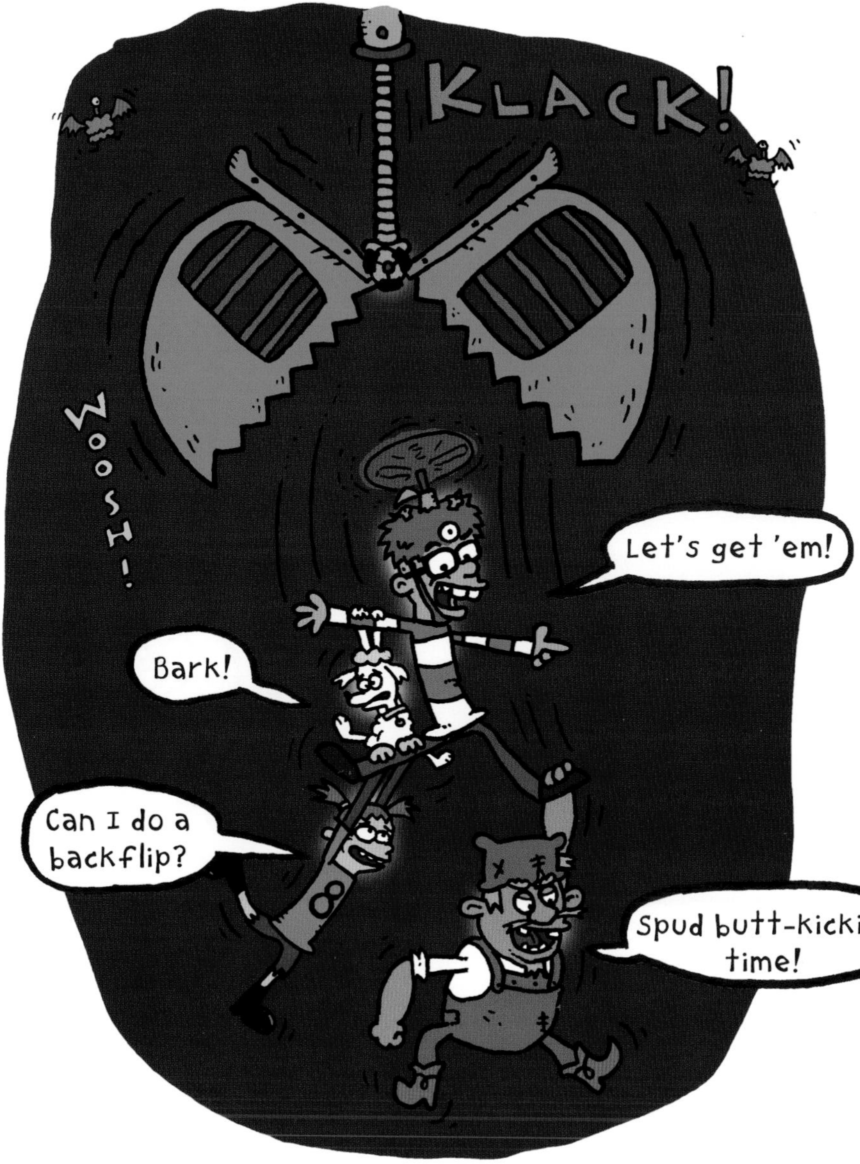
KLACK!
WOOSH!
Let's get 'em!
Bark!
Can I do a backflip?
Spud butt-kickin' time!

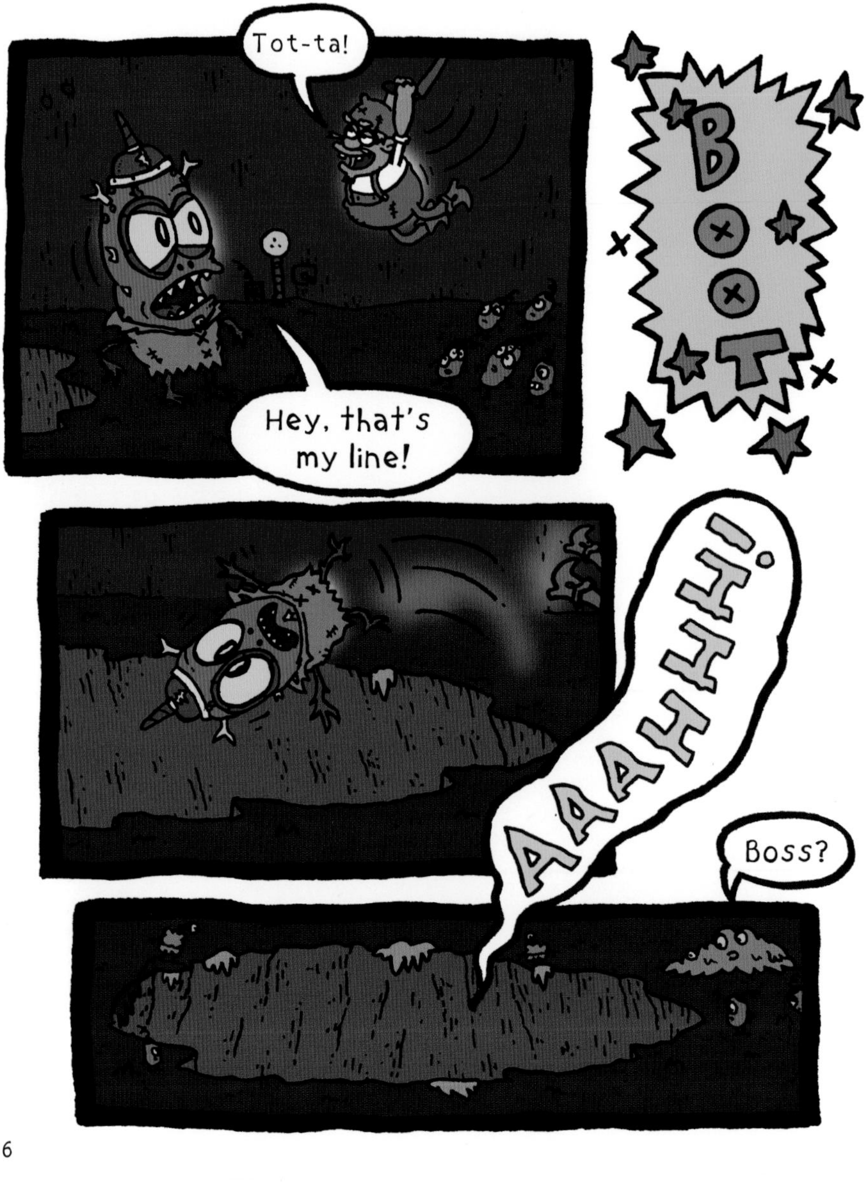
Tot-ta!
Hey, that's my line!
BOOT
AAAAHHH!
Boss?

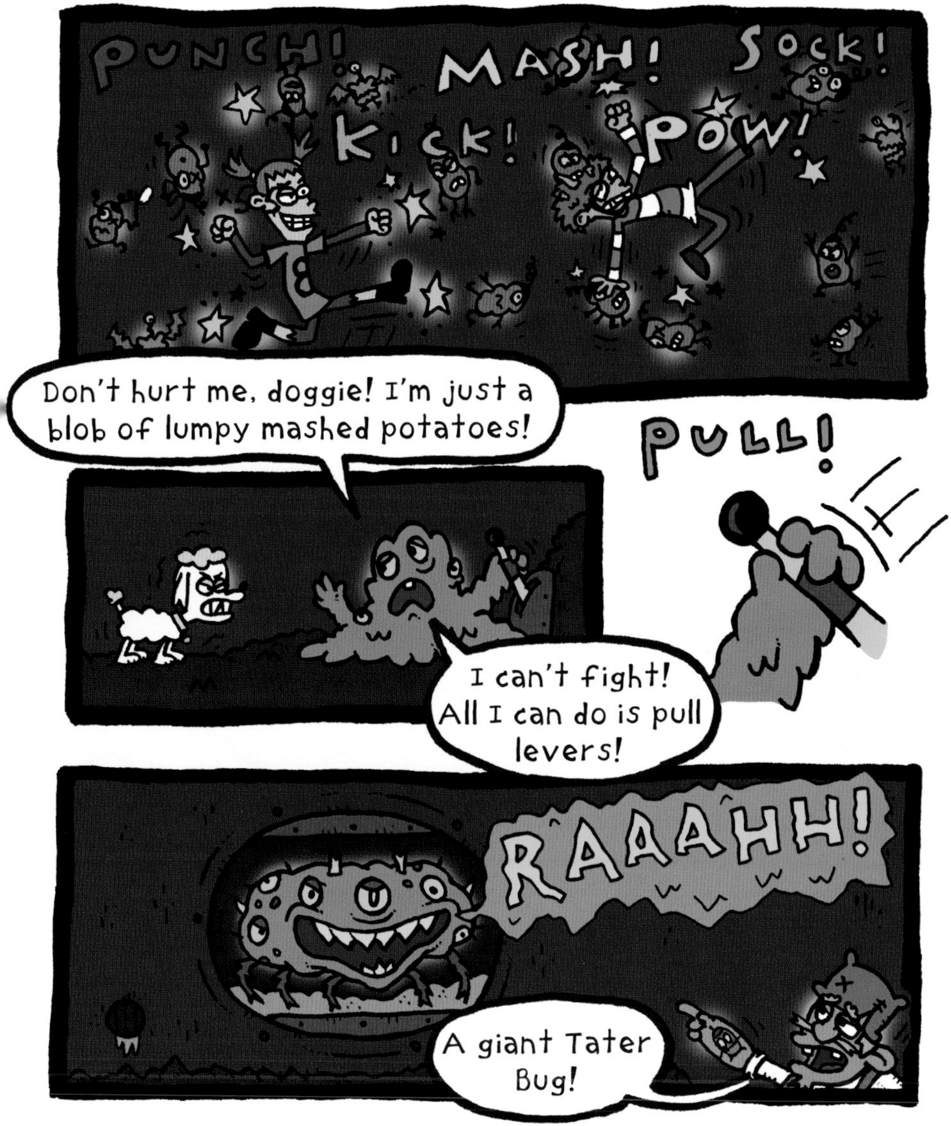
PUNCH!
MASH!
SOCK!
KICK!
POW!
Don't hurt me, doggie! I'm just a blob of lumpy mashed potatoes!
PULL!
I can't fight! All I can do is pull levers!
RAAAHH!
A giant Tater Bug!

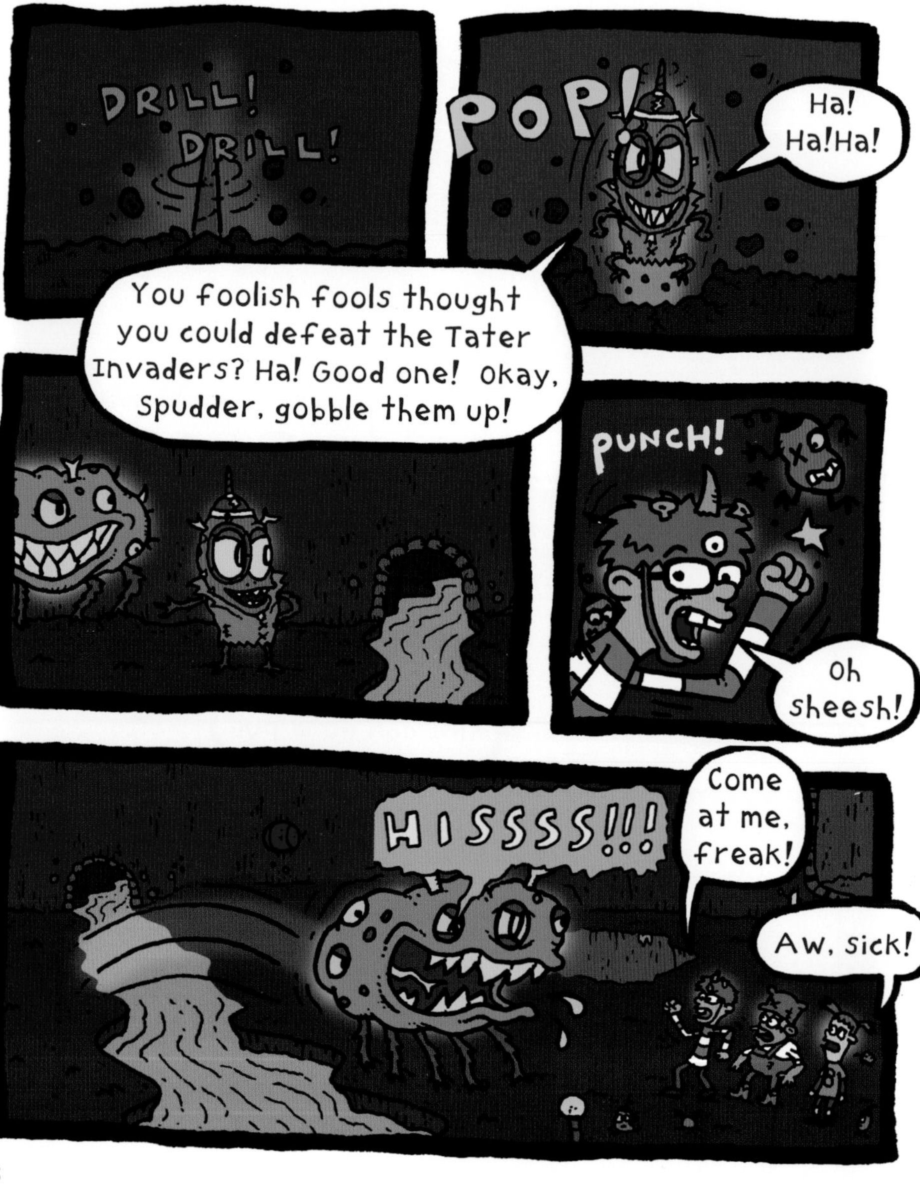
DRILL! DRILL!
POP!
Ha! Ha!Ha!
You foolish fools thought you could defeat the Tater Invaders? Ha! Good one! Okay, Spudder, gobble them up!
PUNCH!
Oh sheesh!
HISSSS!!!
Come at me, freak!
Aw, sick!

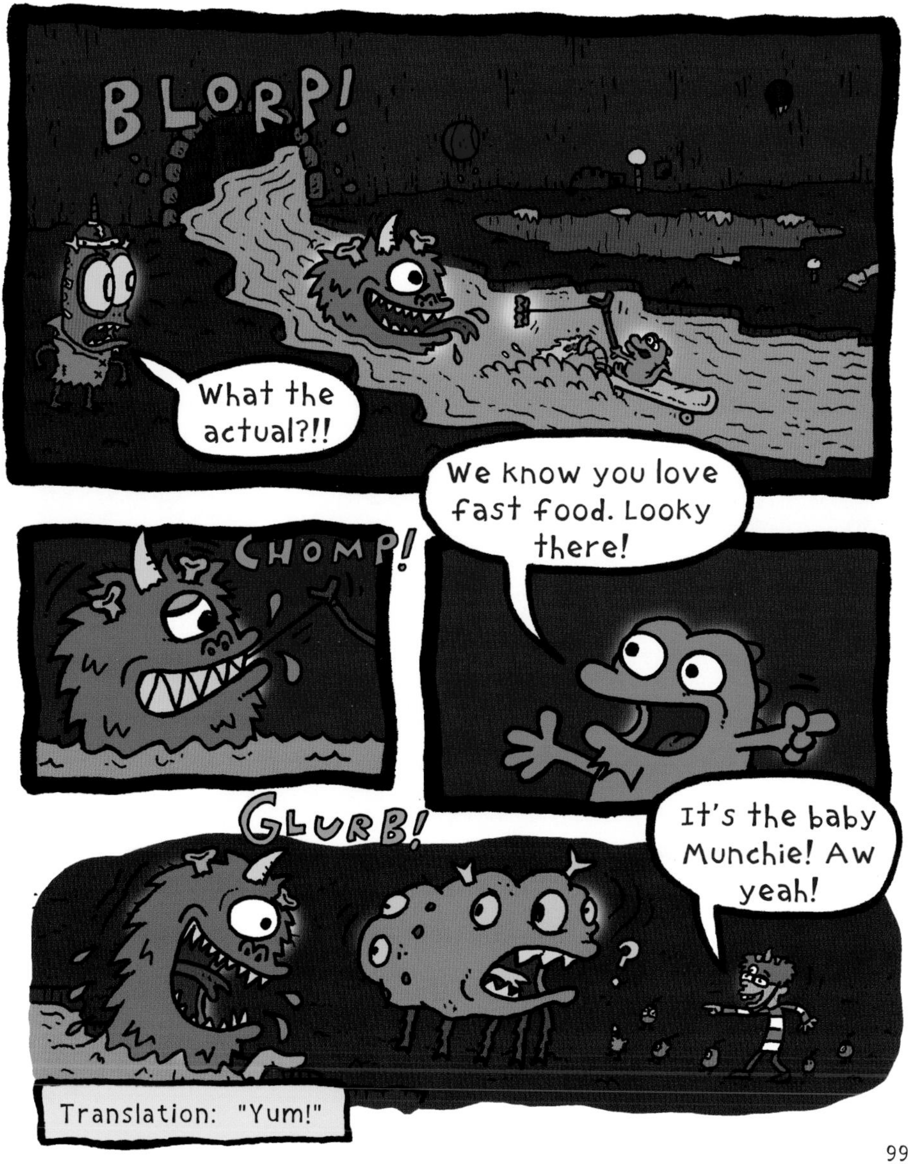
BLORP!
What the actual?!!
CHOMP!
We know you love fast food. Looky there!
GLURB!
It's the baby Munchie! Aw yeah!
Translation: "Yum!"

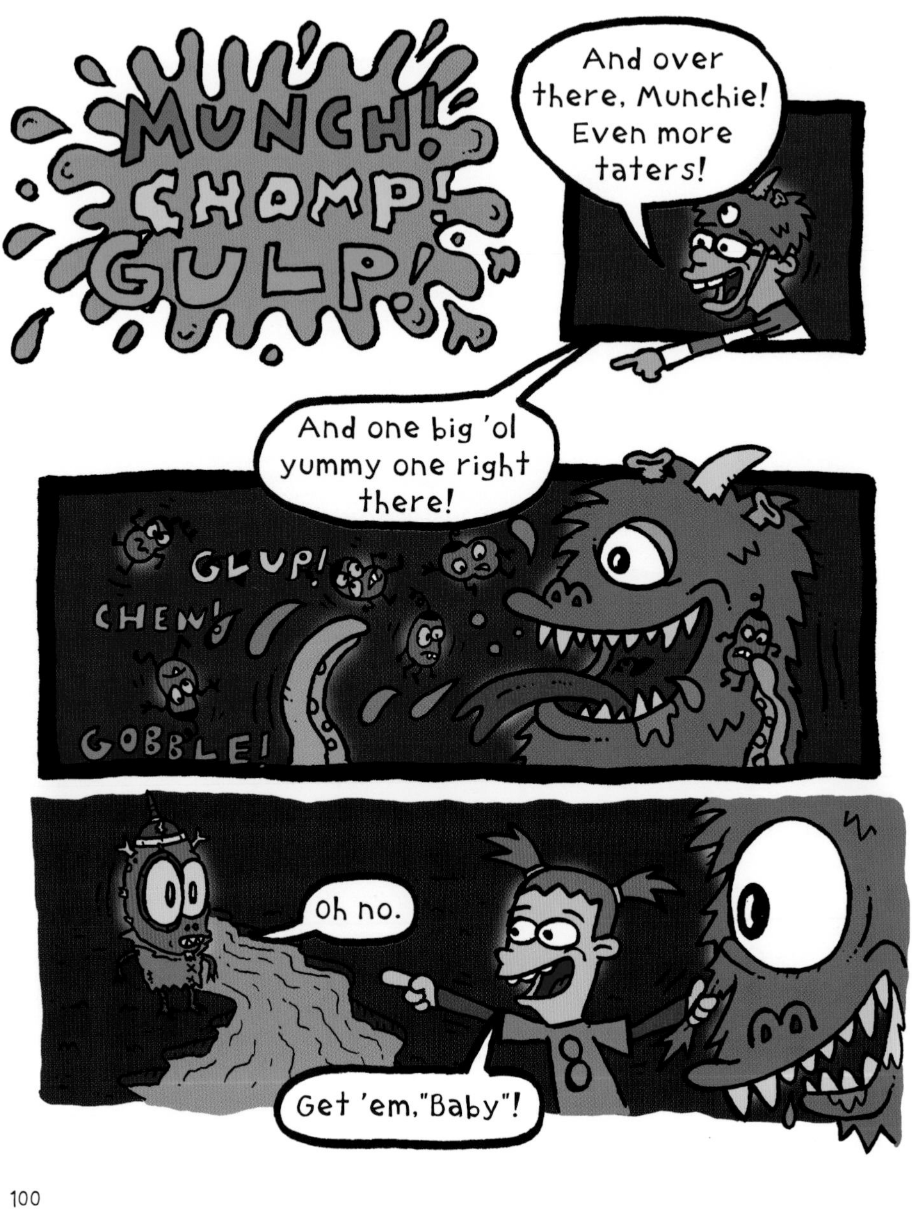
MUNCH! CHOMP! GULP!
And over there, Munchie! Even more taters!
And one big 'ol yummy one right there!
GLUP!
CHEW!
GOBBLE!
Oh no.
Get 'em, "Baby"!

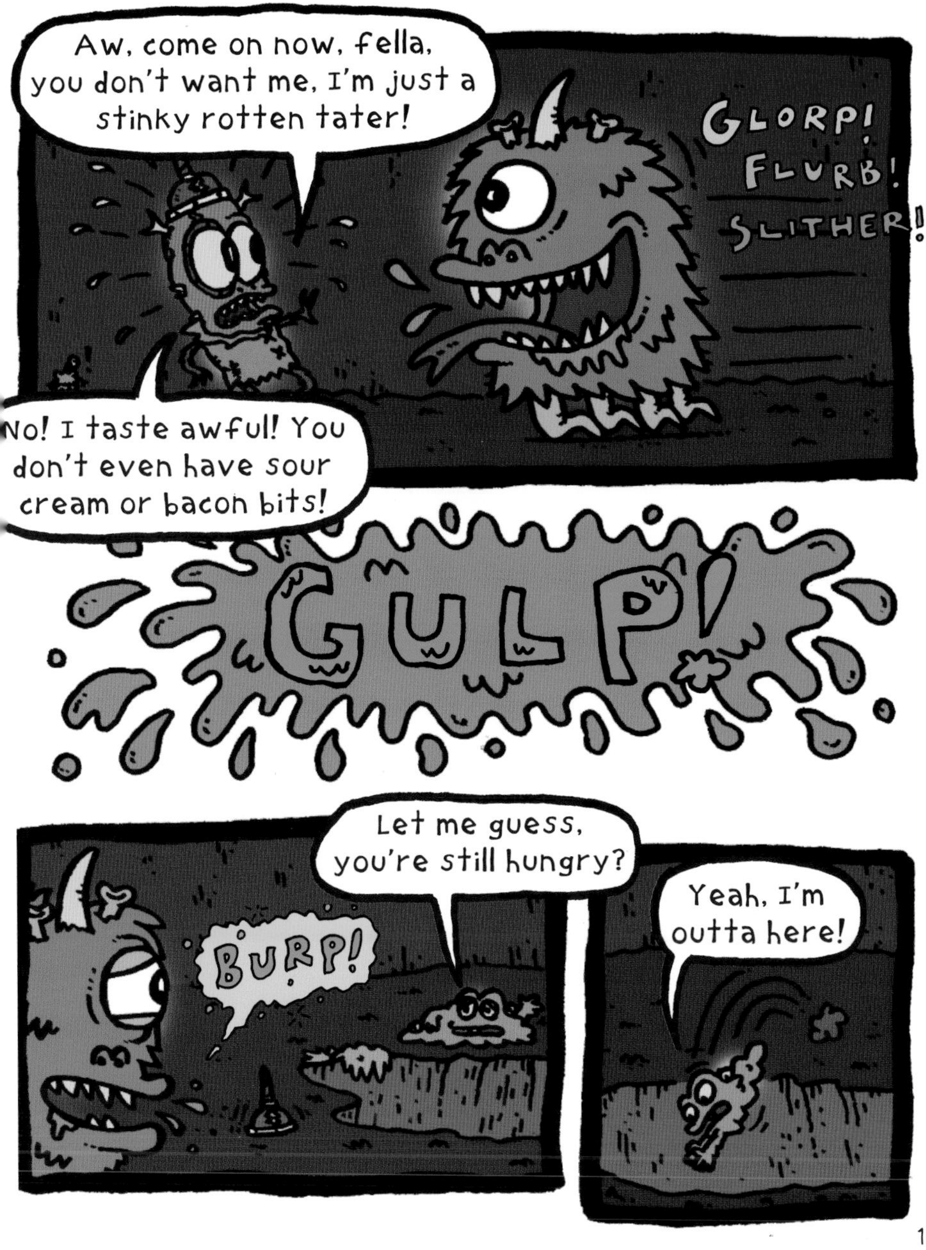
Aw, come on now, fella, you don't want me, I'm just a stinky rotten tater!
GLORP! FLURB! SLITHER!
No! I taste awful! You don't even have sour cream or bacon bits!
GULP!
BURP!
Let me guess, you're still hungry?
Yeah, I'm outta here!

CHAPTER 10

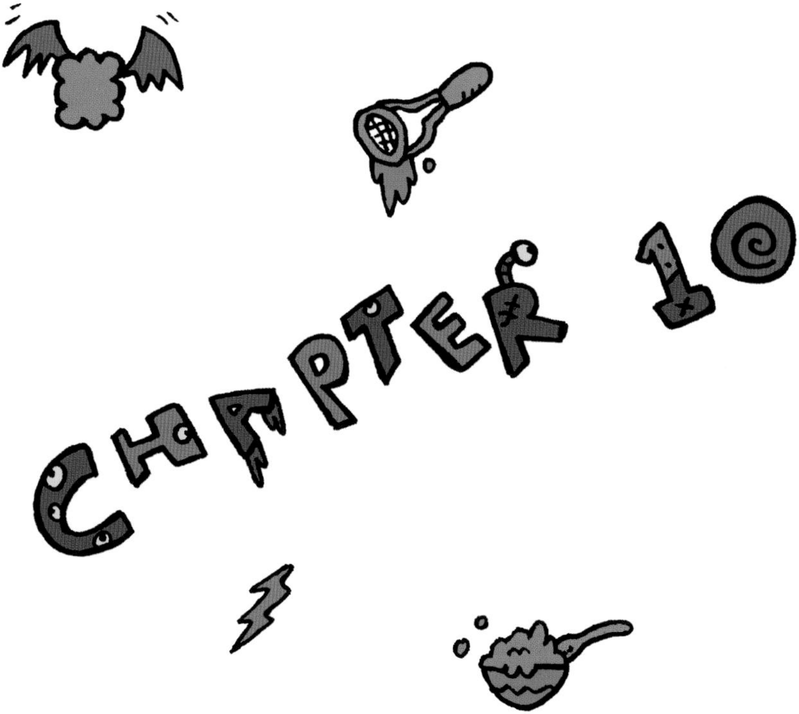

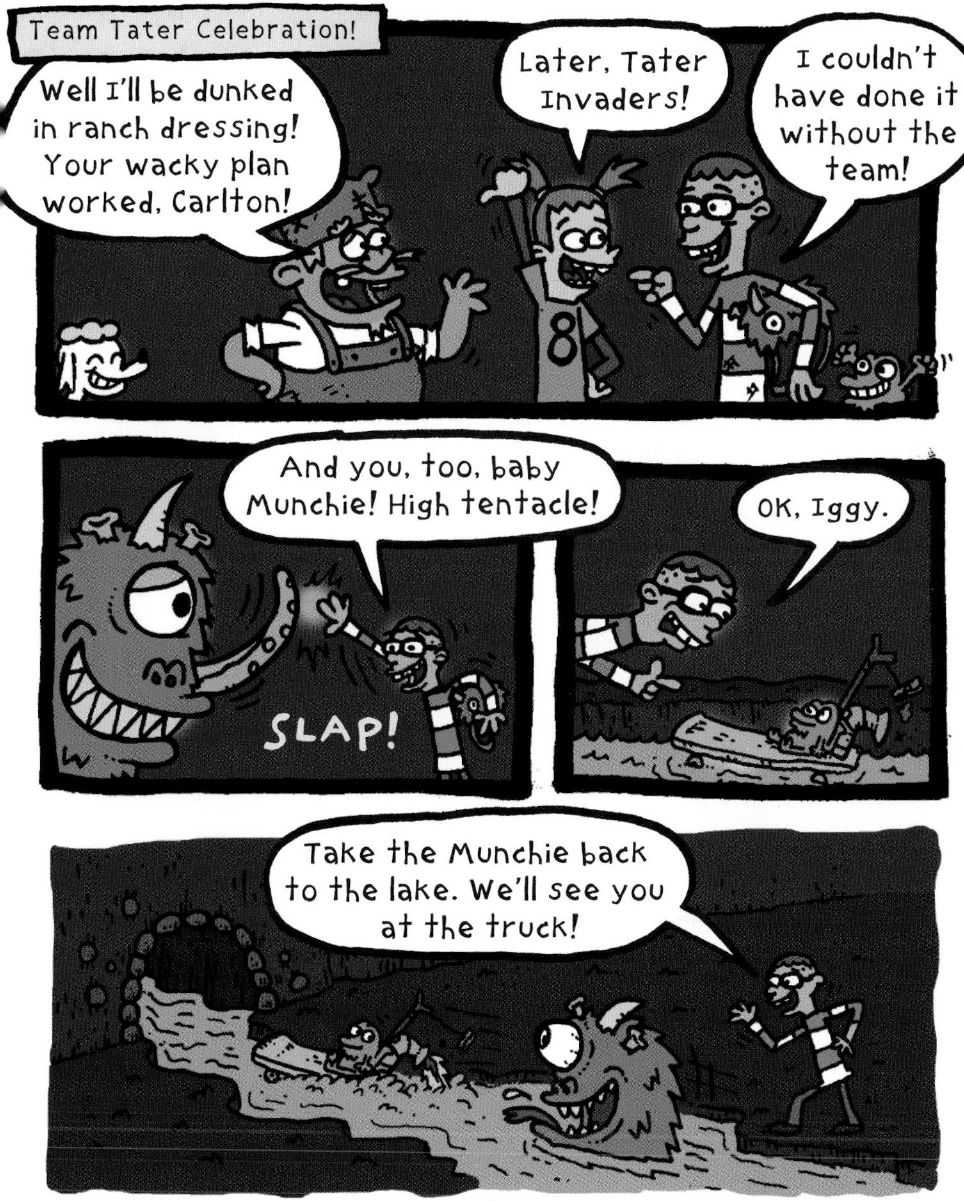

Team Tater Celebration!
Well I'll be dunked in ranch dressing! Your wacky plan worked, Carlton!
Later, Tater Invaders!
I couldn't have done it without the team!
And you, too, baby Munchie! High tentacle!
SLAP!
OK, Iggy.
Take the Munchie back to the lake. We'll see you at the truck!

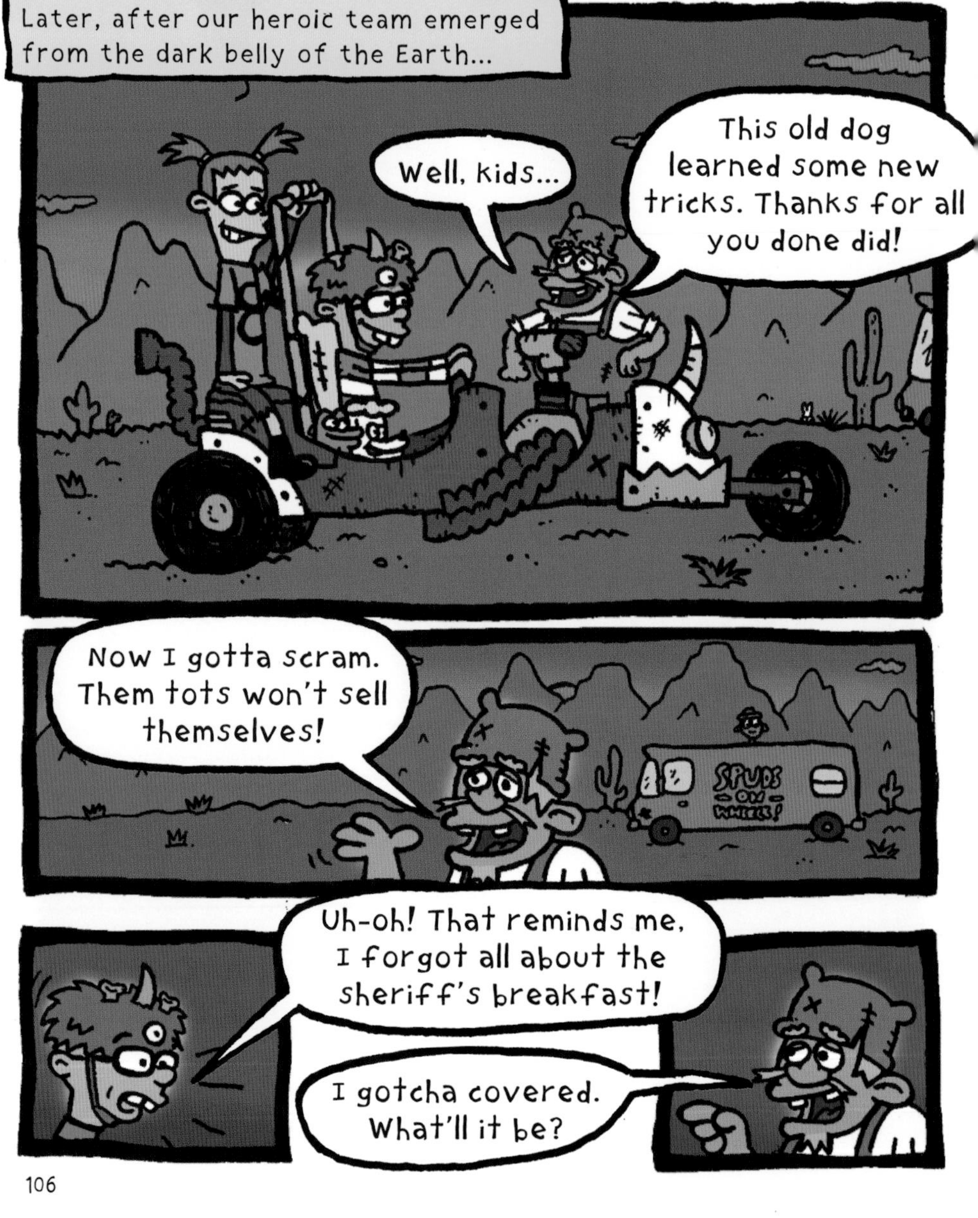
Later, after our heroic team emerged from the dark belly of the Earth...
Well, kids...
This old dog learned some new tricks. Thanks for all you done did!
Now I gotta scram. Them tots won't sell themselves!
SPUDS ON WHEELS!
Uh-oh! That reminds me, I forgot all about the sheriff's breakfast!
I gotcha covered. What'll it be?

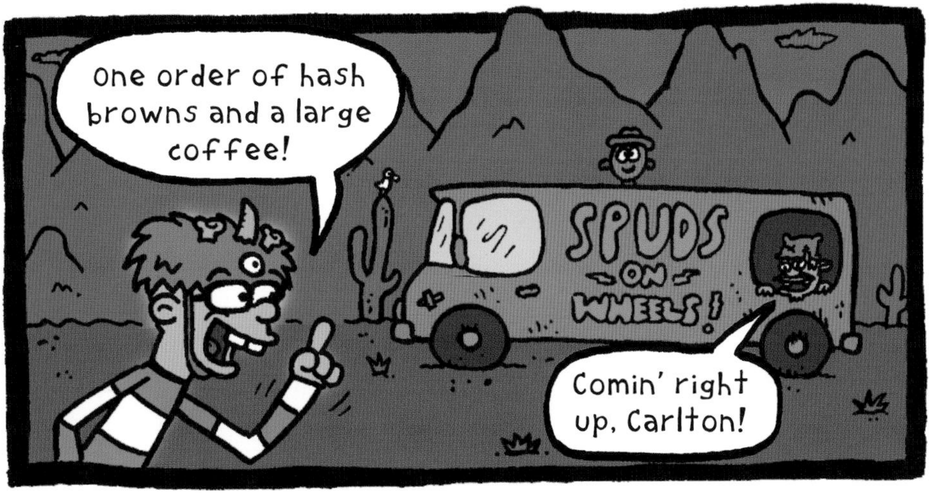
One order of hash browns and a large coffee!
SPUDS ON WHEELS!
Comin' right up, Carlton!

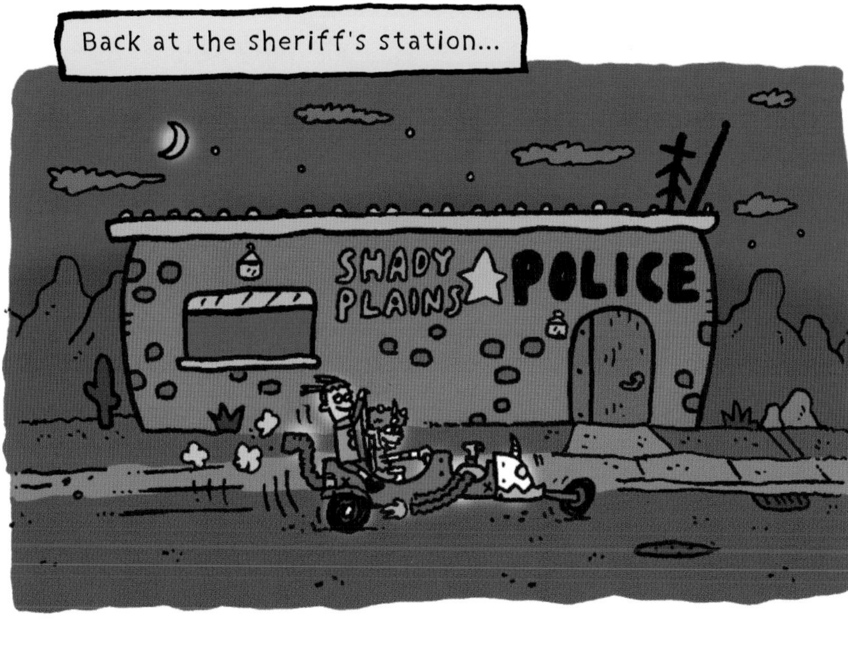
Back at the sheriff's station...
SHADY PLAINS POLICE

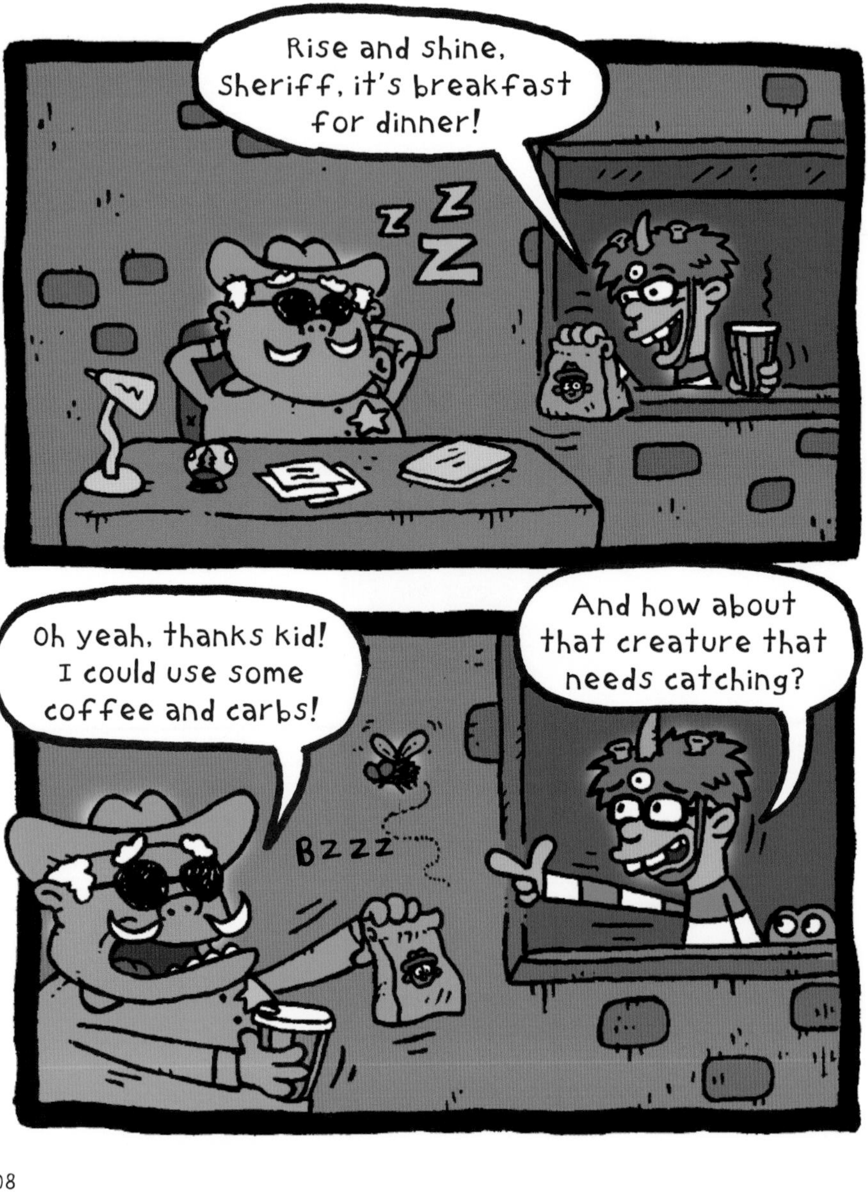
Rise and shine, Sheriff, it's breakfast for dinner!
Z Z Z
Oh yeah, thanks kid! I could use some coffee and carbs!
And how about that creature that needs catching?
BZZZ

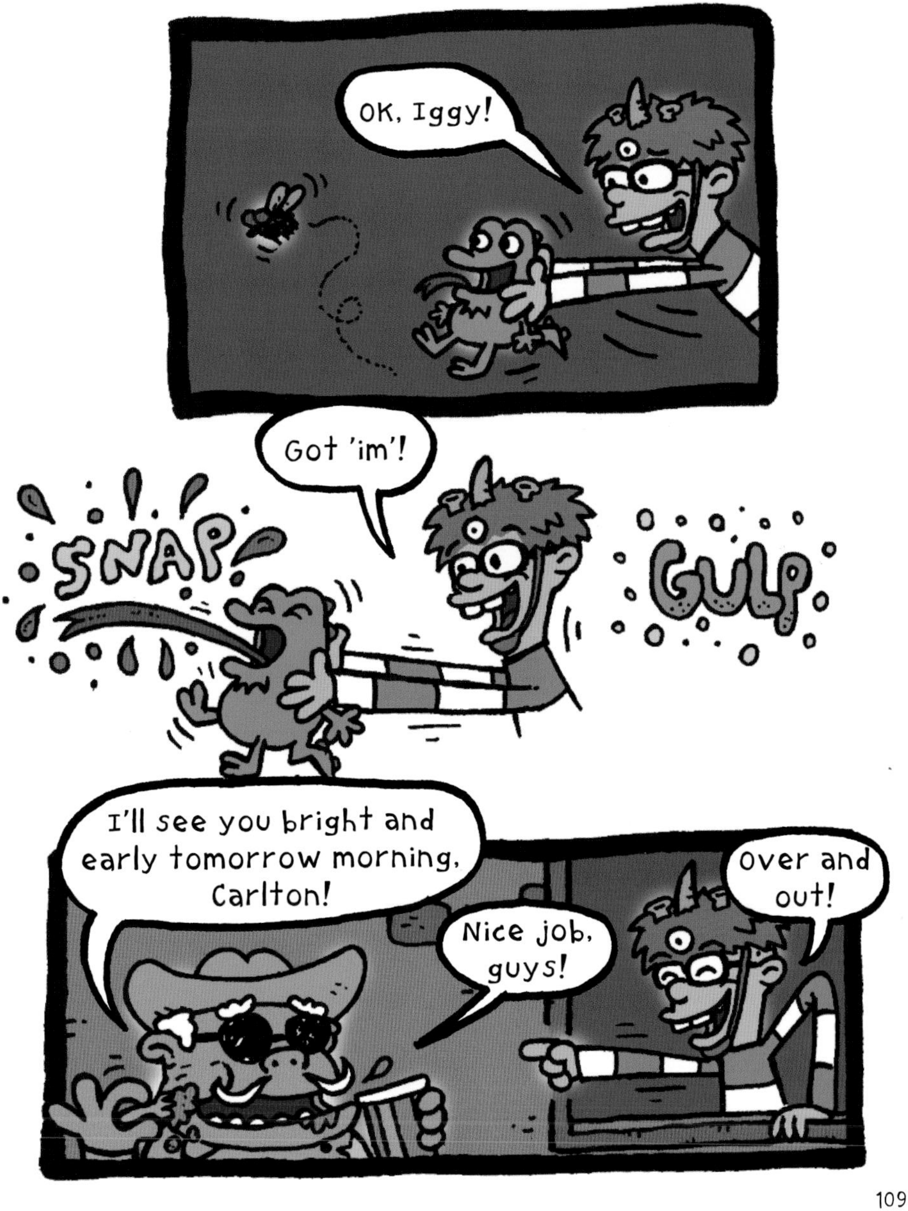
OK, Iggy!
Got 'im'!
SNAP
GULP
I'll see you bright and early tomorrow morning, Carlton!
Nice job, guys!
Over and out!

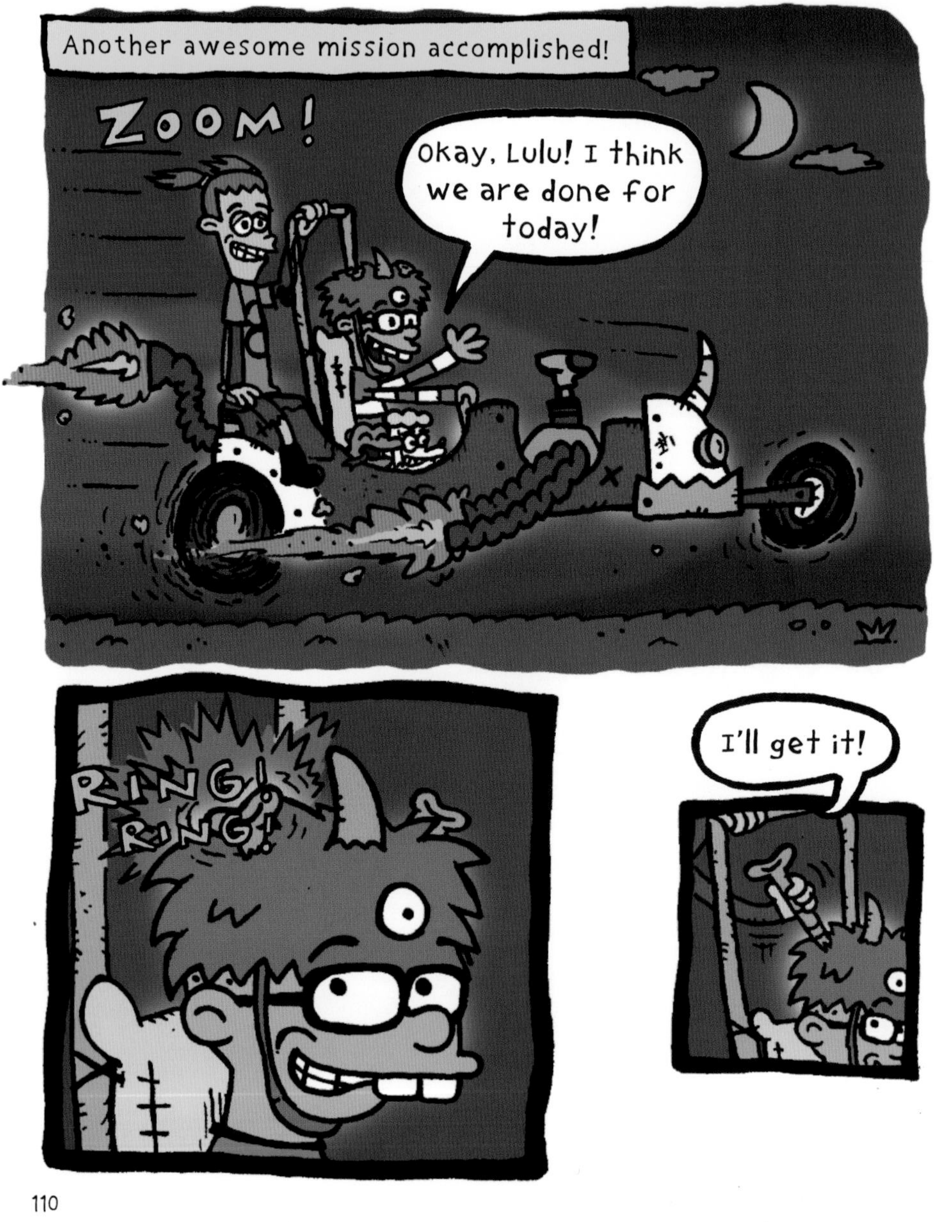
Another awesome mission accomplished!
ZOOM!
Okay, Lulu! I think we are done for today!
RING! RING!
I'll get it!

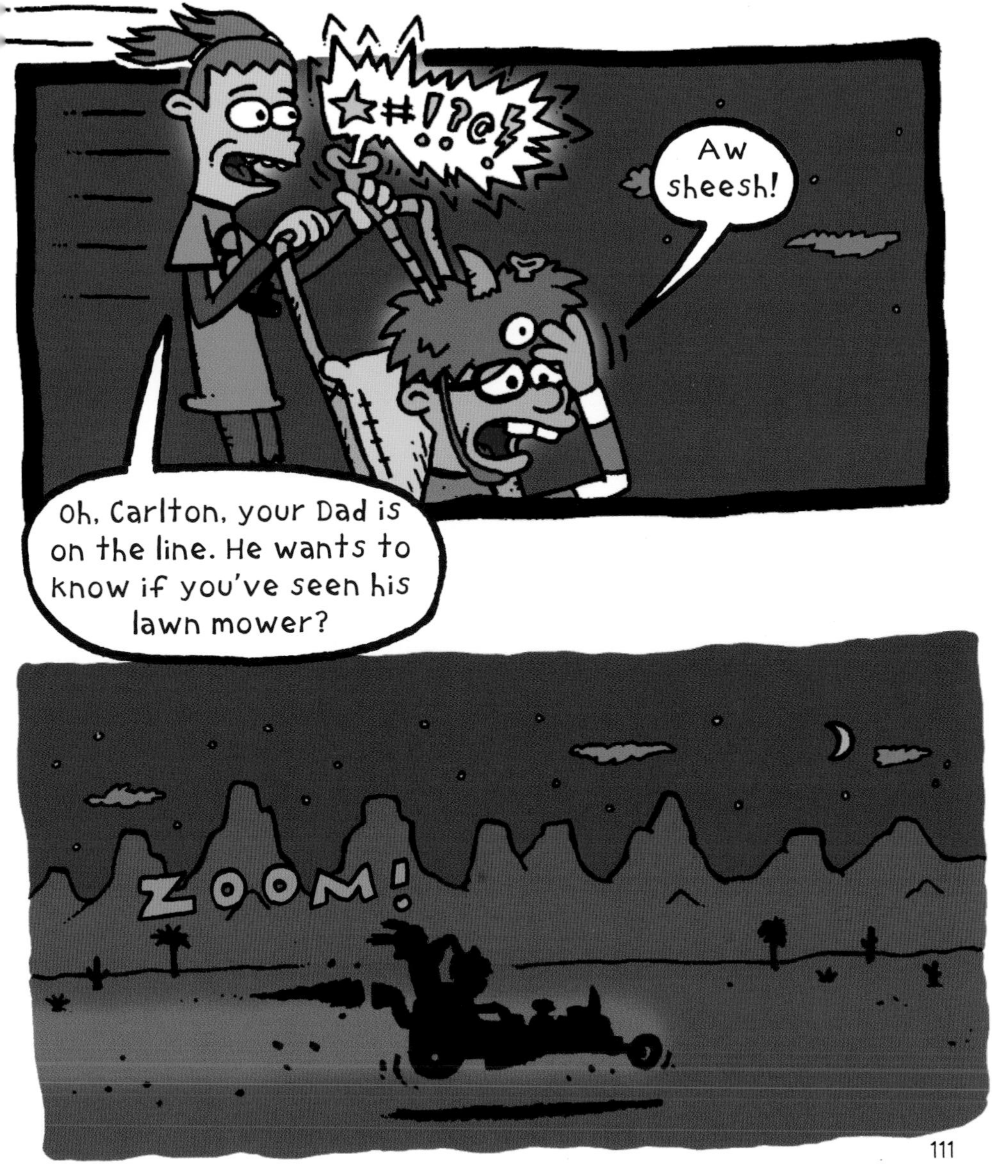
Oh, Carlton, your Dad is on the line. He wants to know if you've seen his lawn mower?
Aw sheesh!
ZOOM!

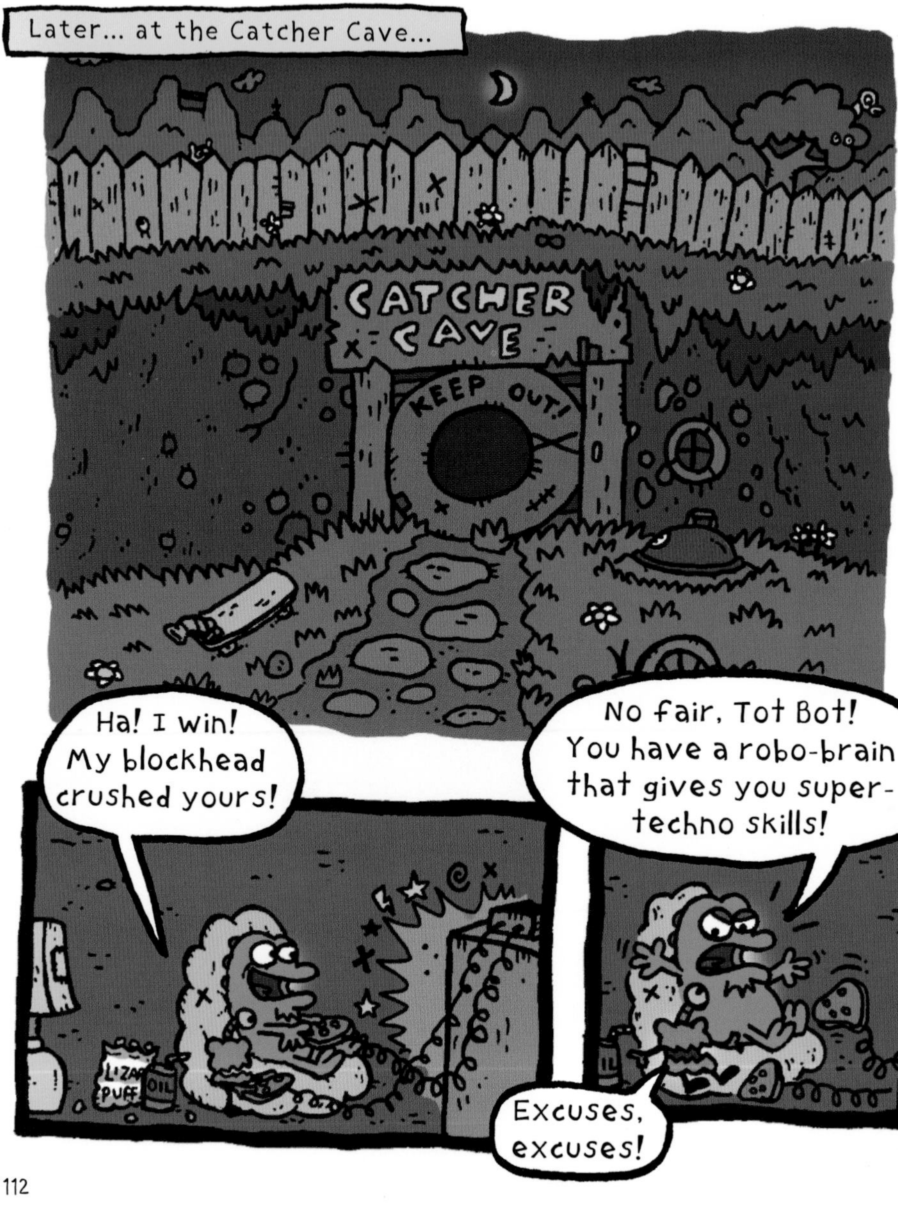
Later... at the Catcher Cave...
CATCHER CAVE
KEEP OUT!
Ha! I win! My blockhead crushed yours!
No fair, Tot Bot! You have a robo-brain that gives you super-techno skills!
Excuses, excuses!
LIZARD PUFFS
OIL

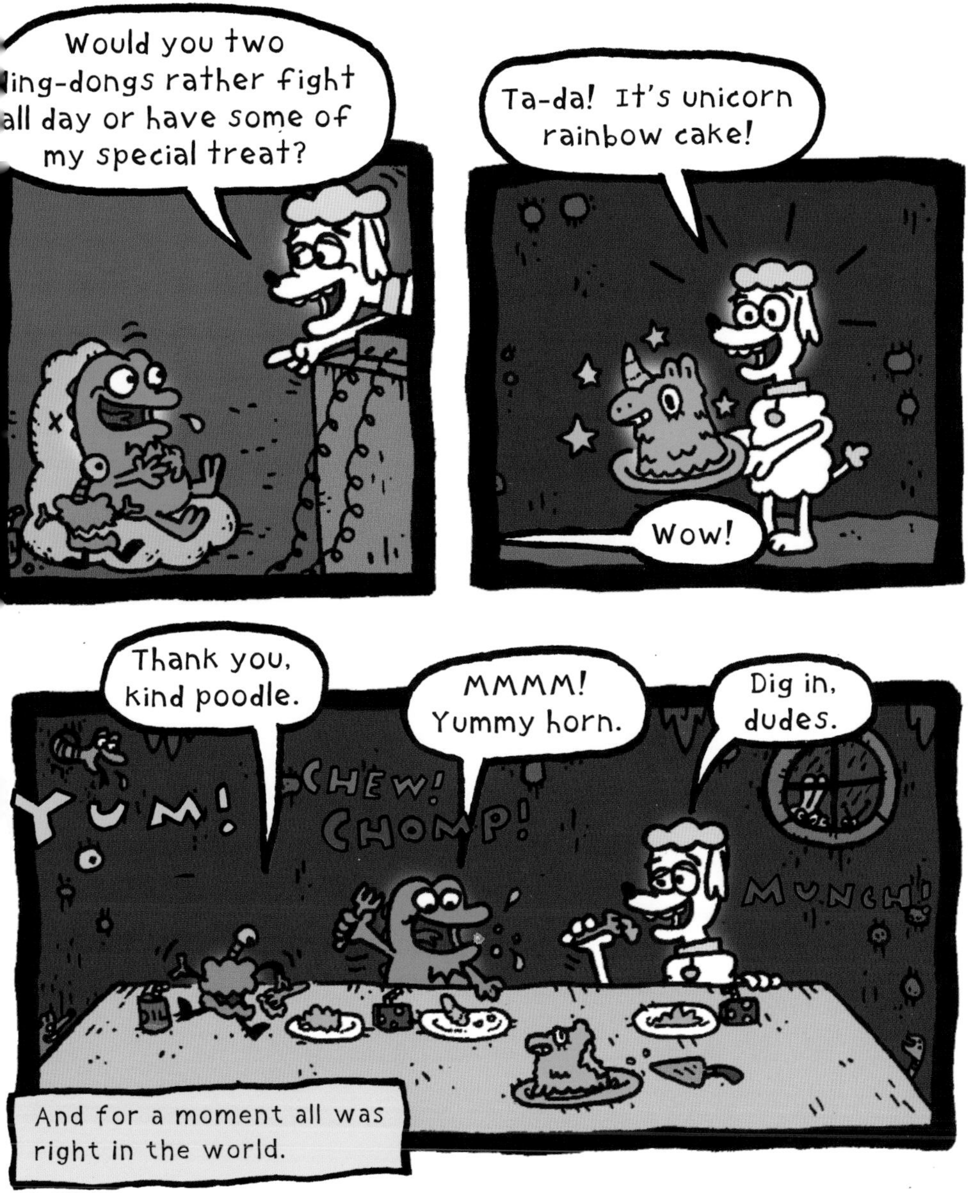
Would you two
ing-dongs rather fight
all day or have some of
my special treat?
Ta-da! It's unicorn
rainbow cake!
Wow!
Thank you,
kind poodle.
MMMM!
Yummy horn.
Dig in,
dudes.
YUM!
CHEW!
CHOMP!
MUNCH!
DIL
And for a moment all was
right in the world.

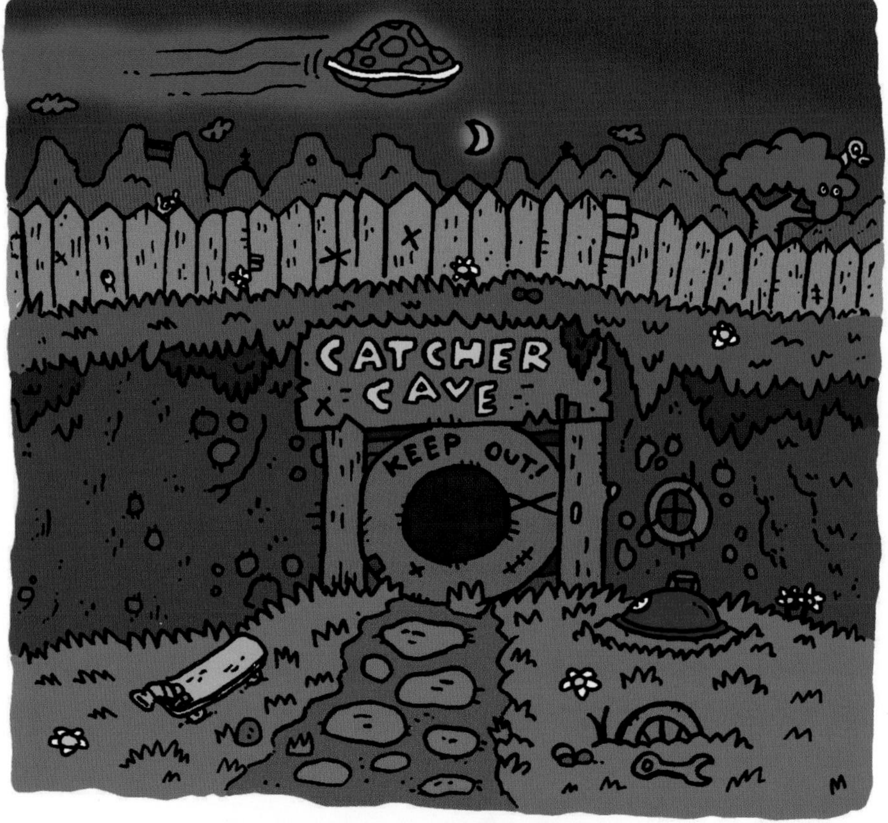
CATCHER CAVE
KEEP OUT!

Uh-oh, here we go again!

Carlton Crumple
Creature Catcher Book 3:
Reptoids from Space!

Carlton Crumple must rescue Poof-Poof and Iggy from the clutches of slimy aliens from space. Zap!

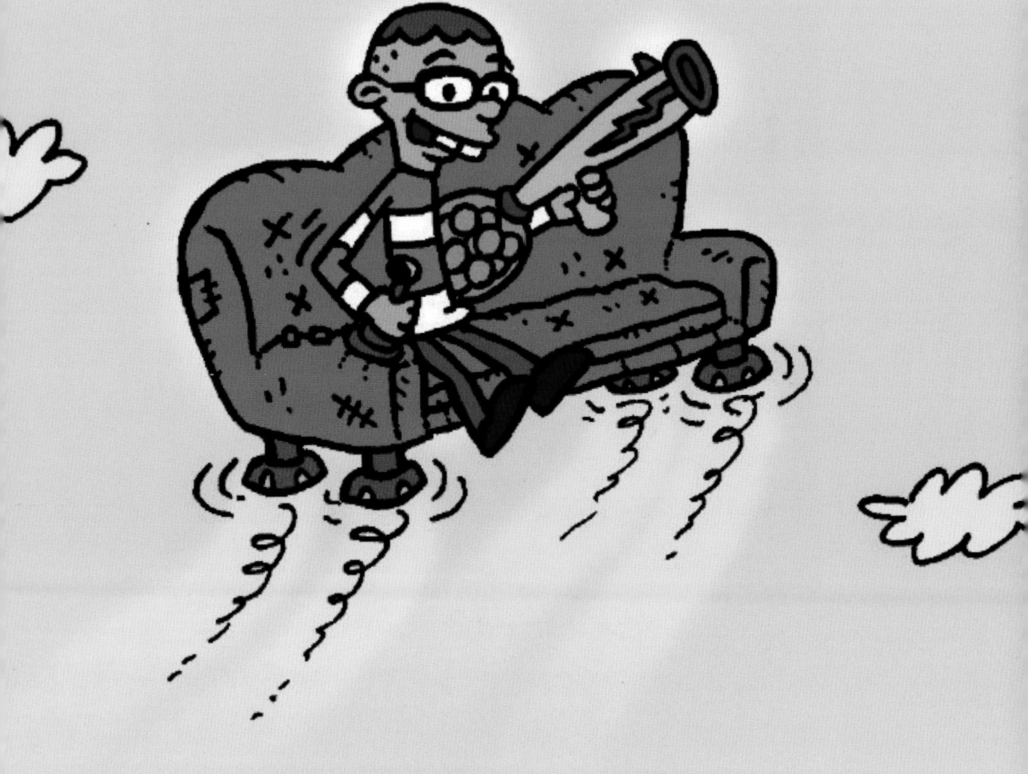

ABOUT THE AUTHOR

DAVID FREMONT grew up in Fremont, California—yep, a Fremont from Fremont! He loved watching *Underdog* cartoons, reading comics, and drawing with his brother. When David was eleven, his cousin Steve showed him a super-cool shark comic that he had drawn, inspiring David to start drawing his own comics. When David grew up, he moved across the bay to San Francisco, where he got a job painting cartoons at an animation studio. While at Colossal Pictures, he created projects for Cartoon Network and Disney. More recently, after moving to Los Angeles, he created a pilot for Nickelodeon and an online kids series for DreamWorksTV, called *Public Pool*. He currently lives in Woodland Hills with his family (and many furry pet creatures!), where he teaches cartooning classes to kids. This is his second book for children.

ACKNOWLEDGMENTS

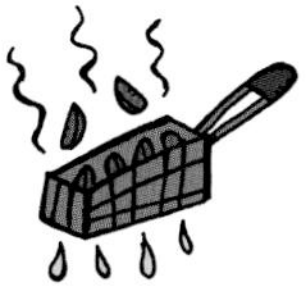

I am eternally grateful for the following people who helped put this book together. Editor-in-Chief Bethany Buck for your hard work and patience and for keeping the Spuds-on-Wheels truck rolling! Color Wizard/Partner-in-Toons Jimbo Matison for going the extra extra (and not getting completely swallowed by that dastardly dog!), and Graphic Artist Sammy Yeun for putting it all together while small children with stuffed monkeys climbed atop your head. Big thumbs-ups to all the kind and hardworking folks at Pixel+Ink, Holiday House, and Trustbridge. Tot-tastic job, team! Special thanks again to Mary Harrington who tossed that first french fry into the lake, and Kyra Reppen who got the Munchies loaded up into the hippie van. For publishing tips and advice, thank you to hometown pal and romance author Julie Anne Long. High fins to Patricia Arquette and Eric White for hosting the Jaws movie pool party and inadvertently helping unlock my writer's block (and of course thanks to Steven Spielberg for making that great film. Quint rules!). Most of the art for this book was created while sheltering in place during the 2020 pandemic and my inspiration and motivation came from many virtual (and six feet apart) connections. Shout-outs to the following podcast people that kept me laughing and crying while I inked potato monsters: Justin White/Outspoken, Marc Maron,

Tom Scharpling, and Dax Shepard. Thank you to Wilco, Cat Power, Radiohead, Thelonious Monk, Deerhoof, and all the other great music that inspires me while I work. Encore to my neighborhood friends for social distance backyard jams. Lesli Simon, Rob Schwartz, and Dustin Penrod, you guys rock! Thank you to neighbor Carol Rees for the handmade masks and beautiful bouquets that would show up at our doorstep and brighten my day. For all the novel writing games via Zoom during quarantine, thank you to the Fremont, Silas, Engle, and Majewski families. You all should write books! Thank you to kind friends Brad Mossman for all the inspiring art you sent, and Robin Scovill for our creative story-writing chats. Tension-freeing hugs to my wife Carol for being my personal copy editor and for your loving support, to my son Milo Wolf for enlightening us with the amazing Spirit Trap music you create and your surprise gifts (new Microns, whaaat?!!), and to my daughter Greta Fox for filling our tum-tums with your amazing baked treats and making us all laugh with your Tik-Tok dances and hilarious Love Island impressions. I love you all beyond words. Thank you so much to all of you Creature Catchers out there who enthusiastically gobbled down my first Carlton Crumple adventure and are eager for more. Your feedback and support mean the world to me! Lastly, but not leastly, thank you to all of the talented and creative students who have attended the cartooning and comic book classes that I have taught over the years and who continue to inspire me. Please don't ever stop drawing, writing, and creating... This world needs you now more than ever!

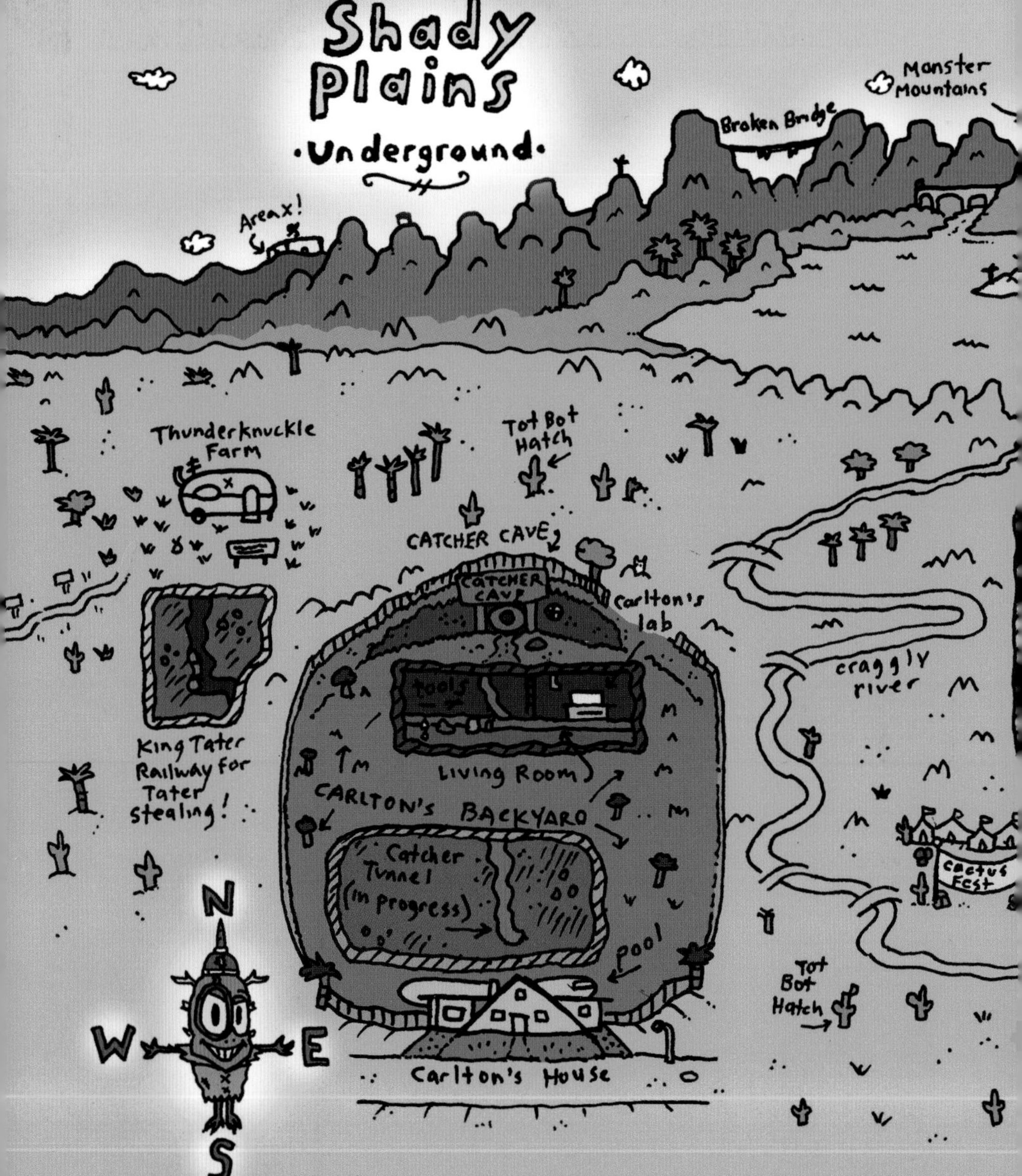
Shady Plains
·Underground·
Monster Mountains
Broken Bridge
Areax!
Thunderknuckle Farm
Tot Bot Hatch
CATCHER CAVE
CATCHER CAVE
Carlton's lab
craggly river
tools
King Tater Railway for Tater stealing!
Living Room
CARLTON's BACKYARD
Catcher Tunnel (in progress)
Cactus Fest
pool
Tot Bot Hatch
N
W
E
S
Carlton's House